THE MEDUSA STRAIN

Chris Holmes

Printed in Canada

For information address:
Durban House Publishing Company, Inc.
7502 Greenville Avenue, Suite 500, Dallas, Texas 75231
214.890.4050

Library of Congress Cataloging-in-Publication Data
Chris Holmes, 1941

The Medusa Strain / by Chris Holmes

Library of Congress Catalog Card Number: 00-2002103006

p. cm.

ISBN 1-930754-22-1

First Edition

10 9 8 7 6 5 4 3 2 1

Visit our Web site at
http://www.durbanhouse.com

Book design by:
Strasbourg-MOOF, GmBH

For Christopher.

No longer beside us.
But always with us.

The
Medusa
Strain

"And they are three, the Gorgons, each with wings and snaky hair, most horrible to mortals whom no man shall behold and draw again the breath of life."

Apollodorus

Achmed Malabee entered the line at Air France's Orly Airport ticket counter with great trepidation, squirming as the sweat ran down his sides and hoping his fear didn't show. To prepare for this journey he had cropped short his black, curly hair and shaved his full, bushy beard, two things normally forbidden by the harsh Islamic law he followed. But his Imam had granted him these special dispensations for his mission. His Western-style business suit, designed to help him blend in with other travelers, was tailored by someone clearly unused to fashioning such clothes; it draped rather than fit him, triggering more anxiety.

The pretty Customer Service Agent smiled at him. "Your final destination is LAX. Is that correct, sir?"

Achmed just nodded and pushed his ticket across to her. The stubble of his beard itched and begged to be scratched. But he fought the urge. "Do nothing—not the slightest thing—to draw attention to yourself," he had been ordered.

"Your passport, *s'il vous plait,*" she requested.

He dug into his flight bag, extracted the French Passport under which he was traveling and wordlessly passed it across to her.

She looked at him, puzzled. "Do you not have any luggage to check?"

"No, just two carry-ons," he said quickly, maybe too quickly. "Two carry-ons, that is all."

She looked at his one small piece of luggage and accompanying flight bag. It seemed very odd. This was an international flight and she'd never before seen a traveler with just carry-ons. But she shrugged and handed him a boarding pass. "Boarding time for Air France Flight 62, non-stop service to Los Angeles, is in about 3 hours at gate number 12. Have a pleasant journey."

As he headed for his gate, Achmed passed a familiar face. It was Ramallah! Though disguised in ill-fitting Western clothes like himself, he recognized the other man instantly. They had spent the past forty-eight hours cooped up together in a small room. But he was under strict orders to avoid unnecessary contact of any kind. So he suppressed the impulse to nod, wave, or say even one word of recognition to his comrade. But under his breath he said, "*I wonder where he is heading?*" and continued on to the boarding area, reviewing in his mind for the fifth time today the details of his mission and how he'd come to be assigned it.

When Rashid Bin Yegal, *al-Qaeda's* chief agent in Iraq, had contacted him a few weeks ago, Achmed had seen it as a call from God. He had known Rashid from the years in Paris when they were both students there, Achmed studying civil engineering, Rashid biology. Rashid knew an Islamic fundamentalist when he saw one, a potential holy warrior for *al-Qaeda*, the terrorist organization founded by Osama Bin Laden. Rashid had had little trouble recruiting Achmed into its ranks.

During his student years, Achmed kept track of *al-Qaeda's* activities through underground publications. But he had heard nothing directly from Rashid since those Paris meetings. So, he had settled down, bored and frustrated, into a job as a bureaucrat in the Iraqi Department of Water and Power in Baghdad.

When Rashid unexpectedly sent him a secret message announcing "I have a mission for you," it was electrifying. Achmed had been waiting—all his life it seemed, bowed over in his prayers, watching the sun go down on one more wasted day—for a call to serve Allah, to serve the jihad. This was it.

The next evening he drove for several hours down twisty desert roads to a secret meeting with Rashid near the northern Iraqi city of Mosul. Under a lustrous moon and a starlit sky he was told he had been selected for this mission because of his facility with languages, most importantly French and English, because of his general level of education and training, and because of his light skin and European features. And, most importantly, because of his devotion to Allah and to His agents, *al-Qaeda*.

The air was redolent with jasmine from a nearby villa. The shadows of the moonlit desert marched away to the horizon in a spectrum of grays, browns and blacks, until they disappeared into the inky void of the Kurdish hills, where no dwelling nor even tree broke the monotony.

Rashid fired up a one-burner camp stove, spread out a blanket on the ground to ward off the desert chill, and offered his young guest sweet tea, flat bread, and *babagenush*, the spicey garbanzo bean paste served as an appetizer thoughout the middle east.

"What is it to be?" Achmed asked excitedly. "A car bomb? An assassination? Where am I to be sent?"

The thinnest hint of a smile crossed Rashid's lips. "Hold your questions. They will all be answered in good time. But first I must know whether you are truly prepared to accept this assignment. It could be dangerous. In fact," the terrorist looked into Achmed's eyes with a stare sharper than a scimitar, "there is a high probability you will not return alive."

Achmed felt his heart turn over. He pulled his rough woolen cloak tighter about his shoulders, cradled his tea cup in his hand, and sniffed the vapors arising from it like some Greek oracle. Finally, he raised a fist to the sky. "Allah akhbar! God is great." If he survived, he would be a hero. And if he died, he would be a holy martyr and sit in heaven next to God Himself.

"Is it true," he asked Rashid, his eyes wet in the lamplight, "that if I am martyred, I will be rewarded in heaven with a harem of seventy-two beautiful virgins?"

Rashid nodded. "At least that many!"

Three days later Achmed found himself, together with five other men, one of whom was Ramallah, in the city of Mosul. They sat around a table in a modern conference room of an old building with a rusty red sign which read *Mosul Chicken Company*. Each man, they were told, had a similar mission but a different destination, though all were headed for that Great Satan, the United States of America. During their stay in Mosul, all six men shared one small room, which contained six cots, one commode, one mirror, and one wash stand.

Days of group training and orientation followed. Then there were instructions for each man. When they were allowed outside for brief exercise periods, they were assaulted by the pungent smell of the chicken processing plant next door, a rank contrast to their sterile briefing rooms and training quarters.

Achmed's own briefings were conducted by Rashid himself. He was told he would fly first to Paris, then, after a brief lay-over, continue on to Los Angeles. Once there, he was to check into a hotel near the airport where a room had already been booked for him.

"A few days after that you will be contacted by another agent. He will give you your final orders and brief you on your mission."

Achmed nodded that he understood and would comply.

"You will be given ample money for food and other expenses," Rashid added.

"What kinds of 'other expenses?'"

"We want you to visit certain places while awaiting your contact. These might include sporting events, the cinema or theatre, and a theme park. You are to blend in with other visitors. Go on some tours. Carry a camera and take pictures like all the other tourists."

Achmed was shocked. "Is this not prohibited by the Holy Koran?" he protested. "Would it not be an offense to Allah?"

"You must trust me on this," Rashid insisted, his eyes cold. "Much good will come of it." He leaned back and spread his hands. "And besides, if you take no pleasure in it, it is not thought to be a sin."

Achmed nodded.

Rashid opened a fresh pack of filtered cigarettes, lit one, and inhaled deeply. His cold eyes watched Achmed. "A small vice. Allah will forgive me." He offered one to his new pupil.

Achmed shook is head.

"American." Rashid took another long draw. "The best kind."

On their last night in Mosul the six men were issued French Passports, U.S. currency, Western clothes and carry-on luggage. Only carry-on luggage. Nothing would be checked. Therefore nothing could be traced. Achmed slept poorly, as did the other five men. Their evening prayers echoed in the small room. Anxiety about his journey weighed heavily on Achmed's mind. In addition, the air in the small room seemed especially stuffy and close this last night. There was a vague, almost nauseating smell to it which he couldn't place. Prayer filled words hung in its cloying grip.

The next twenty-four hours were a blur to Achmed. Just after dusk he and the others were blindfolded and transported over good roads by car for several hours, then by horse carts over bone-bruising paths choking with dust for another three hours, then by car for two hours more.

All Achmed could remember of the journey were the sounds and smells: the sweat and dung of the horses, urged on by whips; the fumes from old cars, one of which regularly misfired; and the sounds of men who guided him along rocky paths. The air changed, from desert heat to a pine-scented cool alive with bird calls and animal sounds. These gave way to city traffic and rotting garbage.

They were given food and water and allowed a little sleep. The food was some type of processed meat and greasy fried potatoes; western food, they were told, to prepare their digestive tracts for what lay ahead. By the time they were put aboard separate airplanes heading for Paris, they were completely disoriented, which was one of the purposes for all the secrecy.

Also, this twenty-four to thirty-six hour period—the time from their last night in Mosul until their departures for Paris— was not accidental. It matched perfectly the time needed for the new, genetically-altered anthrax spores they'd inhaled to germinate in their upper respiratory tracts, incubate there for twelve hours longer, then begin producing symptoms.

It was now time for the final leg of Achmed's journey to begin, the one from Paris to Los Angeles, and he headed down the boarding ramp of the Boeing 747 for what he hoped would be a glorious rendezvous with history. When he showed his boarding pass to the flight attendant waiting in the airplane doorway, he sneezed.

Then he sneezed again.

Then a third time, hurriedly covering his nose and mouth with his hand as he made his way to his seat, 15E.

The first half of the ten-hour flight was uneventful, and Achmed dozed. He picked dutifully at his meal. But then he began to feel unwell. He had developed—out of nowhere it seemed—all the symptoms of a bad cold. He quickly worked his way through a small package of tissues on his runny nose. His congested sinuses gave him a dull, throbbing headache. In addition to the fits of sneezing a cough had developed, a deep, wet cough, which made his chest hurt each time a spasm seized him. He didn't have a thermometer, but he felt certain he had a fever. He had little appetite and refused the on-board meal. He did sip some of the juice which came with it.

His seat mates to the right and left, 15D and 15F, withdrew from him every time he coughed or sneezed, either by turning their heads or visibly edging their bodies away. At first, he muttered apologies. But then he just suffered in silence, hoping he would be well enough to undertake his mission—whatever it was—when he got to Los Angeles.

He reached up and opened his ventilation nozzle full blast then clicked the 'Call' button.

"Please," he said to the Flight Attendant in his heavily-accented English, "do you have any more tissues? And perhaps an aspirin or two for my headache?" He had barely finished his sentence when a fit of coughing overtook him.

The attendant smiled tightly. "I'll see what I can find," she said, hurrying away.

⬤

Flight Attendant Suzette Marie Kelly, a pixie of a girl with a ponytail and bounce, rummaged through the plane's medical kit. "That guy in seat 15E has a really bad cold," she said to a colleague in the galley. "Christ, I hope I don't catch it. I'll be pissed if I do."

She found a bottle of acetaminophen capsules, dumped two out into her hand, and filled a glass with water. Tucking a small packet of tissues into her apron pocket, she headed back down the aisle to Achmed's seat.

Suzette had planned this lay-over in Los Angeles for two weeks. Her boyfriend, a pilot for another airline, had reserved a room for them for five glorious nights at a hotel on the beach in Santa Monica. She'd packed some alluring underthings and made certain to bring along her birth control pills. Five days and nights of good food, good wine and good sex! The thought got her wet.

She handed Achmed the pills, water and tissues and was rewarded for her efforts with a mighty cough. As she turned to go, she caught the eye of the woman next to Achmed, who shook her head in disgust.

"Bastard," Suzette said under her breath as she headed back to the galley, wiping the droplets of Achmed's spittle from her face.

⬤

Saundra Williams, the window seat passenger to Achmed's left, scrunched her head into the pillow she had placed against the window and turned her back to the ill traveler next to her. She was returning from a brief business trip to Paris and was exhausted. She didn't need fatigue and jet lag as well as a cold from this guy sitting next to her. She'd offered Achmed a bottle of nasal spray earlier, but he'd politely refused it, just as he'd been ordered to do. Her husband, two children, and a hot bath were waiting for her in Santa Monica. She just wanted this flight to be over.

Achmed was equally ready for the flight to end. He had not said his prayers for many hours, and though Allah would surely forgive him considering the circumstances, he was a good Muslim and felt guilty about it anyway. He headed back to the lavatory where he hoped to find a measure of privacy and the opportunity to whisper some of the sacred words from the Holy Koran. But even in this he was frustrated. A long line of other passengers waiting for the toilet were in front of him. He had no choice but to wait his own turn, coughing, hacking and sneezing.

In Mosul it was already dusk, and pink-fingered clouds drifted across the evening sky. Mohammed Ali Osman sat alone in his office going over some paperwork. The rest of the laboratory was empty. Since the first phase of their work was now complete, he had given his employees a rest. But in a few days they would return and start production of a new batch of his hybrid biological agent and begin the selection process for the six new agents who would carry it.

Mohammed looked up from his reading and glanced at his reflection in the small mirror he kept on his desk next to a signed photograph of Iraqi President Saddam Hussein. He saw a swarthy-complexioned man in his mid-forties, heavy set but not obese. Cold pools of black for eyes stared out from a round face. His beard was licorice-black. A small mouth, which rarely smiled and never laughed, completed the image in the mirror. Without his lab coat he could have been mistaken for a teacher or a merchant. Or even a physician. Which was what he once had been.

All his distinguished visitors had long since departed for their offices or for the pleasure domes in Baghdad. There was nothing left for Mohammed to do but wait. It was now up to the six infected agents—his plague carriers—now loosed on six U.S. cities. He had taken in private to calling them his 'dark vectors.' Dark because like the original 'Typhoid Mary' they were unaware of what they were carrying. Vectors because they would do what vectors did: transmit disease from one person to another.

"But why send them to America on crowded airplanes?" one of his visitors had asked earlier. It seemed too risky, an invitation to discovery. "Wouldn't it be safer to smuggle them in through Canada or Mexico, or even by boat from Cuba?"

"Since the World Trade Center attack, the Americans have finally tightened their border security," Mohammed said. "They remain very suspicious of anyone who looks Middle Eastern. No, the risk of detection would be much greater from those ways. But American air security has grown sloppy again, overwhelmed by the numbers of legitimate international passengers, business or tourist, who want entrance to their country. Think of it like this, Yasim: you've been on airplanes before, you've seen the crowds of travelers of every ethnic type and nationality. Who pays them much attention anymore? No, our agents will fit right in with these other travelers. And the French passports and other identity papers we supplied them with will allay American suspicion even further. They will blend in smoothly with the rest of the traveling public."

"But what about their symptoms? Won't those draw attention to themselves?"

Mohammed explained, small mouth pressed into a smile. "Have you never sat near someone on an airplane who was ill? Or waited in line at an airport with someone coughing all over you? Many times it has happened to me." He snorted. "More than I care to remember! Haven't you had someone sneeze in your face while you were waiting at the baggage carousel? It happens all the time, right? So who's going to pay attention to another sick traveler with a cold?"

"And one more thing." Mohammed scratched his beard. "Have you never wondered why you got sick yourself so often a few days after an airplane trip? Did you think it was just coincidence that your illness followed so closely to your air travel? Crowded, confined airplanes are perfect places for the dispersal of droplet-borne infections like our hybrid anthrax spores. It's a recognized risk of air travel. It fits our plans perfectly."

Yasim began to see the genius of Mohammed's scheme to start the epidemic in America through infected air travelers. It was diabolical. "And, of course," he noted, "our agents have no idea that they themselves are the real mission. They believe there is some other purpose to their trips. They will assume they've just caught a cold—bad luck!—and will behave like anyone else who is ill, arousing no suspicion."

"Exactly!" Mohammed nodded vigorously. "And there is one further benefit from my scheme. The air in airplanes is drawn in from the cabin, cooled, and recycled back. This means that not only will passengers in direct contact with our agents be exposed to the droplet-bearing spores, but those many rows distant will be exposed as well from the re-circulated air."

Mohammed smiled. "Think of it as an epidemic in a bottle, just waiting to be uncorked when the aircraft taxies to its gate and opens its hatch. Six vectors on their way across the ocean. Six aircraft with six disease carriers. Six epidemics just waiting to be let loose on six American cities."

While Mohammed was busy congratulating himself in Mosul, Achmed's flight had landed at LAX's International Terminal. He headed straight for the foreign visitors section of the U.S. Customs area. When his turn came in the long line in front of the desk, he wordlessly passed his travel documents across and waited.

Without looking up, a bored and tired Customs Agent with the name 'Barney Campo' printed on his badge asked, "what is the purpose of your visit, sir?"

In his best French accent Achmed replied, "to travel and to tour," just as he had been programmed to say. "To see your country."

"Where will you be staying while in the United States?" Agent Campo had turned his attention to Achmed's 'Declaration' card and still had not looked up at the man himself.

"At the Hilton Hotel for a few days." This was true. "It is near the airport, yes? Then I will rent an American car and travel up your coast of California." He said the word slowly, emphasizing each syllable.

The agent automatically stamped the documents and started to pass them back. When Achmed first coughed, then sneezed and blew his nose, Agent Campo hesitated and finally looked up. He saw a man with flushed cheeks and a red nose.

"Are you ill, sir?" the agent asked, suddenly interested.

Achmed daubed at his nose. "A bad cold," he said. "I maybe catch it in Paris before I board the plane."

The agent studied Achmed for a moment and briefly considered referring him for a medical evaluation and quarantine. The Customs Service had the authority to quarantine any person— or an entire airplane—it suspected of carrying a potentially deadly disease. But this was one of many snotty-nosed foreigners Agent Campo had already seen today; he even thought he might be catching something himself. Finally, he just shrugged and pushed Achmed's papers back to him.

"There's a lot of that going around," he told Achmed sympathetically. "Welcome to the United States." He waved him through and motioned to the next person in line.

After a cursory inspection of his carry-on luggage, Achmed was directed to the street outside the terminal. There he took his first breath of United States air, replacing it, when he sneezed a moment later, with several thousand airborne droplets full of hybrid anthrax spores.

Achmed's taxi headed for his hotel a few blocks away. He frowned at the blatant display of 'Adult Entertainment' signs over the Century Boulevard sex shops. He checked into his hotel and immediately visited the gift shop in the lobby to purchase newspapers and over-the-counter cold remedies. Once in his room, he ordered soup from Room Service. Then he covered his head with a small hat, said his prayers, and took a long nap.

When he awoke, he felt better. His nose was less congested, the muscle aches had diminished, and his headache was gone. He still had a wet, croupy cough, but other than that he felt well enough to carry out the instructions he had been given in Mosul.

The next day, along with forty other tourists, he boarded a bus for a trip to Disneyland, that symbol of Western decadence. Neither his fellow bus riders nor the crowds at the theme park paid much attention to this solitary, sour-faced man in their midst who scratched his face and sneezed and coughed a lot.

When he awoke the next morning, Achmed immediately sensed that a drastic change for the worse had taken place in his body. He had never felt so sick before, and his physical weakness was accompanied by a feeling of dread, of impending doom. Alarmed, he dragged himself out of bed, dressed, and made his way downstairs.

"Please take me to a doctor," he whispered weakly to the cab driver. Then slumped back in the seat holding his chest.

Doctor Mohammed Ali Ossman wove his new Mercedes through the traffic on the Saddam Hussein bridge over the Tigris River. His black eyes showed a cold impatience, his small mouth was compressed against his black beard. Mosul, the city he was leaving on the western bank, slowly receded in his rearview mirror, but not before he caught a final glimpse of the rubble left by allied air attacks during the Gulf War nine years earlier. He felt a sudden twinge of pain in the index and middle fingers of his left hand. He relaxed his grip on the wheel and instinctively reached his other hand over to sooth them. But while the pain was there, the fingers were not. Phantom pains, his own doctor had called them, from the two missing fingers which had been blown off in the same bomb blast which killed his new bride. And which gave him yet another reason to hate Americans.

He clenched the steering wheel as humiliating memories flooded back, memories of fist-shaking, impotent rage at the F15's and F16's swooping in for their bombing and strafing runs. Much of the rubble (what the allies had termed 'collateral damage' but which had included schools, mosques, and apartment buildings) had yet to be repaired. It stood as stark evidence of the effectiveness of the embargo on Iraqi oil and a perpetual reminder of Iraqi shame.

He switched on the radio, a local music station. It was playing a popular middle eastern tune, a meandering melody sung by a female vocalist accompanied by a tambourine and a reedy woodwind.

As he drove he said a quick prayer to Allah for the success of Achmed Malabee and his five colleagues, even now on their way to spread terror in America.

Mosul is Iraq's third largest city, located barely 100 miles south of the country's three-corner junction with Syria and Turkey. It sits in the middle of the Kurdistan Plateau, a broad plain sweeping south across Mesopotamia between the headwaters of the Tigris and Euphrates Rivers. A dry, forbidding, hostile land, nothing survives here very far from the life-sustaining rivers. Except the Kurds. And a few petroleum workers on their derricks out in the desert. As much as half of Iraq's oil comes from here.

Still part of the Northern No-Fly Zone, the area around Mosul is patrolled daily by allied aircraft, though they maintain a lower profile now than in those earlier, heady days of Gulf War combat. Originally established to protect Iraq's Kurds from Saddam Hussein's murderous harrassment—just as the Southern No-Fly Zone was developed to protect Shiite Muslims from Saddam and his Sunni Muslim henchmen—there were getting to be fewer and fewer military targets for the airmen and naval aviators. It was mostly boring duty, and the fliers were just glad to finish their missions, leave the monotonous, featureless landscape behind them, and get back to their barracks and beer.

With a last glance in his rearview mirror at the smoke curling up from the campfires of squatters who still called Mosul's rubble home, Mohammed turned north at the end of the bridge and headed for the village of Nabi Yunus, about three miles up a narrow dirt road.

He parked his car and glanced at the clouds. They were all that provided even momentary shade from the September sun. Heat mirages shimmered across the desert as he trudged through the village's dusty main street, oblivious to the looks his western clothes drew from the villagers who stood watching him pass by: stout, heavily-bearded, ruddy-faced men dressed in baggy pants and soft felt hats. These were the Kurds, direct descendents, they claimed, of the ancient Medes, who still spoke a variant of the Persian language and frequently came into the little village from their camps in the hills to the north.

Mohammed, if he had cared to, could have read the history of the Kurds on their weathered faces. The soil of the Kurdish homeland, the actual geography, has been successively conquered by many: Arabs, Seljuk Turks, Mongols, and Ottomans. But not the Kurdish soul. In this century alone their struggles for a "Kurdish State" have been brutally suppressed by the governments of Turkey, Iraq, Iran and Syria. Saddam Hussein used poison gas on their villages and excuted all male Kurds he could find in 1998. Twenty thousand of them perished in that year alone. Though they maintain an uneasy truce with the rest of the populace, the Kurds are still viewed with suspicion by Saddam and treated accordingly. If he had happened to glance their way, Mohammed would have seen in their eyes the resentment the Kurds held toward any authority outside their own, a resentment which periodically built up toward a new outburst of rebellion.

Relieved to be done with Nabi Yunus and its Kurds, Mohammed felt his spirits lifted when, a few hundred yards from the edge of the village, he came to his destination, the ruins of ancient Nineveh. There wasn't much left of what had once been one of the fiercest cities in the world. Remnants of the mud-brick walls which had once been a merchant's store, or a temple, were all that remained. Everything else from the excavations here, as well as from digs at the other great Assyrian cities—Nimrud, Assur, Arbela—were now in England at the British Museum. Mohammed had visited the BM many times during his medical studies in London, staring in awe at the images and reliefs of the great Assyrian Kings, their soldiers bearing the heads of conquered generals as tribute. His fists would ball in anger, his eyes mist with tears, at the pillage of these priceless relics of his heritage by British and other European archeologists. Only revenge would clear such bitterness from his mouth.

As he walked through the ruins, he noticed two French archeologists setting up their survey equipment. They had been granted approval by the Iraqi government to carry out a preliminary assessment prior to undertaking a new dig. They would have slim pickings, Mohammed thought. But now at least, anything they did find would remain in his country.

He walked along the restored eastern wall of the city and leaned against the portico of the Shamash gate, one of fifteen such entrances into this, the cruelest city in an already cruel world. He caressed the warm, crumbly stone like it was a woman's thighs, first stroking it slowly with the gap of his missing fingers, then pushing his cheek against it to breathe in its history. He closed his eyes and imagined himself one of the Lords of Nineveh, racing out this very gate in his chariot to conquer and terrify the rest of Mesopotamia as the Assyrian star burst upon the world in the ninth century B.C., burning like a supernova for more than three hundred years until abruptly flaming out.

Sometimes, when he couldn't sleep, Mohammed fantasized himself as another Sennacherib, the Great King who made Nineveh his Imperial Capitol in 705 B.C., then had dug canals, initiated a massive building program, and filled his palaces with a harem of beautiful wives and exotic concubines. At other times Mohammed imagined he was Ashurbanipal II, who had started it all in the 9th century B.C. by setting out on a course of conquest using—for the first time in recorded history—terror as state policy. Terror to keep in check already-conquered cities. Terror to persuade the unconquered to surrender. And cruelty. Cruelty as deliberate and savage as any Hitler's Gestapo or Stalin's KGB could have devised.

Mohammed knew by heart old Ashurbanipal's boast after one such conquest: how he had burned the town then impaled, flayed alive and beheaded the survivors, covering the walls with their skins; how he had cut off the arms, feet, ears and noses of the soldiers and gouged out their eyes; how he had burned alive young men and maidens, making piles of their skulls, proudly asserting that he took not a single hostage.

Mohammed admired that degree of cruelty and terror. Terror deliberately and systematically carried out was the height of power. He relished the pain and suffering it must have produced. His face twisted as he imagined such treatment in store for, say, the city of London, or New York, or for that bastion of evil, Los Angeles. And if his own plans came to fruition, he would rain down on these modern Sodoms and Gomorrhas more suffering than even old Ashurbanipal could have dreamed possible. He would show the Americans real terror. And it would be more terrible because they wouldn't see it coming. Until it was too late.

Mohammed returned to Mosul just as the sun was setting and the muezzin was announcing the evening call to prayer from the minaret, his ululating song carried away like a sigh on the wind. His visit to Nineveh had filled him with more determination than ever for his holy war, his personal jihad, against the Western infidel. He parked in a dirt lot and entered a one-storied, dilapidated stucco building over which hung a rusting red sign lettered in arabic: *Mosul Chicken Company*. Down the hall to the right was a large warehouse actually engaged in the processing of chickens. On his left, he punched his personal security code into a heavy, windowless fire door and entered another world, a modern, well-lit, air-conditioned one, with immaculately clean, tiled floors, carpeted meeting rooms and offices, and gleaming aluminum-and-glass laboratories.

The human security for the building was provided by a dawn-to-dusk team of armed sentries. There was no barbed wire or other fencing, no high walls or watch towers, nothing to draw the attention of U.S. spy satellites. Only the single human patrol outside, to keep away vandals and nosey intruders. Security inside the laboratory, however, was another matter. It was saturated with state-of-the-art motion sensors, coded door-locks, and silent alarms.

Mohammed quickly washed his face, blew Nineveh's dust from his nose, then ran a comb through his hair and beard. He slipped into a white, starched lab coat and flicked a piece of lint from the lapel. He knotted his silk tie and examined his teeth in the mirror: straight, white blocks of enamel dotted with a few gold crowns, a luxury in this poor country.

In the conference room with its immense rectangular oak table and plush leather chairs, two assistants, also white-coated, waited. They stood and greeted him respectfully when he entered.

"Good morning, Director," said Ramazzan Fahrs, his chief administrative assistant. "We have arranged tea and biscuits on the side table."

"Has anyone arrived yet?"

"Yes, Director, they are arriving now."

The visitors arrived in ones and twos over the next half-hour. Some, like Mohammed, wore expensive Western suits and ties. Others wore military uniforms. Still others were dressed in traditional desert robes and headdresses of the finest silk. Mohammed greeted each one with a slight bow, and, since he was their social equal, by first name as well. They were all professionals, a *Who's Who* of Iraqi science. Like Professors Selim Ali Rahman, a biologist, and Abdul Bin Ahmed, a microbiologist. Yousef Rassan and Ibrahim Assad were physicians and medical school professors. Yasim Abdel Bary was Iraq's top molecular chemist and Mahmud Salmon a recombinant DNA researcher. Other visitors were from the disciplines of public health, genetics and immunology. All, like Mohammed himself, held advanced degrees from prestigious European universities.

Some of these men were skilled researchers engaged in legitimate studies, such as the development of vaccines through recombinant DNA technology, research on new water-sparing grain hybrids, and studies on more effective uses for pesticides. Others were professors at university centers, still others administered Iraq's national health programs. But they all had three things in common: they were members of Iraq's ruling elite and loyal to the dictator

Saddam Hussein; they were totally without scruples; and they were all intent on revenge against the West, especially the Americans.

While he waited for his last and most important guest, Mohammed led the others, now about a dozen, on a tour of his facilities. He pointed out the rooms where thousands of petri dishes and culture tubes full of bacterial colonies peacefully incubated in carefully controlled environments. Further on they passed laboratories where technicians dressed in biosafety suits pipetted cloudy solutions onto agar plates. Other labs contained gas chromatographs, mass spectometers and equipment for agar diffusion, immunofluorescence and PCR techniques. Up-to-date biotechnology hidden away behind chicken processing.

Mohammed was quick to point out the safety features of the laboratory. To prevent any germ-filled air from escaping, all the rooms had negative atmospheric pressures. And the entire building was equipped with a controlled ventilation system. Effluent air had to pass through a series of filters, then a cascade of thirty percent hydrogen peroxide, before it was vented into the community. This was one precaution Mohammed's visitors were very interested in. They all knew about the anthrax epidemic in Russia in 1979 which was proven to have originated from the accidental release of anthrax spores from a nearby military biological weapons facility.

When Mohammed returned to the conference room, his most anticipated visitor had arrived at last. This man was neither a famous scientist, nor a doctor, or a technician. But without his financial backing and spiritual support Mohammed's vision of retribution against the West would never have gotten started, much less brought so close to realization. The visitor was Sheik Khalid Ibn Fahdil, wealthly Saudi businessman, *al-Qaeda* member, and implacable enemy of the Western democracies.

He was accompanied by a single assistant, Rashid Bin Yegal. An Iraqi biologist trained in all the latest research techniques, Rashid had assisted Mohammed in training the original six agents, one of whom was Achmed Malabee. And he oversaw the distribution of Khalid's considerable research funds. He smelled of tobacco.

Mohammed bowed deeply. "May Allah bless and protect you, Sheik."

"Greetings, my son." Khalid embraced him with kisses on both cheeks. "Is everyone else here?"

"Yes, they have all arrived. We are about to begin the conference."

"Very well. But before you go, is there a place we can talk for a few minutes? In private?"

"Of course. My office is just around the corner." He took the man's arm and began to lead the way.

"Rashid sends me glowing reports about your progress," Khalid murmured into Mohammed's ear. "They are most flattering."

Mohammed blushed against his full black beard. "He has been most helpful."

In his office, where tea and biscuits were hastily brought in from the conference room, Mohammed waited until his guest had settled into a chair. Then he briefly assesed the man. Average height. Stocky. He filled out his camoflage fatigues. A high forehead and a long hooked nose revealed semitic ancestry. And his eyes. Unrevealing, impassive. Except when anger flared. Then, it was said, they could pin a listener like an Arabian dagger.

It was rumored he suffered from liver or kidney trouble, and Mohammed searched the man's eyes for telltale signs of jaundice. But he saw none.

"How was your journey?" Mohammed asked.

"Difficult. Tiring." Breath escaped him as he closed his eyes for a moment. "We were constantly on the move. American intelligence agencies have learned how to monitor our phone calls with their satellites and spy planes. Communications with our agents must be by messenger or in person. It takes much longer now and is very dangerous."

Rashid added bitterly, "Since the glorious attack on the World Trade Center, spy planes and satellites search for our agents almost continuously. And many of our most loyal followers have been targeted for assassination by Western operatives infiltrating our few remaining strongholds in Pakistan."

The Sheik nodded. He took a biscuit. "They've tied up much of my financial resources." A tired smile creased his face. "But not all."

Khalid munched on his biscuit and recalled his recent meeting in a seedy hotel in Peshawar, Pakistan with the few Afghan *al-Qaeda* men who had escaped Northern Alliance troops and U.S. war planes during the war on terrorism…

A gray-bearded, stooped old man had leafed through pages of a dossier. "Your family has ties to the Saudi Royal Family, yes?"

"Very distant. But my father's enthusiastic support of King Faisal's oil embargo against the U.S. in 1973 helped the family business."

"Ahh, yes. The oil embargo. Punishment for American support of Israel."

"Yes. I was a teenager then. It was the turning point for my father. He was drawn more and more to Islam. I accompanied him to secret meetings."

"Did the Saudi Royals suspect him?"

"Perhaps. But he used his money, not his mouth, to achieve his goals. By supporting others who believed as he did."

"Such as?"

Khalid sipped some tea. "What does that file tell you? Does it not say that my father was one of the first contributors to Osama Bin Laden when he founded *al-Qaeda* in 1979?"

The other man nodded. "It does."

"When my father died, I resolved to continue his work."

"And you have been a faithful supporter." The gray-beard chuckled. "A 'silent partner,' the Americans would say."

Khalid rubbed his forehead, his face flushed with sudden anger at the mere mention of his enemies. "To see these American troops stationed on Saudi soil is…"

"An insult? A slap in the face to your country?"

"More. Much more. A desecration of the most Holy soil of Islam. Site of the Holy cities of Mecca and Medina. Where the

Prophet Mohammed began His jihad." He slapped his fist into his palm. "I have had to endure the American presence since they first arrived there to fight the Gulf War in 1990. Six thousand of them are still there. To our everlasting shame."

The stooped old man closed Khalid's dossier. "It is a disgrace. But you will redeem Saudi honor if this current operation succeeds. Is it nearly ready?"

"The Laboratory Director assures me it is now operational. That is why I must see for myself."

"You wish to make the journey to Iraq?"

"I must."

"It is very dangerous."

"I must see for myself."

The terrorist looked at his colleagues then back to Khalid. "Very well. We are as committed to this project as you are. We will find a way to get you to that laboratory…"

When Sheik Fahdil had departed, Mohammed returned to the conference room, took his seat at the head of the table and tapped on his water glass for quiet. "Our spiritual leaders urge us to wage holy war on the infidel," he began. "The Prophet himself instructed us in this duty over 1400 years ago. But conventional, ground-based warfare—armies fighting armies—is out of the question for us. We may have the willpower, but we have not the resources for such a crusade."

He scanned the other faces around the table, the finest brains of Iraqi science. Then he abruptly stood and began to pace back and forth at the front of the room. He paused occasionally to punctuate his points.

"We must wage war in secret, a guerrilla war, a war of terror against the population and governmental institutions of the Western powers. We must exact retribution from them for the destruction of our own country and its holy mosques and shrines by their missiles and bombs."

Sweat appeared on his upper lip.

"We must kill them!" he said, his voice rising, "as many as we can, wherever we find them, in any way we can. Kill the American pagans. In their cities. At their workplaces. In their homes. By any means possible. We must make them feel the terror. Only then will our shame be avenged." He looked at each man in turn, his voice suddenly quiet. "Only then will our jihad be complete."

He reached for his glass of water, noting how steady his hand was. His audience watched him. Many, he knew, had also lost friends, relatives and fortunes during the American invasion of their country.

"So," he asked. "How are we to do this? Iraq is a small country; we have no nuclear weapons nor the resources to develop them. The bombings against American targets have been spectacular. But she has quickly recovered. How can we wound her more deeply, more permanently?"

It was Professor Abdul Bin Ahmed, the microbiologist, who answered. "Biological weapons."

Mohammed nodded. "Yes, my friend. That is why we are all here. This is the way to avenge ourselves on our enemies. With maximum killing effect for a small cost of production, these weapons are ideal for us. And we have so many to choose from: cholera, the ebola and hanta viruses, botulism, and plague to name but a few. Each has its own unique advantages and disadvantages. But as you are aware, there is one which is supreme, one which outranks all the others. The Queen Mother of biological agents."

He signalled his assistant, and a slide full of bluish bacteria was projected onto the screen. They looked like tiny box cars lined up in twos and threes.

"Care to comment, Professor Bin Ahmed?"

"Anthrax," the microbiologist said. He paused to let the impact of the word and his gestures sink in. "An ancient pestilence traceable back to early recorded history. The Fifth Plague of Egypt, which decimated their cattle in 1500 B.C., was probably caused by anthrax according to the Book of Genesis. And in 25 B.C. the Roman poet Virgil described the disease in both man and sheep and recognized its transmissibility to man from raw animal hides."

Mohammed nodded and slapped the screen with his pointer. "And in 1876 Robert Koch first saw anthrax under his microscope and made the connection to the disease in animals. To halt an epidemic in sheep which was devastating Europe's economy, Louis Pasteur, in 1881, developed a vaccine against it, a form of which is still in use today."

A bemused voice came from the end of the table. "You know we all know this Mohammed. Did you bring us out here just for a history lesson?"

Mohammed smiled through straight white teeth. He pointed to a colleague seated across from him, a biology professor. "Abdul, tell us about your studies on anthrax."

A wiry little man with a pointed gray beard answered matter-of-factly. "It can occur in three different forms. The skin variety, which arises from direct contact with infected animal hides, is rarely fatal. The second form, the gastrointestinal, comes from eating infected meat. It is almost always fatal. But nearly universal livestock vaccination and strict isolation of ill or dead sheep and cattle before they are brought to market have severely curtailed this form of the disease."

The biologist was interrupted by another impatient voice. "Yes, yes, we all know it's the inhalation form of anthrax which is the most deadly."

Mohammed continued himself. "Exactly so. The breathing in of anthrax spores. Spores which infest the hides or wool products of sheep and cattle and when inhaled cause a devastating and rapidly fatal illness." He nodded again to the little biologist.

"We called it the poor man's atomic bomb," Abdul chuckled. "The spores are so easy to prepare, store, and process. And they are amazingly hardy, remaining fully virulent for generations, even after direct explosions."

Doctor Assad, one of the physicians, leaned forward. "It can kill in either of two ways: by invading the blood stream directly and being carried to the lungs, brain, kidneys and other organs. Or through a toxin which causes hemorrhage and shock, a toxic shock syndrome." He had saved the best for last. "And this toxic shock continues even after the bacteria themselves are killed with antibiotics."

Mohammed pointed to an immunologist named Selim. "What about vaccine protection? What's currently available?"

"We developed and tested our own vaccine. It is identical to the one the Americans use. Six injections are required before it is fully effective. And there is virtually no protection until at least two of these shots have been given."

They sat in silence, each pondering the advantages of this potent bacteria as a biological weapon.

Selim, the immunologist went on. "The spores can be delivered by airplane sprayers or in bombs and missiles, as we did in the Great Patriotic War against Iran."

"But," another voice pointed out, "the problem is delivering them to an enemy half a world away. Even if our agents could smuggle kilogram-sized amounts into the West—millions and millions of spores—and disperse them by sprayers or explosives, for example, at a sporting event or a concert, they would still only cause a few thousand deaths. Unless…" the speaker adjusted his tie in an oddly western gesture "…you want to send a large amount through the mail again."

"Amateurs!" Mohammed sneered. "Those anthrax-laced letters caused, what, a couple of dozen cases and maybe a half-dozen deaths? Hardly worth the effort."

"But the fear and economic disruption were great."

"Exactly!" Mohammed slammed the table then slowly massaged the stumps of his missing fingers. "Imagine if we could turn anthrax into a self-propagating epidemic. Make it truly contagious from person to person. Cause it to spread by itself throughout the entire American country. Think of the number of cases, the many thousands of deaths. The social disruption and economic consequences would be massive."

Abdul, the biologist, shook his head. "Mohammed, we know there is no known person-to-person transmission of pulmonary anthrax. It is infectious only by inhaling the spores. There is no way to introduce an anthrax version of 'Typhoid Mary' into a population and have it spread from one person to another. It's just not possible."

Mohammed stood quite still, cradling his disfigured hand in the other. Behind him the slide of bluish bacteria offered its lethal symmetry. Only the sound of the projector filled the room, its light catching motes of dust.

Professor Bin Ahmed spoke into the silence. "You've done it, haven't you, Mohammed…"

Mohammed said nothing, waiting.

The moment of understanding came as a profound insight into what they were witnessing.

"Gentlemen, we are not here for a history lesson. We are here to make history." Mohammed's face held no emotion.

3

"Life is short,
The art so long to learn.
Opportunity is fleeting,
Experience treacherous,
Judgement difficult."

Hippocrates, on Medicine
Aphorisms

As Achmed Malabee wiped his runny nose and boarded a bus for Disneyland, Gil Martin, M.D. lay in bed staring at the empty vodka bottle. He knew what time it was, because the sun always came around and caught the bottle in prismatic sunlight. Funny, he always positioned the empties like some personal alarm clock. He stared at it. From outside came street sounds, people on the move, on the go, things to do. He lay quite still. His eyes hurt.

He scratched himself and confirmed the time on the clock: just shy of noon. Another drunken night pissed away. At one time, he recalled, he had been so full of energy he had deeply resented the very passage of time itself, took it as a personal insult. He had so many plans and things to do he was bitter he had to sleep at all. But that was then. Now he slept until his head stopped throbbing.

He glanced at the wall calendar: Friday, September 24, three days short of his forty-fifth birthday. Another year spent alone. He couldn't remember when he'd last had even a remotely satisfying relationship with a woman. But since he was impotent now, what did it matter? And his impotence was not just in his lust for women. He'd lost the one desire which had always aroused him: his hunger for work, for medicine. He couldn't get it up for that either. He was nearly impotent for life itself.

He stared at the small suitcase. He despised it. He despised the memories and artifacts of a wasted life secreted away within its fake leather. Diplomas. Fat paycheck stubs. That old photo of young men graduating from medical school, their futures bright. His wedding ring. God Almighty…He rubbed his eyes and listened to the first knocking on walls and moving of merchandise in the porno shop next door. Another busy day. Things to do…

He sat up finally and his eyes drifted to an old family photo taken years ago when he still had a family. A pretty young wife with auburn hair and pouty lips, a beautiful pig-tailed two-year old girl on her lap. Cassie was now a teenager who still loved him unreservedly, her love the only thing in this world he knew still to be true. He'd been apart from them for four years, had seen neither in two. Two summer vacations, two birthdays, two Christmases, all passed with only a card or an awkward phone call. Except for the often-late child support checks he sent every month, and this photo, there was little proof he'd ever had a wife and daughter. He blamed the lack of contact on the great expanse of geography separating Atlanta, Georgia from West Los Angeles, California. But he knew better. As the song said, it was his own damn fault.

He washed out his mouth and used his finger as a toothbrush. If he brushed now he'd throw up. He stared at his reflection but his mind was blank. He had made the journey to his face many times. It was a wasted trip. A fragment of his workday came back. The boy had been young, wanting to become a nurse, not a doctor. What did Dr. Gil Martin think of that?

They had talked…

Gil managed a smile as he threw a used tongue depressor into the receptical. "So you want nursing, not medicine."

"Yessir."

"Nursing can give you added headaches."

"I know. I've accepted that."

Gil shrugged. "Can you accept what goes on here?" he said, waving a careless hand around the ER. He noticed the woman on the bench. Didn't look good. He'd have to get to her quickly, deepsix nurseboy.

"It's all important work, helping, right, Doctor?"

"Treat 'em and street 'em," Gil said. "Colds, runny noses. And don't forget the drunks who break bones falling into gutters. And jaundice from cirrhotic livers. That's not all of it, of course."

"Sir?"

Gil shrugged again. "Stabbings, gunshots, gougings. When people get mean, they get creative. Look, I've got to get back to my patients…" He started towards the woman.

"But you would recommend nursing anyway, wouldn't you." The boy made a statement, something in his eyes.

"Yes. I'd recommend it. Work hard. You'll do all right…"

Gil watched his face refocus in the mirror.

While the water heated, he caught a misty glimpse of his reflection in the shower door. Over six feet tall, with a full head of brown hair flecked with gray, he was skinny to the point of gauntness from too much alcohol and too little food. His thin nose showed English breeding, and a firm jaw testified to an inherent pugnacity, at least before life had beaten it out of him. Sparkly blue eyes as a baby were now gunbarrel gray, though on the rare occasions he found to smile, they could still light up with charm. He pulled down their blood-shot lids and stared at them in the mirror. Hello! Was there anyone still alive in there? He couldn't tell.

It had begun with B.A. and M.D. degrees from U.C. Berkeley, then the Family Medicine Residency at San Francisco General. But in other ways it had begun with Tara O'Reilly, newly minted epidemiologist. It had been sunny, the sidewalk cafe intimate, the conversation easy.

"What?" She looked at him over the rim of her wineglass.

"Your eyes. They light up, catch the sun, match your name."

"And you have a classic nose."

They smiled across the table.

"So, you're going into numerator medicine," she teased.

"Hey—"

"One patient at a time—"

"I prefer to call it traditional medicine. Not denominator medicine, like you. Caring for groups of people. Whole communities."

"Yeah, right. That's what an epidemiologist does."

Gil set his glass down and grinned at her. When he reached for her hand it was warm.

Later they had both given to each other, ravenously, gloriously, until collapsing into each other, sweaty and complete. Her words had been soft, delivered to a finger trailing down his spine. "Do you like children?"

"Yes."

Their daughter Cassandra had followed close on their marriage vows. They had loved and nurtured, grappled with careers and parenthood. The slide down had been subtle, beguiling in its drift, slowly eroding what they had, all of it lost in the intensity of their dual careers.

They had continued down their separate paths. Tara worked in San Francisco's Health Department while Gil joined a group practice in affluent Marin County. But he quickly grew bored with the 'worried well' who wanted drugs for every minor discomfort and seemed unable to make even the slightest changes to their unhealthy lifestyles, expecting instead that he would take out his prescription pad and effortlessly make them all better. And the personal connection with patients he thought would come with private practice—a lure at least as attractive as the money—had, like the money, been an illusion. Managed care and HMO's had seen to that.

He had been in the City, on Ghiradelli Square, wandering without purpose, fed up, when a voice called out to him. He turned.

"Hey, mister!"

"Yes?"

"Wanna see somethin' good? Cost you a buck. My kids love it and so do I."

He was a rumpled little man with expressive eyes. Perhaps they had seen something in Gil.

"So what is it?" Gil said.

The little man gestured grandly to a white painted booth standing off by itself, away from the hubbub and clatter of the square. "Feed in a buck. Go ahead."

Half smiling, Gil fed in the dollar bill.

Immediately the shade on the glass front shot up to reveal a bearded long-haired man. The figure banged with his foot on a drum. He played a harmonica and strummed a guitar. A cacophony of merry sound blasted away at Gil.

"I like the guitar. Watch his fingers, watch his fingers—my daughter likes that. See how they work. Must be hinged or somethin'."

Gil nodded, smiling.

Then the music stopped and the shade suddenly shot down.

"My only complaint," the rumpled man said. "Not enough time for yer dough."

But Gil had loved it, had celebrated in the performance of some metaphor for what medicine had become. "Bang your drum, doc, lessee you strum, and twang that guitar, doc, keep it all movin'. Here's another buck."

Gil shook his head as he stared at the shaded window. When he turned to talk to the rumpled little man, he was gone.

━━

Gil soaked himself in the shower, lathering up, trying to soap off the mood that haunted him. The downward slide of his life became an avalanche, sly and ugly, all of it inhabiting his dreams. Big things, little things. In the end they were all big things. Hot water pounded his skin as he remembered Tara's phonecall.

"Gil?"

"Yeah."

"I don't know quite how to put this, so I'd better just say it straight out—"

"—that usually works."

"I've accepted a position with CDC in Atlanta."

"Oh."

"It will be good for me, Gil."

"What about Cassie?"

"She'll adapt. It'll work."

"So she's going. I wasn't in the loop on that one, was I, Tara?"

"We've gone over this, Gil. You know it'll be for the best. Besides, it'll only be short term."

Lies came easy for both of them now.

"I'll need letters and phonecalls, Tara. Especially with Cassie." Gil hated the anxiety in his voice, but it was there, a living thing, part of the long slide down.

"Of course."

But the letters and phonecalls had dwindled. Tortured thoughts of what she was telling Cassie about him added to the rest of it. When the divorce decree arrived, he put it in the fake leather suitcase with his other diplomas.

He turned off the shower and emerged pink and squeeky clean. At least on the outside. He dressed in his usual attire of tee shirt, jeans, and sandals, and drove to the beach to see what the tide had brought in. Aimlessly, he drifted through the day, which was like every other one, finally falling asleep in his clothes on the sofa.

The next morning, sober, freshly shaved and properly dressed for the part, he paused at the entrance to the Emergency Room for one last look around, like a traveler at the gates of the nether world. He wouldn't see the sky again until well after dark. He glanced up. It was still early, but the inbound flights to LAX were already lined up on final approach above Century Boulevard. He watched a 747 jumbo jet sweep in above the freeway on its way to touch down.

He had barely started the shift, was just finishing the cast on a teenager's fractured wrist, when out of the corner of his eye he glimpsed a sick-looking man being rolled in on a wheelchair from curbside and lifted onto an examining table. It was Achmed Malabee.

The ER crew moved efficiently to take the man's vital signs, undress him, get him into a gown, and record some basic identifying information. Gil was washing his hands when the charge nurse, Kathy Roberts, interrupted him.

"You better see this guy right away, doc," she insisted. "He doesn't look very good."

Kathy was a gorgeous, willowy blonde whom Gil had briefly hit on when he first took the job. But she was married with a couple of little kids and had made it clear he had no chance. His lack of interest in women started at that point, waning like a post-coital hard-on. His relationship with Kathy was now strictly professional. Satisfyingly so.

He walked into the exam booth and pulled the curtain behind him. He could tell in less than the blink of an eye trained by twenty years' clinical experience that Kathy was right; this guy was in trouble. He quickly scanned the ER record and analyzed the data: a weak pulse too rapid by almost double; falling blood pressure; a high fever; and respiratory distress. Even from where he stood at the foot of the exam table he could see that the man was dusky in color. And when he laid on hands, the skin was cool, almost cold, to the touch.

Suddenly the boredom of another ho-hum illness—'nickle-and-dime' medicine he called it—was gone. Like a jolt of electricity to a starter motor, he came to life with a roar, stuck his head out the curtains and yelled—to no one and to everyone: "Alright people, let's get moving! I want oxygen by face mask and a cardiac monitor. And someone start looking for IV access on this guy."

As the staff exploded into activity, he turned back to his patient, giving additional orders to the nurse.

"Kathy, notify the lab we need a complete blood work-up, stat. And tell X-ray to bring their portable machine for a bedside chest film."

"What's going on with this guy?" the R.N. asked as the oxygen began hissing down the green tube to Achmed's face mask.

"He's in shock. No doubt about it. He's got all the signs. A textbook case. When you get that IV started, run in a bolus of fluid. Run it in as fast as it will flow."

He watched the staff hustle to carry out his orders. Satisfied, he began Achmed's comprehensive, hands-on physical exam. As he looked into the man's ears, mouth and throat and felt his belly, he tried out a few simple questions on him.

"Sir, can you hear me? What's your name?"

A semi-comatose Achmed opened one eye and tried to speak, but all that came out was a wet, weak cough accompanied by a reflex clutch at his chest. It had hurt.

Gil tried again.

"Do you have any allergies to drugs or foods? Are you taking any medicines? Do you have any current medical problems?"

No response.

He lightly shook Achmed's shoulder and was rewarded with opened eyes and a weak attempt at speech. But all that came out was the noisy wheeze of respirations.

He listened to Achmed's lungs with his stethoscope and heard the tell-tale signs of fluid in the chest and the characteristic coarse breath sounds of bronchitis. He paused for a moment to watch Achmed breathe: rapid rate, retracted ribs, neck muscles tensed to aid the respiratory effort. The man's distress was worsening by the minute.

He took a sterile, cotton-tipped swab, wiped it deep into the man's nose, and handed the gooey specimen to the lab tech who had just arrived. "Culture this, please, and stain it as well. If you see a heavy concentration of any particular organism, let me know."

He peeled off his exam gloves, pulled down his face mask, and headed over to the x-ray view box just as Fergus Robinson, one of the young ER technicians, flipped Achmed's chest x-rays onto it.

"What do you think, doc?" Fergus asked casually. He didn't expect much of an answer.

"Fluid in the chest." Gil pointed out the shadows he was referring to. "Here…and here."

The tech nodded, grateful for the little bit of teaching. This was unusual from Dr. Martin, who rarely gave him the time of day.

Suddenly Gil looked closer. Something had caught his eye. "Wow, look at those big pulmonary lymph nodes!" He pointed them out to Fergus. "See, here, these lumps. They're normally about a third this size."

"Is he gonna die?" The tech looked worried.

"I don't know. But he's gonna be sick for a while. The oxygen should help his breathing. And if we can get him out of shock with IV fluids, he should stabilize."

Kathy Roberts joined them at the view box. "Do you think he's septic?"

"Definitely. Septic shock. Let's load him up with IV antibiotics."

He turned to the desk clerk, about five feet away. "Is there an ICU bed available?"

"Sorry," she answered. "The house is full tonight."

"No room at the inn, huh?" He grunted and turned to the nurse. "Alright," he said, "he's too sick to transport anyplace else. We'll keep him here in the ER until an ICU bed opens up."

He turned back to the desk clerk. "By the way, what do we know about this guy? Who brought him in? Did he have any ID on him?"

"He came alone, by taxicab. Here's all we found." She pointed to a plastic bag.

Gil picked through the items: a few hundred dollars in U.S. currency; a French Passport with a Paris address; a hotel room key; and the stub of a three-day old boarding pass from Air France Flight 62. For no particular reason—maybe a hunch—he slipped the last two items into his lab coat pocket.

When he returned to Achmed's bedside, the first IV fluid bolus had run in, the labs had been drawn, and the initial dose of antibiotics was being piggybacked into the IV. Achmed's color had improved with the oxygen therapy, his breathing less labored. His vital signs were also better. But he still responded to all attempts at communication with mere groans or grunts.

"See if anyone around here speaks French," Gil said to the desk clerk. "Maybe this guy no *parlez vous anglais*." Then he turned to the pile of new patient charts which had grown into a foot-high stack during the time he'd worked on Achmed. Back to the 'nickels and dimes…'

It was shortly after lunch—a bowl of chili in the cafeteria—when Gil got a call from the laboratory.

"Good morning, doc." It was Luis Gonzales, the microbiologist.

"*Buenos dias, amigo*. What have you got for me?"

"The nasal smear you took is loaded with bacteria. And not just the usual suspects."

"What is it? Strept? Staph? Pneumo? Or one of the gram negatives?"

"None of the above. In fact …well, it's pretty amazing. Why don't you come over and take a look for yourself."

It worried him as he headed through the hallways to 'Micro.' Luis Gonzales, in addition to fifteen years experience in some high-powered hospitals, had spent four years traipsing around the world for the World Health Organization, a microscope and a satchel full of blood agar plates on his back. He wasn't easily amazed.

Gil stared at the bacteria under the 'scope, deep-blue in color from the stain. They didn't look like anything he'd seen before. And he thought he'd seen them all. Big, robust rods, lined up in two's and three's like little boxcars, or better yet, like the double and triple tractor-trailer rigs he'd seen on the open highways of Utah, Arizona and New Mexico.

"What the hell is this, Luis?" He was stymied.

"You won't believe it, doc. I couldn't believe it myself. I've only seen this organism in the flesh once before. In a hospital in Pakistan on a specimen taken from a shepherd with a scabby, black sore on his face."

"Well...?"

"It's anthrax. I'd bet my next paycheck on it."

For about five seconds Gil looked like someone who needed the Heimlich Maneuver: eyes open, mouth agape, no speech coming out.

Finally, he exhaled. "Anthrax? Are you serious?"

"I know, I know. It sounds crazy! But compare this textbook photo with what you're looking at under the 'scope. What do your eyes tell you?" The microbiologist laid open a thick tome under Gil's nose and stabbed a finger at a photograph. Gil looked back and forth between the textbook and the slide. The two images were identical, perfect matches.

"Shit! Where would this guy pick up an infection like this?"

Louis shrugged. "That's your job to figure out, doc. I just identify 'em."

As he turned to leave, Gil poked the other man in the chest. "If you're right about this, *amigo*, you've earned your salary this month. Call me as soon as the cultures grow anything."

On his way back to the ER, Gil detoured to the medical library and spent a quick twenty minutes scanning two articles on anthrax in the textbooks, then asked the reference librarian to perform a search of the current medical literature for him.

Between patients he phoned the hospital's Infectious Disease specialist. But the ID guy wasn't buying it. "Anthrax!" he snorted. "Not you too?" He had been inundated with referrals ever since the two dozen or so east coast anthrax-by-mail cases. But they had all turned out to be something much more common. Staph or strept, usually. He thought he'd seen the last of these referrals.

"I know, I know." Gil was apologetic. "We all kinda overreacted to those terrorist cases, didn't we?"

"Right. Your lab's mistaken. This is another false alarm, some bacteria that's been altered by the staining."

Gil was defensive. "My lab guy's the best there is. And what about those big lymph nodes in the chest? They're characteristic of anthrax, aren't they?"

"Look, Gil, if you've got a new case of anthrax, I'll help you write the article myself because you've got a guaranteed publication. This is probably nothing more than a garden variety of septic shock. Wait for the cultures, you'll see. Besides, your antibiotic coverage is broad enough for everything, even anthrax."

"And it's never been shown to be contagious, right?"

"Abso-fucking-lutely! It cannot be transmitted from person to person. But that's not what your patient's got."

Gil hung up and chewed on his fingernails. They were almost down to the quicks. One was bleeding

Gil worked his way through the afternoon's cases. But his mind kept coming back to Achmed. He checked him frequently. He pulled out the boarding pass stub and hotel room key he'd stuffed into his pocket. He was desperate for more information about this man, which was something quite remarkable in itself. Actually wanting to know more about a patient was a strict violation of his 'treat 'em and street 'em' rule. On impulse, he called the number listed on the hotel room key.

"Was he traveling alone or was someone with him?" he asked the desk clerk.

"He registered as a single guest."

"Did you notice if he seemed ill during his stay?"

"I was on duty when he first checked in. He did appear to have some sort of a cold or flu. He was coughing a lot. I remember one of the bellmen even commented on it. But he was well enough to take a tour yesterday."

"And he's had no visitors or messages? No contacts from anyone? A business associate, a friend?"

"The man kept to himself, spoke to no one as far as I know. Is he going to be alright?"

Gil glanced at the monitor above Achmed's bed. "I don't know," he replied truthfully, "he's very sick."

Before he finished his shift he took one last look at Achmed. He had been holding his own for the past ten hours. That was a positive sign. But there were so many things that didn't add up yet, so many unanswered questions about this guy. He ticked them off in his head: If Luis Gonzales was right and this really was anthrax, what was the source of the exposure? And where had he been exposed? And if those germs he saw under the microscope weren't anthrax, what were they? And what about the man himself? What was he doing in this country alone, without any contacts, a stranger in a strange land? Even solo travelers usually had someone to meet at their destinations. But not this guy.

Like mosquitoes on a hot summer night, these thoughts kept buzzing around in his head even after he stepped outside when his shift ended. Normally, he would stop at a favorite bar on the way home for a few drinks, and be in his cups by the shank of the evening. But not tonight. He headed straight back to his apartment, a stack of medical journals under his arm.

In five other U.S. cities sick Iraqis were beginning to make their way to hospitals, emergency rooms and urgent care clinics. Their symptoms were similar to Achmed's, the puzzlement of their doctors similar to Gil Martin's. The official FBI report would explain the delay and confusion in diagnosing these 'index cases' as understandable, considering that no physician had ever seen anthrax cases like these.

"When he opened the fourth seal...I saw
a pale horse, And its rider's name was
Death, and Hades followed him; And they
were given power...to kill with sword...
and with Famine and with pestilence..."

Revelations 6.7

In Mosul, the sun was high over the chicken processing company and its hidden microbiology labs. Another hot, dusty day.

Mohammed raised his hands for quiet in the conference room. His last comment hinting at a possible contagious form of anthrax had sparked a torrent of questions.

"What do you mean, 'make history?'" Yousef Rassan, a physician whose ego was only matched by his girth, had stood up. "What have you done?"

Selim Ali Rahman, one of the biologists, added his voice to the storm. "Yes, what have you done, Mohammed?" He was clean shaven except for a Hitler-style mustache. But he was unsure of himself, and his eyes darted from Mohammed to others across the table and back again, looking for guidance.

"Such a thing is not possible." Yasim Abdel Bary, a molecular chemist, was trying to be heard over the din, his long unruly beard sticking out like a bundle of copper wires. "Anthrax is simply not communicable. There's no way to make it so. We've tried ourselves in my own laboratory for years, without success. The bacteria are too fragile. They disintegrate during transmission."

"Patience, patience. It will all become clear to you shortly."

Mohammed finally got them quieted down.

He slid a cassette into a VCR on a side table, switched on a large overhead television monitor, and dimmed the room's lights.

"Watch the video," he said quietly. "See for yourselves. Nothing is impossible when the will is strong enough."

The first image to appear was a panoramic shot of a small barracks-type room with six cot-like beds, one stainless steel commode, and one washstand. There were no windows to be seen. No pictures or shelves broke the monotony of the four walls. A large mirror was mounted on one of the walls. It was a two-way mirror, and behind it stood the video camera which had recorded the scene Mohammed and his guests were now watching.

The sole occupant of the room was a man sitting on one of the beds. At his feet was a tray of dishes, all empty except for a few scraps of food. He was young, full-bearded, and dressed in the Kurdish fashion: high-topped boots, baggy woolen pants bloused over the boots, and a khaki shirt. A soft, bowl-shaped hat rested on the night stand next to his bed. A monitoring device above his head continuously displayed his blood pressure, heart rate, respiratory rate and temperature. Mounted next to the monitor was a microphone and next to it a small speaker. Similar monitors, microphones and speakers could be seen above the other beds.

From off-camera a sugary male voice asked, "How do you feel today, Abdullah?"

The man jumped to his feet and stared at the speaker above his head as if it were alive.

"How do you feel?" the voice asked again, this time more insistent.

The man hesitated, his eyes darting about the room. "I am well. What do you want with me? Why am I here? What are you going to do…" The flood of questions continued until there was a click. Then they abruptly ceased. The audio had shut off but the video continued to roll.

The off-camera voice narrated over the silent visual. "Abdullah is a local Kurd. He is taking part in our experiment. When he first arrived, he was examined from head to foot to be certain he was free of disease. Then monitoring leads were attached to his body, and he was fed. No drugs or medicines were used on him."

Mohammed paused the tape and looked at his visitors. Most now showed mild curiosity on their bearded faces, though a few still registered impatience.

"Six hours prior to what you are watching," he began, "I sprayed 50,000 anthrax spores into that room and circulated them around with a small fan. Four hours later I completely ventilated and disinfected the room and tested it for residual spores. I detected none."

"So, Abdullah was exposed to the spores for only six hours?" the portly physician, Yousef Rassan, asked. His professional curiosity was piqued, but he felt no moral concern about this human experimentation.

"Correct." Mohammed fast-forwarded the videotape. When it stopped, the man was lying on his bed holding his head. The food in the tray at the foot of the bed appeared to be untouched.

"Here is Abdullah 24 hours later," the narrator continued. "He doesn't feel so well anymore. His pulse rate is elevated, he has a slight temperature, and he is breathing faster than normal. He also complains of a headache and has lost his appetite, though he drinks the soup and juice we provide."

"What do you think, Yousef?" Mohammed asked.

"The start of a common cold, maybe." The physician's eyes narrowed. "Or the flu-like phase of anthrax. I've seen that one many times before. In Iran."

Mohammed looked back at the television monitor. The videocamera now centered on a new face. This second man was sitting on the bed opposite Abdullah's. "Let me introduce you to

Cyrus," said the narrator, "Abdullah's new roommate for the past two hours. How do you feel today, Cyrus?"

The man just shrugged.

"And what about you, Abdullah?"

The answer was a sullen, "I'm okay." But Mohammed's guests could see he clearly was not.

The VCR whirred forward again. When it stopped, the narrator explained. "Here is Abdullah two days later." The man was now prostrate on the bed, his face ashen, his breathing rapid and shallow. He coughed weakly and held his chest with one hand. It hurt.

"His blood pressure has dropped, his heart rate risen, and he is in respiratory distress," the narrator pronounced as if he were describing a travelogue or a news documentary. "He is in shock and close to cardiopulmonary collapse."

The other man, Cyrus, had withdrawn to a corner of the room, as far away from his roommate as he could get. "Cyrus is still symptom free," the voice went on, "as you can plainly see. His health has not changed from the day we first put him in with Abdullah."

Mohammed stopped the tape. "Abdullah died eight hours later. We collected blood cultures from him just prior to death. They all grew out heavy concentrations of anthrax. Cyrus, on the other hand, showed no symptoms of anthrax. He remained completely disease free until we blindfolded him and released him into the Kurdish hills several days later."

"Alright, alright, Mohammed." Yasim Abdel Bary was impatient, his copper-colored beard jutting and bobbing as he spoke. "You've demonstrated that you can aerosolize anthrax spores and deliver them in a high enough quantity to kill. And you've also shown that anthrax does not spread from person to person, even with very direct contact. This is nothing new. Did we come here just to see what we already know?"

"Watch!" Mohammed stabbed a finger at the video monitor. "Watch and see." He rubbed the aching stumps of his missing fingers.

The new VCR image was of the same room, empty but for one person again, this time a woman. Covered from head to toe—except for the moon of her face—in the black *chador*, she sat on the edge of her bed. She was trembling and wringing her hands.

"Good morning, Serina," the narrator said. "How do you feel?"

She glanced over her shoulder at the loudspeaker but said nothing. Tears rolled down her weathered, makeup-less face.

"Serina is fine," the narrator assured his listeners. "Disease free and in her usual state of good health. As with Abdullah, 50,000 anthrax spores were sprayed into this room six hours earlier. Four hours after that the room was completely ventilated, tested, and found to be spore-free. Oh, yes, one more thing…there is something very different about these anthrax spores."

Mohammed fast-forwarded the tape and continued the narration himself. "It's twenty-four hours later now. Serina, like Abdullah before her, is beginning to feel unwell. But there are clear differences between their illnesses. Can anyone spot them?"

Ibrahim Assad, another of the physicians, with a pronounced hook to his long semitic nose, leaned forward. "Serina has a very runny nose. She's constantly blowing it into her handkerchief. And she dabs and rubs her eyes frequently. A conjunctivitis, maybe? I think we did not see these things in Abdullah."

Professor Bary was now sitting forward in his chair, no longer bored. "Abdullah had only a mild, dry cough. Hers is wet and productive. And she sneezes often. Abdullah didn't sneeze even once."

Mohammed nodded. "Any other differences?"

"Her fever's higher and she's breathing faster. Does she have pneumonia?"

"No, there is no pneumonia."

"She seems to have a sore throat," someone else offered. "See how she winces when she swallows."

"Correct," Mohammed said. "Anything else?" He waited a few moments. "No? Then can we all agree that Serina's illness is more typical of a common cold than of inhalational anthrax? A garden variety URI?"

Everyone concurred.

"This is unlike any human anthrax case I've ever seen," one of the physicians said. Several others murmured agreement.

"Watch again," Mohammed said. "I'm jumping ahead twenty-four hours."

The monitor flickered then resumed the video. Now the little room was full of people, three men and two more women. They were all Kurds, all milling about and talking with one another. All except Serina. She had taken to her bed. Her temperature indicator now read 104 degrees. She had lost the color from her face. She was breathing heavily and rapidly. Her heart rate had climbed to nearly double its resting level.

Mohammed listened to the murmurs from around the table. His guests were all sitting up straighter now, some on the edges of their seats. This was definitely a highly unusual way for a simple cold to progress in a healthy young woman. Something else was going on here. A few had begun to guess what it was.

Mohammed fast-forwarded the tape again. "It is now forty-eight hours later," he announced. "As you can see, Serina's illness is beginning to take on similarities to Abdullah's course of anthrax. Her sudden collapse into shock, for example. You wouldn't expect this from a simple URI, would you?"

Serina was now comatose, her face almost blue. Her breathing had become so slow and shallow it was barely detectable.

The other Kurds in the room were avoiding her, clinging to the walls as far away from her as they could get. They too were now all sneezing, coughing, rubbing their eyes, and blowing their noses. And the vital signs on their monitors were beginning to change for the worse as well.

"These are the last images you will see," Mohammed announced, stopping the tape. "Serina is gone. She died five days after the onset of her illness. Anthrax was grown from her blood cultures.

The five others will all be dead within twenty-four hours. From the same shock-like state as Abdullah and Serina. Anthrax will also be grown in heavy concentrations from their blood cultures."

He clicked off the monitor, brought up the lights and ejected the videotape from the VCR. "Place this in my office safe," he ordered one of his aides.

His diminutive assistant, Ramazzan Fahrs, took the tape carefully, cradling it in both hands like a newborn infant. He bowed stiffly and hurried out.

"Well?" Mohammed asked.

His question met with only stunned silence. It was a full minute before anyone could find his voice.

"Is this true?" someone finally asked. "Have you actually found a way to make anthrax communicable?"

Mohammed's triumph was a religious fanaticism, an ugly rictus. "Allah akhbar!"

"May God help us," Dr. Rassan whispered. "What have you done? How is this possible?"

"It is possible. I have done it. Created a new weapon, a plague to destroy our enemies. Just as the Prophet commands in the Holy Koran. I will unleash this new pestilence on them, and they will know real terror." Visions of Ashurbanipal and his raging Assyrians danced before Mohammed's eyes.

"And now," someone demanded, "you will tell us how you accomplished this."

Mohammed went to a chalk board. "Of course. And you will be amazed how simple it was."

When he finished describing how he had created a contagious form of inhalation anthrax, Mohammed answered a variety of technical questions about the process. Then excited chatter spread throughout the room. Mohammed allowed it to go on. Rashid Bin

Yegal, the *al-Qaeda* agent, caught his eye and nodded approvingly. Sheik Fahdil's investment was paying off handsomely.

Mohammed walked to a large photograph of Saddam Hussein. He wiped dust off the glass with the sleeve of his lab coat and frowned at one of his assistants.

When the chatter began to ebb, he tapped on the table for quiet. "There is one problem with my new anthrax hybrid. The production process for this germ is very inefficient. I was only able to produce a small amount of it."

"How much?" someone asked.

"Enough for six of our agents."

"What about the anthrax vaccine?" Dr. Rassan asked. "The Americans will use it for certain."

"Ha!" Mohammed spit out the word. "It's only given to their military, and even they have been very slow about it. No more than 150,000 troops are fully immunized. And now I hear they've run into production problems. The whole program has ground to a halt." His eyes narrowed like a hooded snake's. "Of course, their civilian population is completely unimmunized and susceptible."

Ibrahim Assad rested his elbow on the table, cradled his chin in his hand, and curled a finger around the hook of his nose. He was shaking his head slowly.

"What is it Ibrahim," Mohammed asked. "What troubles you?"

"I fear you've created a Doomsday weapon. Your epidemic will sweep around the world and end up in our own backyard, destroying us as well as the Americans. It will be a pyrrhic victory."

"Nonsense." Mohammed gently tapped the table. "The very embargo which keeps us in keeps others out, including anyone carrying my new germ. We are an isolated nation. That will be our salvation."

"Ironic, isn't it?" someone observed drily.

"What is?"

"That our worst humiliation—the American embargo and No-Fly Zones—will be our greatest protection."

Mohammed nodded.

"So now that you have developed this wondrous new biological weapon," Doctor Assad asked, "what have you done with it? You said something about six agents? What is your plan for them?"

Mohammed didn't mention Achmed Malabee or any of his other agents by name. But he described their missions in detail. "What I have done," he began, "is this…"

While Mohammed explained to his audience how he had infected and secreted his six 'vectors' out of the country, right under the noses of the allied air patrols, Ramazan Fahrs, his cringing white-coated assistant, slid the videotape he had been given into the safe in Mohammed's office. Then he clicked it closed and spun the dial. The copy he had made, just a few minutes earlier behind the locked doors of his own small office, was safely tucked into a concealed pocket of an ordinary-looking sports bag. He would smuggle it out of the lab later that evening.

"What do you want from us?" one of the scientists asked.

Mohammed opened his hands in the age-old gesture of the supplicant. "My friends, my facilities here are small. I have perfected this process. But I cannot produce the germ in anything like the quantities I would like."

"You want us to duplicate your process in our own laboratories?" one of the biologists asked, scratching his beard thoughtfully.

"Yes. And help me recruit, train and disperse many more agents." His black eyes glowed. "Think of the terror we could unleash on the infidel. Not just America, but all their allies as well. The entire Western world."

His guests chewed on this in silence. They could almost smell the revenge.

"When do you expect to know whether your current six agents have succeeded?" someone else asked.

"A week. Maybe ten days. No longer."

"Call us when you know. If you are successful, we will join your jihad."

Mohammed raised both hands to the heavens. "Allah Akhbar!"

Later that evening, in his apartment above the dirty streets of Mosul, Ramazzan Fahrs turned over in his hands his secret copy of Mohammed's videotape. Then he crossed the room to a small sideboard table, picked up a yellowing photograph in a cheap wooden frame, and caressed the image of a woman in Kurdish dress with the same hollowed cheeks and sunken eyes as his own.

"Soon, mother," he whispered in Kurdish. "Soon." He would somehow find his own revenge on that bastard he worked for. "It won't be much longer now."

"So, tell me again why we're going to see this guy?" the younger man asked. "What's his name?"

"Gardner," his partner replied patiently. "Dave to his colleagues, Rusty to close friends. Dr. David Gardner to you. And we're going to see him because he's about the smartest guy I know when it comes to biological warfare."

"'BW.'"

Oscar nodded. "That's what we call it, buddy boy."

The two CIA agents from the Counter Terrorism Unit had left Langley, Virginia an hour ago and were heading north on U.S. 270, their destination: Fort Detrick, close by the town of Frederick in the foothills of Maryland's Catoctin Mountains. They rolled on through the lush, green valleys and ridges in the stifling heat of this mid-September morning. The names on the rural mailboxes they passed testified to the area's German heritage, and the landmarks and historical markers spoke to its American Revolutionary War and Civil War history.

"And why is this Gardner guy at Fort Detrick, a military facility?" Chip Reed persisted.

Nuggets! Oscar Bentley, the veteran, mused. Nuggets. That was what they called all newly-trained CIA agents. They had promise. But they were worthless until shaped in the forges and fires of experience.

"Because that's where USAMRIID is located," Oscar said. "And that's where Rusty Gardner works."

"Ahhh. U-S-A-M-R-I-I-D. I know that one." Chip Reed reeled it off. "United States Army Medical Research Institute of Infectious Diseases."

"Right. It's the U.S.'s—and arguably the world's—premier laboratory for studying the medical aspects of biological weapons. It's only been around for about thirty years."

Oscar glanced at the red bi-plane crop duster about a mile off to his right. It swept down a row of soy beans, let loose its steamy cloud of pesticides, then climbed on its tail and made a sharp 180- degree turn to get ready for its next pass. A group of farm workers stood well back by the roadside, arms crossed, staring at the plane in silence.

Oscar looked back to the lean, fresh-faced youth sitting next to him, then down at his own growing paunch. He had to admit he'd lost a step or two in the past few years. The gray hairs and wrinkles were piling up as well. And he knew some of the younger guys—probably his partner as well—had started referring to him as 'Pappy' behind his back. He didn't mind the label. It was a lot better than the one he'd picked up in Vietnam.

"So how do you know this Gardner guy?" Reed asked. He tore open a candy bar and began chewing on it.

"We go back a long way. To Nam, in fact. We were there together. He was a young battalion surgeon. I was a green Army chopper pilot. Then, after graduate work in microbiology at Berkeley, I was assigned to Fort Detrick to work with him on the development of an anthrax vaccine for military use. We hit it off immediately. He invited me to a weekly poker game he and his lab buddies held every Friday night. They smelled fresh meat! But I walked away a winner every time. The key to poker is in the betting, buddy boy, not in the playing."

Reed was impatient. "Come on Pappy—I mean Oscar. How did this guy get so smart about biological weapons?"

In '95, I was detailed to UNSCOM…"

"…United Nations Special Commission. It sent the U.N. inspection teams into Iraq after the Gulf War to look for chemical and biological weapons."

Oscar was pleasantly surprised. "You know about that, huh? My job was to recruit, then lead, the BW team. Naturally, I thought of Rusty. At my request the Army assigned him to me. For the next two years we were all over Iraq, poking around in every nook and cranny, every goddam tent and yurt, looking for BW or the equipment used to make it. But the buggers had either hidden it or destroyed it; we couldn't tell which. We tried to go back in '98 and have another look. But they kicked us out. The U.N. just stood by and allowed them to do it. God was I pissed."

"Anyway, during all our travels together I got to know Rusty Gardner even better. I also had access to his Military Service Record and saw what an amazing guy he was: M.D. and Ph.D. degrees from Harvard; an M.P.H. degree from Yale; board-certified in both Infectious Diseases and Public Health; about a hundred military decorations and citations. Including the Silver Star."

"Really? That's like the second-highest award, isn't it? Where'd he get that one? Nam?"

Oscar nodded, closed his eyes, and allowed the scenes to build in his memory. "He was in a Huey on the way from a Battalion Aid Station to a Field Hospital, hitching a ride with a young captain, a rifle company commander. It should have been a routine mission. But the chopper developed hydraulic trouble less than half-way there. They tried for the nearest Landing Zone. Unfortunately, the infantry company defending the L-Z was engaged in a nasty firefight with NVA regulars. The L-Z was extremely narrow, barely wide enough for the chopper's skids. The nervous pilot missed it, the chopper oscillated briefly from one skid to the other, then went slipping, sliding and somersaulting down into the jungle and the fighting."

Reed watched him. He had the last of his candy and stuffed the wrapper into the ash tray.

"Rusty survived the roll-over with only a few bruises and minor cuts. But everyone else was all busted up. The pilot was dead, the co-pilot had a head wound, a broken arm and three broken ribs, and the young captain had a leg so badly shattered that the bone was sticking out. In addition to several broken ribs, and a head wound bleeding all over him. One of the waist gunners was unconscious, the other one was relatively intact. But he was the only one other than Gardner able to fight and defend their Huey.

"Rusty was stunned at first, unable to believe this was happening to him. He had barely three months left on his tour of duty. What finally snapped him into action, he told me over a beer many years later, was the sound of the Huey's mini-gun going off next to his ear." Oscar snorted. "That'll get your attention in a hurry, really rattle your brains, I can tell you!"

"What did Gardner do?"

"That's Colonel Gardner to you, buddy boy," Oscar said, but with a smile. "Since action was preferable to just sitting there, he looked to the nearest wounded man, the young captain, put a pressure dressing on his open fracture, splinted the leg, gave him some morphine, and started an IV. He moved to the co-pilot, got some portable oxygen flowing on him, started an IV, and covered him with a blanket. He continued to treat the wounded and check the other bodies for signs of life.

"Between patients, he even found an M-16 and started blazing away at the advancing enemy. Fortunately, other gunships arrived and held the NVA back until rescuers could hack their way through the jungle and reach them."

"That's a hell of a story," Chip Reed said. "Is it really true?"

Oscar held up his right hand. "As God is my witness."

"How do you know so much about it? From his Service Record?"

"No, from real life. I was the Huey's co-pilot. Rusty Gardner saved my ass." Oscar chuckled. "And that's where I got my handle."

"You mean your call sign?"

"Correct. You don't choose it. It's assigned to you by the rest of the guys in the squadron."

"What was yours?"

"Bullethead."

"Bullethead!"

"When Rusty got me back to the field hospital, he X-rayed my noggin. A piece of bullet-shaped shrapnel was embedded in the bone, right here." He thumped his head above his right ear.

"But there was no harm done? You were alright?"

"Yeah. Except for the scalp wound, which was stitched up. But the surgeons decided to leave the shrapnel where it was. It was too risky to go after."

"'You're just gonna have to live with it,' Rusty told me. What could I do? 'Just call me bullethead,' I said. And it stuck. 'Bullethead Bentley it is,' Gardner said."

"And you couldn't change it?" Reed asked.

"The more I protested, the harder it stuck."

"You must be a lot of fun to watch going through airport security checks."

"Oh, yeah." He thumped his head again.

Oscar heard his stomach growl. "Let's find a place for lunch. I'm hungry."

They pulled off at the next exit and started checking out local eateries.

"So, what else?"

"What, about Gardner? Well, when the UNSCOM mission to Iraq collapsed, Gardner was re-assigned to work on anthrax again at Fort Detrick. He's become the world's expert on BW, especially anthrax."

They had stopped at a small roadside diner and were getting ready to order.

"A regular army type, huh?" Reed asked. "A lifer?"

"Was. He retired as a full colonel a couple of years ago, but the Army kept him on as a civilian researcher and consultant on BW agents. He's still the top advisor on anthrax research to USAMRIID. He pioneered using recombinant DNA technology to make better vaccines and faster ways to diagnose BW agents.

Most of his effort has been aimed at military applications. But some of that basic research applies to civilian populations as well."

Reed was wolfing down his cheeseburger, french fries and soda. "That all you havin'?"

Oscar stared at his thin soup and salad. "Gotta get my cholesterol down."

"So, when you headed the UNSCOM team in Iraq, what did you find?"

Oscar wiped his glasses with a napkin. "Those bastards were awash in biological weaponry. And I'm as sure as I'm sitting here that they were prepared to use them against our troops, against the Israeli's, or against anybody else they took a disliking to."

"Yeah? How were they going to do that?"

"Christ, buddy boy, don't you read the briefing papers?" Oscar spooned his soup then shoved it away.

"The Iraqi's had started serious BW research and production as early as 1985 at Salmon Pak, a laboratory near Baghdad. Anthrax was their principal agent, and by '89 we estimated they had 8000 liters of the stuff in slurry form. Since each milliliter holds about a billion spores, and since it only takes 5000-8000 spores to kill a person—well, you do the math. Anyhow, they used 6000 liters of the slurry to fill various weapons and stored the rest of it at their Al Hakam plant on the Euphrates."

"How were they going to deliver the spores to their targets?"

Oscar waited until a counterman had moved out of earshot. "They bought about 800 SCUD missiles from the Russians. They were deployed in railway tunnels and at sites along the Tigris. At least two of the missiles were loaded with anthrax spores. They also had airplane-loaded bombs with spore payloads."

Reed stopped eating.

"Got your attention, huh? Saddam had also purchased several hundred Italian-made pesticide sprayers, originally designed for agricultural use. But the Iraqis modified them for the anthrax slurry and fitted them under aircraft wings or attached them to land vehicles."

"What finally happened?" Reed asked, as they walked back to the car. "Did the Iraqis ever use any of their BW weapons?"

"No. Saddam was terrified we would retaliate with nuclear weapons if he did. And we would have. Nuked him back to neolithic times. And in the end, we won the Gulf War, we kicked their butts! When it was all over, the U.N. ordered the Iraqis to destroy their BW stores and dismantle the plants. When Dave and I first snooped around in '95 and '96, most of the missiles had been destroyed. Ditto the spores at Salman Pak. As for the equipment, that was a different story. They claimed they were using it for legitimate vaccine development and other peaceful purposes. The U.N. wimped out and bought this bullshit."

"Do you think they have any BW capability left? Could they have re-stocked their depots?"

Oscar looked around. They were alone except for a woman buckling her toddler into her car. She was out of hearing. "That's the big question, isn't it, buddy boy? Since the UNSCOM inspection teams were kicked out two years ago, we have no way of knowing. Satellite imaging, an occasional spy plane mission, and a couple of deep cover agents on the ground are all the intelligence resources we have left. That's it. The Iraqis could be armed to the teeth again with BW agents and we would be none the wiser."

"Christ!" Reed had finally begun to see the bigger picture. He tore open another candy bar.

"Gimme."

"What?"

"Gimme the candy bar. You saw my lunch."

"What about your cholesterol?"

"Fuck it. Gimme."

The young agent was silent for the rest of the trip, and Oscar was content to leave it at that. Let his partner handle this new information while he let his candy bar digest and caught a few zzz's.

When he awoke, they were just pulling into the USAMRIID parking lot.

"Bullethead, you old spook!" Dave Gardner smiled and stuck out his hand. "How in the hell are you?"

"Hi, Rusty. How ya been?"

"Y'all played any poker lately?"

"Gave it up long ago. Same for drinking and chasing women."

The two men shook hands in the doorway of Gardner's office. Oscar noted his friend's closely-trimmed salt-and-pepper beard, a recent addition. But the cool eyes were the same.

"When are you gonna give up the cloak and dagger stuff and get a real job, Oscar?" Gardner led them towards a small table in the middle of a well-appointed office. Walls and shelves were covered with photographs, diplomas, certificates and other memorabilia from a lifetime of medical adventure.

Oscar introduced Chip Reed then studied his old friend. Over six feet tall, Gardner stood ramrod straight, his belly as flat as a frying pan, his gait as springy as a cadet on the drill field. He remembered his friend's life-long credo: 'die young…as late in life as possible.' One look told Oscar he still practiced what he preached. Though sixty-one years old, his sandy graying hair—which he still wore soldier short—hadn't receded from when Oscar worked with him twenty years ago in this very building. He still looked every bit the military man.

"The beard's new," Oscar said.

"Yeah. I figured it went with my suits and ties."

"You'll always be Army green to me, Rusty."

Gardner nodded, eyes serious, catching the respect in Oscar's words. "Thanks."

There was a fourth person in the room. She waited patiently for introductions. Oscar might be paunchy and grey, but his observing powers were still acute. He studied her as she offered her hand. Auburn hair, lips a little pouty, lovely eyes that caught the sun streaming in through the blinds. No wedding ring, but no white band of flesh either. Divorced, but it had been a while.

"Put your eyeballs back in your head, Oscar," Rusty said. "Tara Martin, I'd like you to meet an old friend and comrade in arms, Oscar Bentley."

"Hello, Oscar—or should I say Bullethead?"

Her smile washed over him. But there was a sadness to it, some hidden tug. Divorced for sure. He winked at Gardner. "Someone's been talking out of school." He grinned at her and shook her hand.

Rusty sat down at the table. "Tara's a top epidemiologist. She's senior EIS at CDC, so don't go snortin' about security."

"If you say so, Rusty." But he looked at his friend, eyes questioning.

"Her ex is an E.R. doc in L.A."

Oscar relaxed. No husband, even better for security. "Nice to know you, Tara." She wore a gold pin, elegant against her business suit. Oscar guessed she had bought it for herself. Divorce was hell.

Agent Reed nudged Oscar. "EIS?"

"Epidemic Intelligence Service. A branch of ops at CDC."

"You name it, we've done it, Agent Reed," Tara said. "Legionaire's, AIDS, ebola, hanta virus. We monitor infectious disease trends around the world. And investigate outbreaks whenever called."

Gardner was ready to get down to business. He looked at his old friend over the tops of his half-lens reading glasses. "Alright, Oscar, show us what's gotten you worked up."

The veteran CIA agent laid out a stack of photographs. "These are satellite reconaissance images of northern Afghanistan taken over the past week." He turned them over one by one. "Nothing out of the ordinary so far. The National Reconaissance Office— the NRO, they run our spy satellites—images this area regularly, even at night with infra-red cameras. Normally they don't see much. Maybe some local movement through these mountain passes." He pointed to some green dots. "Like here...and here."

"But these were what really got their attention." He turned over another series of photos. "See, here...and here...and again here, see these specs heading westward out of the mountains? This is not just local movement to and fro. Here they are again, crossing through northern Iran. And finally here, coming out of the mountains into northern Iraq. When they saw these images, the guys at NRO sent them to the experts at the National Photographic Interpretation Center—the NPIC—for analysis."

Chip Reed picked up the briefing, since this was the technical part of the job he most enjoyed and had been trained for. "When the pros at NPIC first noticed this, they asked NRO to re-program some of their satellites to provide round-the-clock surveillance of the area. That's when they discovered that this little group moved only at night, and only along poorly-traveled roads through remote passes. They never stopped for more than a few hours, and never anywhere even slightly inhabited."

Gardner set down his half-glasses. "What have we been dealt here, old friend?"

Oscar grunted. "*Al-Qaeda* terrorists. I'd double any bet on it you'd care to make. And the folks at NPIC can't come up with any other explanation either."

"Where y'all think they're headin'?" Gardner asked. "And why?"

"Must be to some place very important to draw them out of their Pakistani lairs."

"That's only part of the story," Chip Reed added. "Our sources inside Iraq have sniffed out a lot of movement going on there over the past few days also. Particularly by Iraq's top scientists. It looks like they're all heading for the same place, the town of Mosul"— he pointed to the map—"here in the north on the Tigris River."

"Doc," Oscar said to his friend Gardner, "we ran into some of these same bastards during our tour with UNSCOM. You should remember them." He read off a list of names.

Gardner whistled. "How could I forget those guys, the way they stone-walled us when we pressed 'em for information about their anthrax research." Gardner looked down the list of names. "These were the ones who developed Iraq's BW program before the Gulf War. I always thought they'd float to the surface sooner or later. Like bilge in sea water."

"It's my bet they're back up to their necks in BW."

"This one"—Gardner pointed to another name—"was their top anthrax guy at Salman Pak, wasn't he?"

"Right."

Gardner looked worried. "Oscar, what's going on here? Some of the world's worst bad guys and Iraq's entire BW team all headin' for the same place? Obviously for a get-together. But for what purpose?"

Oscar grunted. "We don't know. And why would *al-Qaeda* agents travel all the way from Pakistan under cover of darkness, then attend a meeting in a major city? Why not just meet at a secure hiding place, maybe somewhere outside the city up in the Kurdish Hills?"

Gardner shook his head. "This is bad. There must be something *in* Mosul they all want to see, something that's drawin' 'em there like flies to fly paper."

"That's how we figure it," Oscar agreed. "But what? We never uncovered any evidence of BW production or research in Mosul; that all went on further south, around Baghdad. And neither our ground assets nor the satellites have detected even a whiff of new BW activity going on in the north at this time. We're in the dark on this one."

They sat silent, thinking, turning over the photos again, searching for any detail, any scrap of information which might have been overlooked. Tara stayed out of it. This was not her area of expertise. She doodled quietly on a legal pad. Finally, Gardner got up, took off his jacket and leaned against the back of his chair. His chronic backache had started up again, and the stretch felt good. He glanced out the window and had a stab of nostalgia for his boyhood home in Virginia's Shenandoah Valley, and for the hikes with his father up on the Blue Ridge Mountains.

"Y'all remember, Oscar," he said, removing his glasses, "when we were in UNSCOM, we focused like snake-eyes on the military aspects of biological warfare? This stinks the same, but I think the turd's different. Sorry, Tara. This is a brand new game called bio-terrorism, a whole new gig for us."

Tara was ready. "But there are projections about the effects of bioterrorism on the U.S." She looked at Oscar. "Are you familiar with the 1970 WHO report?"

"Of course." He knew it well, had in fact studied it extensively and could recite its salient points from memory: "fifty kilograms of anthrax spores are released upwind of a city with 500,000 people, perhaps by a crop duster or maybe a pilotless drone. 125,000 people become ill, 95,000 of them die."

Tara nodded. "That's about right. It was that report which finally galvanized our government to develop an anthrax vaccine for military use."

"Rusty, didn't you model some BW scenarios yourself here at Fort Detrick?" Oscar said.

"Yup, but it was very limited. In our game we looked at bio-terrorist attacks on three large cities, the spores introduced via the air vents of the subway systems. We estimated several hundred thousand people would be exposed in each case. We also looked at a scenario where the spores were sprayed upwind of San Francisco. In that case, the entire city got a lethal dose."

Everyone at the table knew these 'models' were purely hypotheticals, 'what ifs.'

"I know that study," Oscar said. "It speculated there would be a high death toll, made worse by communication failures, turf battles between the various public health agencies, failure of the city's ER physicians to diagnose the disease early, inadequate stores of vaccine and antibiotics, and inefficient use of medical resources."

Tara nodded. "And that scenario was confirmed to some degree by the spate of anthrax cases in 2001."

"Refresh our memories, Tara," Gardner said. "How many cases were there?"

"Twenty-four total, of which eleven were inhalational, thirteen cutaneous. Five of the pulmonary cases died."

"All related in some way to the postal system, right?"

"Right. Although in a couple, that link was never conclusively proven."

Gardner persisted. "Certainly that recent experience has made our physicians better in diagnosin' the disease?"

"To some degree," she said. "They'd get it right. But it would take a while; they'd miss some cases at first. But it's not their fault. After all, prior to those few 2001 cases—all on the east coast—there had been less than one U.S. case of anthrax reported per year for twenty years. And even those occurred sporadically, and were almost always of the skin variety, usually in farm workers who had direct contact with ill or dead animals, or in industrial workers processing highly contaminated animal fibers, especially goat hair. Before that, you have to go back to a 1976 case from imported Pakistani wool."

Gardner shook his head. "This ain't good."

"Ironically," Tara continued, sunlight gleaming off her amber hair, "foreign physicians have had much more experience than we have. In Africa, anthrax epidemics in cattle occur regularly, often closely followed by human outbreaks. The largest of these, in Zimbabwe in 1979 and again in 1985, caused ten thousand human cases, mostly of the skin variety. But in Chad in 1988 an outbreak in donkeys caused over seven hundred human cases, with 88 deaths from the pulmonary and gastrointestinal forms of the disease."

A pall of silence descended on the room, broken only when Gardner asked his old friend, "Oscar where do we go from here?"

"I'm not sure, Rusty."

"I've got a bad feelin' about this. Those *al-Qaeda* boys just don't know when to quit. Cut off one head, another pops up."

"What do you mean?" Tara asked.

"Take the WTC attack on September 11, 2001. That was the second attempt to blow the towers up."

Oscar nodded. "That's right. The first was what—February, 1993? They tried with a car bomb. But it failed. So, eight years later they flew two airplanes into them."

"And remember the *Cole*? Blown open in a Yemen harbor in October, 2000?"

"How could I forget," Tara said.

"Well that was also a second attempt to kill our servicemen in Yemen. The first was in 1992. At the Gold Mohur Hotel there. The target was over 100 U.S. troops. But our guys had just left for duty in Somalia when it blew. Two hotel workers and five tourists were killed."

Tara put down her pad and eyed Gardner. "Let me get this straight. You think those anthrax-by-mail cases were a fizzled first attempt? And *al-Qaeda* is gearing up for something bigger? Something connected with this new information Oscar's shown us?"

Gardner said nothing. But his face was grim. He turned to Oscar. "Can we get any more information from the satellites or from your Iraqi agents on the ground?"

"We'll keep trying, of course. But that may be tough."

Tara looked up from her doodling. "We should notify the Office of Homeland security."

"Of course." Oscar rubbed his chin. "And the FBI. I know just the man there."

"I'll contact the National Institute of Allergy and Infectious Diseases," Tara volunteered. "Get the current recommendations for treating anthrax infections. Dave, what about the Surgeon General's office?"

"I'll handle that one," Gardner replied. "I know the Deputy SG personally. She's perfect."

"Let's meet again in a week," Oscar suggested.

Everyone agreed.

But Tara wasn't finished. "What about the White House. Shouldn't they also be included?"

Gardner shook his head. "Nope, I don't think so, Tara, not yet. We still have very little to go on except our suspicions. And if we're wrong, our careers could become as rough as a stucco bathtub. Besides, we might be all wet on this. I don't want to cause a false alarm."

Tara's eyes flashed and she stuck out her jaw. "I wish there had been more of a sense of alarm about terrorism in this country the day before the terrorists hit the World Trade Center in New York. Our guard was down. It was disgraceful."

The tension between her and Gardner was measureable. They were eyeball to eyeball and neither would blink.

"Alright, then," Oscar said, sensing that now was a good time to stand up and head for the door. "We'll see you all in a week or so."

Gardner patted his old friend on the back as he departed. "Call me immediately if you develop any new leads, Bullethead."

"That's affirmative, Rusty."

As Oscar left he wondered about Tara's fire, her guts. Maybe her ex-husband hadn't been strong enough. Anyway, it was none of his business.

"She's a looker, Oscar," Agent Reed said.

"Leave it alone, junior," was all Oscar said.

6

"The doctor's character
Can influence the patient's recovery
More than any medicine."

Paracelsus (1493-1541)
Medieval chemist and physician

In West Los Angeles the cloud cover was finally clearing. Freeway traffic was light but steady. It was Sunday, Gil Martin's day off. At least partially. His ER shift didn't start until that evening. Usually he would begin a day like this not as most people do, with coffee and the morning papers. Instead, he would read the back of a tomato juice can while he finished off the first of two or three Bloody Marys. Then he would loll about his apartment, maybe wolfing down a sandwich with a couple of beers for lunch, until it was time to get ready for work.

But today was different, very different. For one thing, he had awakened with an erection. He couldn't recall the erotic dream which had produced it, but he was both surprised and grateful. It demonstrated he wasn't completely dead down there after all. Or maybe it was just the changing weather which had raised his spirits and his dick. Sunshine replaced the clouds and plastered the walls of his drab living room. Or perhaps it was the birthday card he received from his daughter yesterday. It evoked a mental picture of her standing in his doorway right now, fresh-faced, wide-eyed and innocent. Or maybe it was the interesting patient he had seen last night—Achmed—which had aroused his professional libido from dormancy. Whatever the reason, he felt something today he had not felt in a very long time: a lust for life and for work again.

As he sipped strong, black coffee, his thoughts returned again and again to Achmed. Like an itch under an orthopedic cast, the questions he had left the ER with last night kept coming back. The first one, how the man had contracted anthrax— anthrax, for chrissakes! he still couldn't believe it—was the most intriguing of all. Since he had nothing better planned for the day, he decided to do a little snooping around on his own.

He started by calling the Los Angeles County Health Department. He wanted to know if there had been other anthrax cases reported recently. Was this another flare-up of mailroom bioterrorism? He'd read nothing about it in the morning newspaper. Besides, Achmed hadn't even been in this country until a few days ago. It didn't add up. Must be just a solitary case of contaminated wool or wool products. But what kind?

Ten minutes on the phone to the health department got him only a voice mail menu which, when he punched the number for 'Epidemiology,' produced a sharp statement that today was Sunday and the office was closed. It was followed by an admonition to hang up and dial 911 if this was a medical emergency.

Undaunted, he logged onto the Air France web site, navigated his way to the flight schedules, and discovered that Achmed's flight, AF 62, was a daily non-stop Paris-to-Los Angeles run. Next he tried the phone number for the Air France business office in L.A. He wanted to get the passenger and crew manifest for AF Flight 62 on the day Achmed had been aboard. All he got was another voice message.

While he waited on the phone, he doodled on a scratch pad. Circles, interconnecting circles running to the edge of pad. Sometimes, when he was pissed, it was sharp, ugly slashes forming rectangles and triangles. Today it was just circles.

He tried another tack. He phoned the U.S Customs office at LAX. Representing himself as a 'public health official' (sort of true, right?), he was put through to the duty supervisor. The man assured him that although the records for that AF 62 flight were not readily available, it was routine for the luggage of all foreign visitors—especially any who might appear to be of Middle-Eastern ethnicity—to be thoroughly inspected. Since the 2001 WTC disaster, racial profiling had returned to the Customs Service's manual of standard operating procedures.

"In fact, sir," the supervisor added, "we recently received a notice to be on the lookout for raw wool and other sheep products coming in from Middle Eastern countries."

"Found any?"

"No, sir. And I would know if we had."

"What about the passengers themselves?"

"What do you mean?"

"Suppose any had raw wool in his carry-on luggage or on his person?"

"We would find it and confiscate it."

"Hmmm."

"Is there anything else, sir?"

"Suppose a passenger looked ill, what would you do?"

"We would quarantine him—or her—and send him for a medical evaluation."

"There's no doubt about that?"

"No sir. Our procedures have gotten much tighter. Nothing like you're talking about would slip by us."

Gil had come to a dead end it seemed. Leaning back in his chair, he let his eyes fix on the pile of clutter on his desk. Achmed's hotel room key edged out from it. He'd forgotten about it. Still itching with a curiosity he hadn't known since medical school, he stared at it until he had a semblance of a plan. There were risks, but the potential benefits were large.

He drove to Achmed's hotel, by-passed the front desk and elevator banks and took the stairs. No one was around. He donned a pair of latex gloves and slipped into Achmed's room. He placed the 'Do Not Disturb' sign on the outside doorknob, put on the surgical mask he had brought, and looked around the room.

At first glance, there appeared to be little of interest: one small piece of luggage, probably a carry-on. There was neither a claim ticket nor a name and address label attached to it. The bag was open and contained only cheap, casual clothes, mostly cotton or cotton-polyester mixes. Made in Turkey, according to the labels. No woolens. Similar clothing was hanging in the closet.

He turned to the smaller flight bag. Its contents seemed equally unpromising: some reading material in French, a Mickey Mouse cap from Disneyland, a cheap 35mm camera, some toiletry items, and a well-worn copy of the Koran with Achmed's name printed on the inside cover. As he thumbed through the holy book, a Turkish Airlines boarding pass stub fell out. It was for a flight from VAN Airport to Paris on the same day as Achmed's Paris-to-LA flight. Gil didn't have a clue where VAN Airport was. But at least it was clear now that Achmed had not started his journey in France but from somewhere else. From Van. Wherever that was.

He fished through the flight bag again, hoping to find a return airline ticket. There wasn't one, and he'd found none in Achmed's clothes at the hospital either. That seemed odd, a foreign visitor with a one-way ticket.

As he turned to go, he rewound the film in the camera, popped it out, and slipped it into his pocket along with his mask and gloves. Retracing his steps, he left the hotel without raising suspicion. A wicked little shiver ran up his spine as he made his getaway. This must be how cat burglars felt, at least the successful ones.

It was late in the afternoon, but still two hours before his ER shift began. He dropped the film off at a fast photo developer and waited for the prints. They turned out to be just bad pictures of Disneyland sites, rides, and crowds. Typical tourist stuff. He put them into his pocket then did something quite extraordinary. He went to work early. Early.

Ten miles away at UCLA Medical Center an ambulance, emergency lights still flashing, pulled into the ER entrance. Scrub-suited personnel scrambled to assist the EMT's who were giving chest compressions and mechanical ventilations to a middle-aged woman. It was Saundra Williams, the Seat 15D passenger on Air France's Flight 62. Achmed's airplane neighbor.

According to her husband, Saundra had first become sick two days ago with mild symptoms of a URI. But the illness had worsened to a deep cough, raspy breathing and a high fever. Alarmed, the man took her to their family physician yesterday. He diagnosed pneumonia and started her on antibiotics and a full-liquid diet, intending to see her again in twenty-four to forty-eight hours.

She seemed slightly better this morning, her husband said, but as the day progressed she deteriorated swiftly. When he last checked on her, she was unresponsive, ashen in color and breathing hard. He called 911 immediately.

She was admitted from the ER directly to the Intensive Care Unit, with a diagnosis of septic shock from bacteria yet to be identified. They were reported by the lab technician as blue rods in two's, three's and longer chains.

To add to the Williams family's distress, the rest of them seemed to be coming down with bad colds themselves.

When he got to the hospital, Gil headed straight for the laboratory. It was quiet, not much going on. Luis Gonzales had taken a couple of days off. Phil Byrd, the senior technician, was on duty and greeted him with a wave.

"Anything growing yet?" Gil assumed Byrd had been briefed about Achmed's case.

"It's been thirty-six hours since we plated the blood cultures. This is what we have so far." He held up two petri dishes. There was visible, heavy growth on both.

"Anthrax?"

"Yes. I stained a colony from one of them. There's no question about it."

"You're certain about this?"

"Yup. I snapped some photographs of the plates themselves and photomicrographs of the stains." He handed Gil several rolls of film.

"Thanks." Gil turned to go. It was time for his shift to begin.

"By the way, doc," the lab tech said, "I hear your patient's going to make it."

"I'm on my way to see him now. He's in ICU?"

"Right."

Gil was gratified to see Achmed looking better. His color was more toward pink than blue now, though he was still breathing rapidly. The telemetric data on the monitor at the nursing station showed that the rest of his vital signs were better too.

"How's he doing?" Gil asked the R.N.

"He's out of shock. And his temperature has come down."

"Has he said anything yet?"

"Not really. We've occasionally gotten a few words out of him, but they were unintelligible to us."

"Were they in French? The man was carrying a French passport when I admitted him."

"No. One of the interns is fluent in French. He couldn't understand it either. He thinks it's some middle eastern dialect." She looked at Gil. "You don't speak Persian do you, doc?"

He chuckled. "Are you kidding? I barely speak English." He started to leave. "Let me know if he gets more communicative, will you?"

Gil returned to his load of patients, thankfully light tonight, still so preoccupied with Achmed's case that he had trouble concentrating on the routine 'nickel and dime' ones. What brought him out of it was Kerry Summers, the other R.N., tugging at his elbow.

"We've got another sick one, doc." She handed him a clipboard.

This time the staff had anticipated him. The patient was already hooked up to a cardiac monitor, oxygen was flowing through a face mask, and an IV was in place in the patient's left forearm. X-ray and lab had been called and were on their way.

The patient's name, the record stated, was Suzette Marie Kelley. Her occupation: Flight Attendant.

Gil put down the clipboard and looked at her. She was petite, very pretty, and very sick. A good-looking young man was sitting at the head of the bed holding her hand.

"And who are you?" Gil asked.

"Dennis McCarthy." He looked frightened. "Her...her...friend."

"When did your friend first become ill?"

"About two days ago. We thought it was just a cold." He held a handkerchief to his face to catch a sudden sneeze.

"Gezundheit!" Gil said automatically.

The man smiled weakly. "Must be getting something myself."

Gil auscultated Suzette's lungs. Pleural fluid again. Just like Achmed. That was odd. Two cases within forty-eight hours. Both in young, robust people. Suzette's throat was red, her nose raw and runny, and she had conjunctivitis as well.

"But this morning," the boyfriend went on, "she refused to eat anything. I went to a drug store for some cold pills. When I got back, she was so drowsy I could hardly arouse her. That's when I called 911."

"Why didn't you take her to someone sooner?"

The man lowered his head. "Doctor, this was just a—you know, a fling, a fun way to spend a long lay-over between flights. It's pretty common in the airline business. I thought she would get better. When she didn't, I got scared." He looked up, his eyes red and puffy. "I'm married."

Gil nodded. He asked him to have a seat in the waiting area then continued examining Suzette. When he tried to turn her head, her neck was so stiff her whole body turned with it. She moaned in pain.

"Oh, oh! Kerri," he said to the nurse, "you'd better set up for a spinal tap."

"It's cloudy," he announced when the first few drops of milky spinal fluid dripped out of Suzette's back into a test tube. "Meningitis. Kerri, everyone who comes in here wears gowns, gloves and masks from now on."

He handed the specimens to the lab tech. "All the usual tests," he ordered, "including a stain."

He pulled off his gown and gloves, ordered antibiotics for Suzette, and began writing the progress note.

The boyfriend appeared at the doorway, hesitant to enter. Gil waved him in and told him what he knew so far. Intent on his writing, he casually asked the man, "what airlines does she fly for?"

"Air France."

"Air France, did you say?"

The man nodded. "Yes, she has the Paris-to-LAX run twice a week."

"AF Flight 62?" Gil was incredulous.

"Exactly. How did you know?"

Gil's pen had stopped in mid-sentence. He put the clipboard down. "When was her last flight?"

"Three days ago. Why, is that important?"

The same date as Achmed's. They were on the same flight.

He dropped his clipboard, mumbled an apology, then dashed off to the lab.

"Have you got anything on that spinal fluid stain yet?" he yelled, racing through the door.

Phil Byrd was astonished. He'd never seen Dr. Martin this animated, certainly not about a patient.

"Why, sure, doc, I just put it under the 'scope. Haven't even looked at it yet myself. What's the big deal?"

Wordlessly, Gil sat down at the microscope and twisted the focus knob slowly in and out until the image was clear. There they were. Big, blue box cars, some in two's and three's, others in longer chains. Just like Achmed's. Christ!

Then like a punch it hit him. He'd had it all wrong. He'd assumed Achmed had been exposed *before* he boarded the flight from Paris. But Suzette's case changed everything. There must have been something on that flight to which they were both exposed. A 'point source' was the epidemiologic term for it. Epidemiology. For an instant Tara's face shimmered then was gone. But if it was a point source, it meant that others on that flight might have been exposed as well. Might even now be getting sick.

He hurried back to the ER and called the Infectious Disease Unit of L.A. County/U.S.C. Medical Center. The resident physician on call was first incredulous about Gil's clinical diagnosis, then dubious about the bacteriological findings.

"Lab error," he said.

Like most House Officers at high powered medical centers, the resident had little respect for the diagnostic acumen of 'local' physicians like Gil Martin.

But Gil stood his ground and finally got through to the staff physician in charge. The other doctor accepted Suzette for admission. He promised to arrange transport from his end, but it would take an hour or more to complete.

Gil made another call to the County Health Department. This time he wasn't after information; he had some to give. He left a more urgent voice message describing Suzette's case and his belief that something on AF Flight 62 had now caused anthrax in two passengers. Two! He recommended that all other passengers and crew be contacted immediately.

Kathy Roberts, the charge nurse, was waiting for him when he hung up the phone. "This disease—anthrax—I've never seen anything like it before. Now we've had two cases within forty-eight hours. It's pretty scary. It's almost..." She searched for words.

"Biblical?" he volunteered.

"Yes, biblical."

"Well, it's not. It is pretty scary, I agree. But it isn't some supernatural plague out of Genesis; it isn't the Black Death. It's just a disease, like any other. It has a cause and a natural course. It's a little more scary because of how fast it kills. Our job is to stop it before it does."

She looked around the room, worry lines etching her pretty face. "What about the rest of us? Should we start taking something...?"

"Kathy, anthrax is not contagious. There's no risk to the staff."

"Doc, I've got two small children..."

He looked at her hard and no longer saw just a beautiful, efficient nurse in front of him. He now saw her as a worried mother and wife as well. He relented.

"Alright. I'll write orders for all of us to begin prophylactic antibiotics. A 30-day course. Like they used for those anthrax-by-mail contacts in 2001."

She patted his arm and whispered, "Thank you, Gil."

He just nodded but felt a warm rush spread up his body. It wasn't desire but something else. Then he realized he was blushing. He couldn't remember the last time he'd blushed. What was happening to him?

The nurse went back to her duties, leaving him to mull over other questions about the two cases, ones for which he didn't have such ready answers.

I need to talk with someone a lot smarter than I am about this. An Epidemiologist.

And he knew just who that person was. He even had her number. But he put it off. Maybe it was too late in Atlanta. He glanced at the clock: 8:30 p.m. Yes, it was late, but not too late.

He dialed the number. While he waited for the call to go through, he started doodling. This time it was a sailboat, a sloop outlined in soft, broad strokes. Not so much a doodle anymore, but a sketch of a memory. A sunny afternoon on San Francisco Bay, when things were still right between them...

Serendipity drove a wedge of wake across San Francisco Bay, her spinnaker ballooned out and straining to the whip of canvas.

"Bring it in!" Gil yelled.

"Let her run!" Tara cried, her body stiffened out over the gunwale, a sunvisor trapping her auburn hair, her face wind and sea splashed.

Gil watched her, the joy in her taut body as she leaned out. For a moment her wedding ring flashed gold in the sun. He had removed his, along with his class ring, watch and other loose items that could cause trouble while crewing a sailboat. But Tara would not give up her wedding ring.

Serendipity bounded before the wind, her bow driving into the seas. Tara's triumphant cry sounded above the slap of waves and crack of canvas. She had never looked lovelier...

Gil bit his lip as he listened to the phone ringing in Atlanta.

While Gil was getting connected to Atlanta, Fergus Robinson, the ER technician, was also on the phone, a pay phone in the lobby. But his call was to a location much closer than Gil's, the City Desk of the *Los Angeles Times* where his brother-in-law worked as a reporter.

"Manny," he whispered, cupping his hand around the phone, "I've got a story you might be interested in. What's it worth to ya?"

"Tell me what you've got, kid. Then we'll talk money."

After he took Fergus's report—and agreed to a small monetary reward—Manny Reyes immediately called back Gil's ER. The desk clerk confirmed the information he had gotten from Fergus.

The next day, Monday, the following story appeared on page five of the *Times*' 'Metro Section,' below the fold.

> West Los Angeles. Anonymous sources have confirmed two cases of deadly anthrax infection at a West Los Angeles Hospital. Have terrorists struck again? Not likely, hospital officials speculate. These cases are probably related to raw wool or other animal products carrying the anthrax spores. There is no known person-to-person transmission of the disease, and therefore no public health risk. Citing their right of privacy, the hospital is withholding the patients' names.

Reuters News Service picked up the story and immediately distributed it on its web pages and wire service.

Suzette Kelley died at L.A. County Hospital forty-eight hours after being admitted there, despite the heroic efforts of the staff to save her life. The diagnosis of anthrax was confirmed by blood cultures shortly after her death.

7

A pale harvest moon filtered through the grape arbor of Tara Martin's suburban Atlanta home. It should have been a leisurely evening. But her mind was in overdrive following her meeting with Dave Gardner and the CIA man, Oscar Bentley. She tightened her mouth in censure about Oscar. He had looked too closely into her. Maybe that was part of his job but she resented it. Perhaps she had come on too strong with her own comment about the World Trade Center attacks. . .

Tara shoved aside her legal pad with her notes from the National Institute of Allergy and Infectious Diseases. Notes that covered the current recommendations for treating anthrax. She needed to get them to Gardner, but right now she was watching Cassie, her thirteen year old, who had just discovered bras, boys, and new body bulges this year. As well as the principle reason for girlfriends: to have someone other than mom to talk with.

"Cassie, get off the phone! I need it."

But mom and daughter had played this game many times before. Daughter knew she still had a ways to go before mom's patience ran out.

Wordlessly, Pat held up five fingers. Cassie nodded and mom went back to her papers, wondering if she indulged her daughter too much. But Cassie was her only child. She did well in school and knew right from wrong. Wasn't that about as much as any parent had a right to expect? The only flaw she'd seen in her was an inexplicable devotion to her father. She didn't understand it, nor did she try to undermine it. She'd long since gotten over the bitterness of the divorce and was now comfortably content with her life. Professionally fulfilled if romantically lonely.

She went to the kitchen but lingered at the door to her bedroom with its big, empty bed. A twinge of remorse. A twang of regret. The bed was so lonely. Memories of physical love-making appeared then were gone. She caught herself. She'd had many offers for a tumble in that bed since the divorce. She'd turned them all down.

She had continued to work for CDC which, if not the cause, was at least the stimulus for the break-up of her marriage to Gil. When she first applied for a two-year fellowship after internship and her MPH degree, she had no idea she would still be here twelve years later. But she was hooked on it, lured by the excitement of worldwide travel, the magnitude of the problems—often worldwide in scope—and the chance to make a difference on a grand scale. When disagreements with Gil became a rift, which led to a schism, then to a chasm, and finally to a divorce, she steeled herself against further romantic entanglements and dedicated herself to her career and to raising her daughter as a single mother.

She remembered the tension her move to Ann Arbor, Michigan had caused with Gil...

"Michigan," he said quietly. "What's there?"

"A Doctorate in Public Health."

"How long will that take?"

"Three years."

He said nothing.

"Then back to Atlanta," she said.

"And Cassie? What about her?"

"The schools are excellent in Ann Arbor. She'll make new friends."

"Yeah?"

Her temper flared. "Gil, what difference does it make? Atlanta or Ann Arbor. We never see you as it is. What's the big deal?"

He remained silent.

When she was calm, she said, "I've accepted a regular commission in the Public Health Service."

"So you won't be coming back this way, will you?"

It was her turn to say nothing...

Since her doctorate, she'd had many assignments, had traveled extensively during her CDC career. But for Cassie's sake she had always maintained her home in Atlanta. Now a senior, supervising EIS agent with a pay grade equal to a Navy Commander or an Army Lieutenant Colonel, her most recent project had been to assist local health officials recognize and begin control measures for West Nile Encephalitis, a disease new to the Western Hemisphere in 1999.

She looked at the clock over the mantel and fumed. "Cassie, that's enough. Off the phone."

When mom used her nickname with that tone of voice, Cassandra knew she was near the edge. But there might be a teeny amount still to go. She had to try for it.

"Mom, please! It's Joanna. She's heard the new boy in school is sooo cool! He's a French foreign exchange student named Alain. He's, like, totally cute, and he starts classes tomorrow." She held up two fingers, pleading with her eyes.

Tara shook her head. "Now!" she ordered. Mom's line had finally been crossed.

Minutes after her daughter hung up, Tara received in quick succession two phone calls herself, one from the EIS agent in New York, another from a colleague in Chicago. Their reports were shocking. Her third call was even more professionally disturbing and personally unnerving.

***

"Hello, Tara."

His words spun down the wire and touched her with more memories. She hated it, she fought it, but it always happened. "You sound sober, Gil." Fight back.

"How are you?"

"What is it Gil? This month's child support check coming late? A plea not to report you to the D.A.'s office, again?"

The words spun down, steady and trying for calm. But he wasn't calm. She knew him too well. But he was trying. At some primitive level it unnerved her.

"The check will be there on time this month. And from now on. But that's not why I called."

Tara swallowed, casting around. "Cassie's asleep. Tomorrow is a school day and—"

"No. Listen to me. I'll talk with her tomorrow and thank her for the birthday card—"

"She sent you—"

"Tara, I need your advice."

His words poured out. They rang with tension.

"What?"

"Anthrax. I need your advice on anthrax. I've just diagnosed two new cases."

"Jesus, Gil." She held back her own work, the phonecalls about cases number three and four. "Tell me."

"Both are inhalation cases. One has improved, is hanging on. The other is near death with meningitis. I have positive blood cultures on the first, a strongly suggestive spinal fluid stain on the other."

"Do you still have the blood cultures?"

"Yes, on the first case. Also photographs and photomicrographs of the stains on both cases."

"Could either of them be connected with mailrooms or the U.S. Postal Service?"

"I don't see how. They're both foreigners, don't even have U.S. addresses."

"Did you save any of the original specimens?"

"Yes. Blood, urine and throat swabs on both patients and spinal fluid on the second. But there's more."

"More?" How could there be more!

"The two cases are related. They were both on the same Paris-to-L.A. flight just before they got sick. I'm convinced there's a source of anthrax spores somewhere on that aircraft. Or maybe someplace in the Paris airport. Perhaps a home-spun wool or goat hair article of clothing. I've tried getting the flight manifest from Air France, but no luck. And I've left messages at our county health department. That's about all I could think of. Anything else I should do?"

"Already you've done a lot."

"Thank you. But there's something else."

"Yes?"

"Both cases had some very unusual symptoms. At least I couldn't find a description of them in the literature. Maybe they're just atypical presentations. I thought you might know."

"What are they?"

He described the URI findings he had noted in both Achmed and Suzette. The runny noses, coughs, sneezing and red eyes. "It's like…like they had bad colds at first. Plain old URIs. Then suddenly died of anthrax."

She sat bolt upright. One of her previous callers had described identical findings. Like her ex-husband, he had also dismissed them as unique to his own case.

Tara considered what she had so far: four cases of inhalational anthrax in foreign visitors reported from three cities. All within forty-eight hours of each other. And three had strange but similar URI findings which didn't match any previously-reported cases she'd read about. And she'd read them all. And all this just when the CIA was ratcheting up its concern about biowarfare and bioterrorism again. It couldn't all be coincidental.

She thought about whether to let Gil in on what else she knew. He could be helpful. And he was trustworthy. Probably. At least when he was sober.

"There's more to this than you know," she said.

"Like what?"

"I'm on a government team looking into anthrax as a bioterrorist agent, and we…"

"Bioterrorism? Again? Who this time?"

"Don't start shouting, you always start shouting and—" She caught herself. "I don't have those answers."

"What do we do now?"

She decided to let him all the way in. "Can you get to Washington, D.C. on Tuesday, the day after tomorrow?"

"I'll have to find some ER coverage, but I can probably arrange it. Why? What's going on there?"

"I'm pulling the emergency cord and calling a meeting of my anthrax working group. I think they should hear directly from you. You've done more than anyone so far. Hell, you've had direct patient contact with this new version of the disease, have actually felt the flesh of it!"

She was taking a chance, inviting him without checking with the others. But never mind that, they needed to hear from him. Besides, there was something else. She had a hard time admitting it, but he sounded different, changed in some way. And she needed to know why. If only to protect herself. Maybe a woman, some woman who had helped straighten him out…

"I'll be there," he said, breaking through her thoughts. "Where should I go?"

She took another risk, a more personal one. "I'll pick you up at your hotel. Call me when you've got your flight schedule and room reservations. And bring everything you can get your hands on: case descriptions, your progress notes, any slides you have, the photos and photomicrographs—bring 'em all."

"Okay."

"Can you think of anything else?"

"What about prophylactic antibiotics?"

"For the other passengers and crew on that Air France flight? Absolutely, as soon as we find out who they are. But it may already be too late. If there were anthrax spores aboard, they've already been exposed and are at great risk of getting sick." She stopped for a moment then asked, "Is there anything else, Gil? I need to move on this."

"Yes, there is. How are you? And tell me about my daughter. How's she doing?"

"We're well, Gil. Later, alright?"

"Alright."

The line clicked dead.

Tara set down the phone and stared at it.

"Was that daddy?" Cassie asked.

"Yes."

"Has he money problems again?"

Tara shook her head. "No, he wanted my advice. Professional stuff."

"Did he get my birthday card?"

"Yes, he did. He'll be talking with you. But right now he's working on something very important."

"You got a bit excited, that stuff about shouting—"

She turned on her daughter. "Cassie, don't you ever listen in on my phone conversations again."

"Hey, okay. Don't get mad—"

"I mean it, Cassie. Ever, you hear me—ever!"

Cassie backed away. "Okay, mom."

"Cassie?"

"What?"

"Your daddy said he loved you."

She nodded, then left the room.

In her bedroom Tara stared again at the massive empty bed. Another woman, was that it? Someone who had succeeded where they had failed? Where *she* had failed? When the tears came she jammed the bedcover against her mouth so Cassie wouldn't hear.

Gil spent the following day in his apartment arranging ER coverage for his absence, getting a last-minute afternoon flight to D.C., making hotel reservations. Next he called the hospital lab and authorized Luis Gonzales to send blood and urine samples from Achmed and Suzette to the health department and to Tara at CDC.

"By the way, doc," Luis added, "we sent sera on Achmed to UCLA for an ELISA test. It was positive. I thought you'd like to know."

"Thanks, Luis. I never had any doubts. Fax a copy of the report to me at home and I'll take it with me to my meeting in D.C."

ELISA was not just the name of an eighteenth century London flower girl—Elisa Doolittle—immortalized in the movie *My Fair Lady.* It was an acronym for "Enzyme-Linked Immunoabsorbent Assay." This daunting mouthful was a test to detect antibodies against a bacteria or its toxin. It could be done rapidly and was highly specific. This positive result, Gil was certain, would convince any remaining naysayers.

He had the hospital's record room fax copies of Achmed's and Suzette's medical records to his apartment. He bundled them up and stowed them in his flight bag.

Finally, he phoned the ICU. ""How's my anthrax case doing? How's Achmed?"

"Better," the charge nurse answered. "And by the way, what he was babbling before was in Farsi, an Arabian dialect."

"Really? How'd you find out?"

"One of the food service workers is Iranian. She heard him when she delivered his tray and knew exactly what it was."

"Has he said anything more?"

"Actually, no. In fact, now that we have an interpreter, he's clammed up, defiantly so. Hasn't uttered another word."

Gil nodded. *Now what was this all about?*

To the nurse he merely added, "Thanks. I'll check with you later."

By early afternoon he was packed, had informed Tara where he would be staying in D.C., and was on his way to LAX.

He hadn't had a drink all day. Or the day before. He looked at his fingernails. The bleeding had stopped.

Tara spent her day on the phone and at her CDC computer. Other case reports were coming in now. In additon to the four from last night, Philadelphia, Denver and Washington, D.C. had reported cases. She had seven in all, in six major U.S. cities. The other members of her group—Oscar and Dave Gardner—agreed this was not just coincidence. They arranged to meet the next day. For ease of travel, a government conference room in downtown Washington, D.C. was selected.

She briefed her own bosses at CDC and invited a couple of other staffers to tomorrow's meeting. Then she alerted—by flash e-mail traffic—the nation's principal epidemiologic laboratories. They were to get ready to analyze biologic specimens for possible anthrax, including ELISA and PCR testing. In 1999 Congress had allocated $121 million to expand and upgrade this laboratory system. Tara hoped it would prove to be money well spent. She had a premonition it was about to be tested.

Finally, she notified the FAA administrator and the Head of the U.S. Customs Service and requested them to provide expanded medical screening exams for any foreign visitor who appeared ill. They should contact the local health department for further management of suspicious cases. Despite grumbling from both agencies that this would introduce even greater passenger processing delays into an already over-stressed system, they agreed.

When she finished at her office, she worked late into the night at home, finally collapsing into bed around midnight, her alarm set for 5:00 a.m. Just enough time to get ready for her own flight to D.C. Tight with excitement about this new epidemiologic challenge, her stomach also churned at the thought of seeing again the man she had once loved so much, had been so hurt by, and who had finally become a harmless ghost. Until tomorrow, when the apparition would turn to flesh and bone again.

In downtown Los Angeles, Jerry Essminger, the health department's EIS agent, was still recovering from a delightful weekend at the beach. Music. Dancing. Good food. A stunning blonde. But his thoughts were cut short by his boss, Dr. Michelle Goad, L.A. County's Epidemiologist. She motioned him into her office.

"Listen to this," she said gravely.

She played the two phone messages Gil Martin had left on the answering machine over the weekend, messages alerting her to his two anthrax cases.

Jerry copied down the details on a notepad as fast as he could write. "He sounds alarmed."

She nodded. "Now read this." She laid out a copy of the *LA Times* on her desk and pointed to Manny Reyes's small article about the two anthrax cases. "Reuters has picked it up as well. The story's half-way around the world already, but we're still in the starting blocks. Get on it right away. Let me know before the end of the day what you've come up with."

Michelle Goad was not a woman not to be trifled with. A lean, flinty Texan, with a face as weathered as an El Paso prairie, she ran her department with a velvet-covered iron fist, backed by impeccable academic credentials and extraordinary 'shoe leather' epidemic investigative experience. She drank her scotch neat, could swear with the best of them, and, in her younger days, had smoked a pipe.

Essminger, still a rookie at this business of medical detecting, was terrified of her. He muttered a "yes, ma'am," and hurried out.

By midafternoon, he was ready to brief her on what he had found so far. Yes, he told her, there had been two recent cases of anthrax in L.A. County.

"One patient is already dead, the other might pull through. Interesting, definitely interesting."

He would start his formal investigation tomorrow. Try to find out where the two patients had been exposed. "I don't think it was on the Air France flight. I don't think that was the source of the spores," he said. "Customs would have found and confiscated any possible items of contamination."

Essminger was pleased with himself and what he had discovered. He thought his boss would be also. He smiled expectantly.

She shook her head slowly for a long time, toying with a pen she kept on her desk. A graduation present from her father, it was one of the few keepsakes she had of him. That and the old photo on the wall of her as a five year old mounted on a pony, him standing beside her.

She looked at Essminger through owl-shaped glasses, one eyebrow arched. "Tara Martin called from CDC. There are other anthrax cases in other cities. All are suspiciously related to recent foreign travel." Then she looked over her glasses and fixed him with a withering stare. "I suggest you get out to the airport right away."

Essminger swallowed. Her 'suggestion' was clearly an order. It had what young EIS agents referred to as 'drop-dead time': if it wasn't done within that time, you might as well drop dead. Because that's what your career would be. "I'll get right on it," he promised.

He barely had time to get to Air France's LAX office before it closed. The staff dug up a copy of the passenger and crew manifest for Flight 62 on the date in question; Achmed's and Suzette's flight. After some arm twisting, they produced ticketing information on all the pasengers as well.

Essminger spent the rest of the evening at his computer. He created a master list of the names, addresses and local phone numbers for every person on that flight, including the flight crew members and the L.A. hotels where they were usually billeted. He would start contacting them all first thing in the morning. Hopefully it wasn't too late for prophlylactic antibiotics.

In five other U.S. cities, EIS agents and county epidemiologists were scrambling to compile similar lists of passengers and crews. The nation's epidemiology service was bestirring itself.

In Mosul, Mohammed Ali Ossman listened to the muezzin's call to morning prayers and sipped his tea. The phone rang. It was a very excited Yousef Rassan, one of the scientist visitors at his conference a few days ago.

"Did you see it, Mohammed!?"

"See what?"

"In the *London Times*. A Reuter News Service report of two cases of anthrax from Los Angeles. You have succeeded!"

"Allah akhbar!" Mohammed shouted, jumping to his feet and shaking his fist. When he had settled down again, Yousef read him the wire service report in its entirety. Mohammed copied it down verbatim.

"I have personally spoken with President Hussein," Yousef gushed. "He adds his congratulations to my own and authorizes me to tell you that when you are ready to begin increased production of your new germ, he is ready to assist you in any way the government can."

The next call was from Rashid Bin Yegal, the *al-Qaeda* agent. "It's started Rashid," Mohammed exulted. "We've succeeded."

"You mean you've succeeded. This was your project. Sheik Fahdil instructs me to assure you that his strong support will continue. He wants to know when the next group of agents will be ready for their missions to America."

"What did you tell him?"

"That we had already selected the six men and will begin their training soon. And that you were within thirty days of producing your next batch of germs. That's correct, isn't it?"

"Yes. We'll be ready by then."

Rashid's voice suddenly changed to one of concern. "Our agent in Los Angeles has been following the news about Achmed. Very discretely, of course. It appears he might actually survive the disease."

"What!"

"The other five men have already died. But not Achmed. His American doctor was apparently very good and very quick with him."

"What shall we do? They should all have died. We planned on it. Even though we kept much from them, they still know much." Mohammed rubbed his temple. He was getting a headache. "Our agent knows what to do if Achmed continues to improve?"

"Yes."

"Can he be trusted?"

"He's lived in Los Angeles for many years—a 'sleeper,' we call his type. Although he's adopted the customs and dress of the infidel—to maintain his deception—he remains Allah's faithful servant. He will do what we order."

"When will you give that order?"

"Soon. If Achmed continues to improve, very soon."

Mohammed received more phone calls in rat-a-tat succession from his scientist friends.

"You've done it, Mohammed," one of them said grudgingly. He had been one of the skeptics at their conference. "Just as you said you would."

He basked in their glowing words. But Achmed's failure to complete his mission—to die—nagged at him like an old crone.

After an extravagant luncheon for the laboratory staff, paid for out of his own pocket, Mohammed gathered all his employees in the conference room. He read the Reuters report, praised their work, and exhorted them to continue their efforts.

Ramazzan Fahrs listened to his Director in silence, his face a mask of attentiveness behind which his rage roiled. The time had come to act. As soon as he could manage it without suspicion, he slipped out of the lab and headed across the river. Mohammed was not the only one interested in the ruins of ancient Nineveh.

Jacques Moray picked through his instrument bag for an archeological map of the ancient Assyrian capitol. He and his partner Henri de Villancourt had almost finished their preliminary survey. Soon, he hoped, they would be digging into the dirt to uncover the remnants of Sennacherib's palace, which, if their measurements were correct, should be buried ten feet or so below where they were now consuming a lunch of cheese, flat bread and olives. And the last of the wine they'd had smuggled in by diplomatic pouch.

When he glanced in the direction of the little village of Nabi Yunus, Jacques saw a figure coming toward them, little puffs of dust kicked up from his boots accurately marking his progress.

Ramazzan Fahrs greeted the two Frenchmen, introduced himself, and offered them tarts and other sweets he'd saved from the luncheon at Mohammed's laboratory. After a few minutes conversation about their planned dig—where Ramazzan demonstrated his own considerable knowledge of Assyrian history and archeology— he casually pulled out a copy of the Reuters report on the new American anthrax cases and handed it to them.

"Have you seen this?" he asked.

The two archeologists read the short news item, looked at each other, then back at Ramazzan. They were mystified.

Jacques shrugged. "I don't understand. What does this mean? And what has it to do with us?"

Ramazzan smiled mysteriously. "I must return to work. Perhaps we will meet again. I often come here about this time of the day. Goodbye."

As he turned to leave he pointed to a heap of dirt and crumbling mud-bricks in the distance. "Some think the canal which brought water into the palace is buried right over there."

Then he was gone, disappearing back down the dusty road toward the village.

The Frenchmen looked at one another, then at the Reuters report again.

"I think he was trying to send us a message," Henri offered.

Jacques agreed. "But we're either too stupid or have been away too long to know it. We'd better notify Baghdad."

By "Baghdad" he meant the French Affairs Section there, a small, three-person unit headed by a *Charge d' Affairs* officer located in the Romanian Embassy. The sleepy little mission, with normally not much to do, was about to loom large in world affairs.

8

Gil was waiting curbside at his hotel when Tara, ever punctual, picked him up the next morning. They drove in uncomfortable silence for several blocks, neither one sure how to begin.

The weather had changed. An autumn wind with a whispered promise of early winter blew chill out of the north, stirring up piles of leaves here and there. People would be spending more time indoors from now on, buttoned up in their own closed environments.

"Where are we going?" Gil finally asked.

"DOJ." She quickly caught herself. "Sorry. Lots of 'government speak' in this city. DOJ is the Department of Justice. We have a small conference room there."

After two more blocks of silence, Tara added, "Cassie says hi. By the way, you're not the biggest man in her life right now. A new French exchange student has pre-empted you. The girls are going ga-ga over him and his accent."

"Life goes on," was all he could manage.

They drove several more blocks before Tara gave him a quick appraisal. "You look thin. Have you been eating?"

"I've been eating," he shrugged. "Maybe not great, but I've been eating."

"You look like you haven't been eating."

It was so easy to fall back into old patterns.

"Get much sleep last night?" Gil asked.

"Why, do I look out of it?"

"No. I was thinking about what we're dealing with."

"Anthrax epidemics or us?" She looked directly at him then back at the road.

"Both, I guess."

"It cost you to call me last night, didn't it?"

"Frankly, yes. But you're the best in the business. I needed help. I'm glad I called."

Tara slid the car around a slow moving truck. "You look pretty good, Gil. Thin but good."

"Thanks."

"You must have met someone."

Gil smiled. "Why do you say that?"

"Come on, let's face it. You were down the tubes, riding the vodka express. I—I didn't know how to handle it, Gil. Obviously someone did."

Gil studied her. There was a touch of gray in her auburn hair. Her face was young and serious. "There's no woman in my life, Tara."

"Hey, I'm not prying."

"I know."

"So what's caused this return to stability, to being a sharp doctor again?"

"Anthrax. This patient who came into the E.R. I got fired up. But I like to think I was straightening out anyway." He looked at his fingernails. "Cassie okay?"

"I shouted at her after our phone conversation. First time in a long time."

"Did you say I'd call and that I liked her birthday card?"

"Yes." Tara hesitated. "You're doing good work on this epidemic, Gil."

"Maybe so. I'm glad I have your help."

"I—I notice you don't have your ring on."

"Neither do you. Seems inappropriate after the divorce papers."

"What did you do with it?"

"I have this beatup small suitcase. It's in there along with my diplomas, certificates—and divorce decree." He watched her. "What about yours?"

"It's in my jewel box. With my mother's favorite broach."

There was no time for anything else. Tara pulled the van into the parking area. Piles of leaves swirled up from their passage.

When they got to the conference room, Tara was amazed at the number of people there, double the group's initial size from Dave Gardner's office. Half were strangers to her.

Dave Gardner detached himself from a small knot of people, greeted Tara with a kiss on the cheek, and was introduced to Gil.

"My ex-husband," she said. "The other Doctor Martin."

"Double the fun, eh?" Gardner reached for Gil's outstretched hand. "This is your show, Tara, you called the meeting. Let's get under way, shall we?"

When everyone was seated around the table, Gardner rapped on a water glass with his pen. "Y'all know why we're here. Let's begin. He pointed to Tara. "What's the count so far?"

"When I checked with my office"—she glanced at her watch—"about an hour ago, we had twelve reported cases of anthrax, all of the inhalation type, from six cities. As the epidemic investigation goes forward…"

"Hold on a minute," someone interrupted sharply. "Who says this is an epidemic? We'd better be careful about using terms like that until we're certain. Don't want to cause a panic."

Tara didn't recognize the speaker, a bespectacled man with a paunchy stomach and a poorly-fitting hair piece. She looked to Gardner for help.

"Meet Andrew Cardigan, Deputy Administrator of FEMA."

Tara nodded to him then said gently, "Sir, the generally accepted definition of an epidemic is an increased rate of disease above normal. We now have twelve cases when there shouldn't be any. I think that meets the definition. But if you prefer another term, perhaps 'outbreak' would suit you better. It's your choice. For most of us, however, this is an epidemic."

The man did not appear chastened.

"Why are you here?" Gardner asked the FEMA man. "And what do you see as your role in this?"

The answer was automatic, as if he were reading from a brochure describing his agency. "FEMA is charged with the overall control and direction of disasters." In other words, he expected to be in charge.

"Not so fast, Andrew." The new challenge to his authority came from a short, stocky, woman—mid-fifties, Gil guessed— dressed in a sparkling white, creased uniform with four rows of ribbons over her left breast. Everyone else seemed to know her.

"Deputy Surgeon General Carolyn McCormick," Gardner whispered in Gil's ear. "Head of the Commissioned Corps of the U.S. Public Health Service. And, incidentally, Tara's ultimate boss."

"This is not an earthquake or a tornado or a flood," the Deputy SG pointed out sharply. "Or even an outbreak." She eyed Tara. "This is an epidemic, the term I also prefer. What does FEMA know about vaccines, antibiotics and blood cultures, or how to get public health services to sick communities?"

The meeting was barely five minutes old and already turf wars had begun.

"Children, children," Gardner said drily. "Play nice now. I agree with the Deputy SG that this is chiefly a public health show. But FEMA (it came out 'Fimah') can help out by providing equipment and facilities for command and control, for communications, and for food and transport. For the infrastructure needed to deliver health care to large groups of people."

The portly bureaucrat wasn't willing to let the matter end there. "My boss may have something more to say about this. He does have direct access to the White House, you know."

"So does my boss." the Deputy SG shot back. "He's the Surgeon General, you know."

Gardner was not willing to let the meeting deteriorate into a shouting match over turf. "Listen, y'all, can we just settle down long enough to let Dr. Martin finish what she was saying?" He glanced at Tara.

Tara summed up her information. "Here's what we know so far about our twelve cases. First, there is no age predeliction; they span a range from a teenager to a sixty year-old. About equal numbers of males and females."

"What about ethnicity," someone asked. "Is any particular race over-represented?"

"Possibly. The six initial patients all appear to be of Middle-Eastern descent, though their actual countries of origin are still unclear."

She held up a map showing the distribution of the twelve cases, each one marked with a red thumb tack.

"From the dates they were first reported, it appears all patients became ill within four days of one another. In fact, the initial six cases were reported within forty-eight hours of each other. All twelve have been identified as passengers on Air France flights from Paris to the U.S. two to three days prior to the onset of their illnesses. The conclusion seems clear, doesn't it? We have not one but *six* point-source epidemics taking place, all clustered around those international flights."

"Could it be coincidental?" Oscar Bentley asked, looking not at Tara but at Gil, his eyes carrying a private humor.

"Not likely," Tara said, "not when six cities separated by hundreds of miles are involved."

"Any idea how many additional cases we might get?" the Deputy SG asked.

Tara pulled out a notepad and flipped through it until she found what she wanted. "I've already done the calculations. Assuming an average planeload of 275 passengers, there would be 6 x 275— or about 1500 people—who will need antibiotics, not counting the flight crews. But I can't predict how many of these will get sick."

"What's the antibiotic of choice?" Gardner asked. "And do we have enough of it?"

"The current recommendation is for Ciprofloxacin or doxycycline for thirty days. But since doxy has more side effects—especially skin rashes—it should probably be reserved for patients who are allergic to Cipro."

"Do we have enough Cipro for a full thirty-day course for all 1500 passengers and crews?" Gardner asked.

Tara took out a calculator. "Let's see, 1500 times 2 doses a day, for 30 days duration, right? I get 90,000 doses. About 16,500 for each of the six cities."

Gil winced. "That's a big demand all at once."

Tara nodded. "But pharmacies share supplies with one another. If we notify the manufacturers right away, they can direct extra doses to those six cities."

"I'll handle that one," the Deputy SG said. "And we have another source for just such emergencies: the National Pharmaceutical Stockpiles. They should have enough antibiotics for ten million people for six weeks."

"Who's authorized to release 'em?" Gardner asked.

"I am."

Gil Martin looked worried.

"What's on your mind?" Gardner asked, looking at him. "Speak up, we're all friends here."

"Thirty days of prophylactic therapy is a long time," Gil said. "Many patients will quit after a few weeks. What happens when the course is cut short? Or the medication is taken only intermittently?"

"It's pretty clear, Gil," Tara replied. "Shorter courses only delay but don't prevent the disease." She waited a moment for questions then said, "I'd like to ask Dr. Gil Martin, who has had direct experience with two of these cases, to give a brief report." She smiled at her ex, then looked oddly embarrassed, only to find herself looking at Oscar, the CIA agent. She colored and looked at her papers.

Gil's report was concise. Using the few slides he had prepared, he described the clinical course of his two patients.

"What do you make of those unusual cold-like symptoms?" Gardner asked. "They've shown up in all twelve cases, more in some than in others. Highly unusual for pulmonary anthrax, wouldn't you say?"

"I don't know what to say," Gil answered. "I've just seen these two cases, so I didn't know what to expect. But I got back some interesting results from the viral tests I ordered on my two patients."

"Like what?" Gardner was leaning on his elbows.

"An adenovirus."

"What does that mean?" someone asked.

"Adenoviruses are just one of many kinds of viruses which cause the common cold," Gil explained. "We were all infected with one or more of them during childhood. But since there are over forty varieties, we're still highly susceptible to some of them."

"Suppose we find this same adenovirus in other cases as well?" Oscar asked. "Does that mean these people simply had colds when they were exposed to the anthrax spores?"

"I suppose," Gil admitted hesitantly. "Why else would they have a URI then anthrax? One after the other."

Oscar persisted. "They were just unlucky enough to have a cold at the same time they were exposed to anthrax, huh?"

Gil shrugged. "I guess. Just bad luck."

Oscar's microbiology background had clearly raised his curiosity, and he pressed further. "But suppose they all had the *identical* strain of adenovirus? What would you say about that?"

"I don't know, Oscar. What would you say about that?"

"I'd say it looks mighty suspicious."

"I agree. Mighty suspicious."

The two men looked at each other and wondered if they were both thinking the same thing. They were. But neither was prepared to say anything more about it yet.

Gil sat down. His part was over. Or so he thought.

Dave Gardner was still trying to understand the significance of the adenovirus infections in Gil's two patients when he noticed his old friend Oscar fidgeting in his seat.

"Oscar you look as restless as a cat over water. Do you want to say something?"

"Yeah. Could we turn to a couple other important questions?"

"Like what?"

"Like where did this germ—whatever it is—come from? And how did it get into the country?"

"I agree, *amigo*. After the attack in New York, I thought our guard was up a little higher now. Got any ideas?"

"I do. I definitely do. We know that the first six cases of anthrax all arrived from Paris within hours of each other. They were the source of the spores. And equally clear, it wasn't coincidental. That notion kept buzzing around in my head, that this wasn't coincidental. Those six men weren't innocent sheepherders bringing in home-made sweaters for their relatives. They were terrorists. The first question, then, is where did they come from? And how did they get to Paris for their flights to the US.?"

"Alrighty," Gardner said, scanning the table, "anyone care to start off?"

"Can't we assume the men were all Iraqis, since they're the only ones in the Middle East with the technical capability to do this?" someone asked.

Oscar gave the questioner a thumbs up. "That's how I figure it, too. But how did they get out of a country with air travel restricted from Baghdad and absolutely blockaded in the north and south No-Fly zones?"

"What do your sources tell you?" The same person asked. "Didn't you turn up some unusual goings-on around that city in the far north? What was its name?"

"Mosul. And yes, we've had the city under surveillance. But we've detected no flights out of it or from the nearby military airfield. The region's completely bottled up."

"What about ground transportation?" A representative from the FBI asked. "Could they have gotten out overland?"

Oscar leaned back in his chair. "I suppose. But the satellites have only detected the usual traffic heading south out of Mosul toward Baghdad." He rubbed his chin. "Though about a week ago we did track four vehicles heading north toward the Turkish border. It was odd because they were traveling in caravan formation in the middle of the night, a moonless night at that."

"What was so odd about that?" Gardner asked.

"That's a very dangerous road at night. It's unlit and winds through rugged hills and river gorges. Bandits prowl it after sunset. It would have to be very urgent business to bring a traveler out on that road after dark."

"Or a great desire to avoid detection," the FBI agent observed, "when the risk might be justifiable. What happened to that convoy?"

"It halted at a remote site near the Turkish frontier, lingered there for about twenty minutes, then headed back the way it came."

"And its passengers? Any trace of them?"

"None. We lost contact."

"Excuse me," Gil Martin said quietly.

No one paid any attention to him.

"You have something, Gil?" Tara said.

All heads turned his way.

"Where is Lake Van?" he asked Oscar.

"Southeastern Turkey." The CIA agent went to a wall-mounted map and pointed to the area. "Why?"

Gil pulled out the stub he had taken from Achmed's hotel room. "I found this on my first patient, one of the original six." He passed it forward to Oscar. "It appears to be part of a Turkish Airlines boarding pass for a flight from Van Airport to Paris on the same day as AF Flight 62 to LAX. Could this be connected to your midnight caravan?"

Oscar traced his finger along the map from Mosul into Turkey. Suddenly, he stabbed at the spot marked "Van". "That's it! That's how they got out. A heavily-escorted and well-armed caravan from Mosul to the Turkish border, infiltration across the frontier, then separate transportation to Van. Once there, they got their tickets for their flights to Paris, and then on to the U.S...."

Tara Martin watched her ex-husband. "If that's true, it only explains how the spores were smuggled out of Iraq. But how did they get *into* the U.S.? No source of spores was found in the luggage or on the bodies of any of those men. And none on any of the airplanes."

"She's right about that," the FBI agent observed. "Border security is now tighter than a virgin's asshole—oops, sorry ladies! Besides, wouldn't this be a very inefficient way to wage biological warfare? Since the Iraqis have spore delivery systems of every type and sophistication—missiles, bombs, sprayers—why resort to this method, to humans hauling around wool vectors for the spores?"

Gardner agreed. "If those six agents were carrying the spores in some way we ain't figured out yet, they'd represent a big effort for a very low yield. Even if half the passengers on those planes became infected, that's still only a few hundred potential casualties at most. Considering what the operation must have cost, it would have to be history's littlest bang for its biggest buck. Like manuring a wheat field with sparrow shit." Gardner made no apologies for his colorful language.

"Perhaps they plan to repeat the process and send over more agents," Tara suggested. "They did it once. Maybe they think they can get away with it again."

"I disagree," the FBI agent said. "They know we'll be on to them sooner or later. They won't succeed a second time. I still say we're missing something." He looked at Oscar. "Can't you get any more ground resources into Mosul?"

Oscar put his finger to his lips. "That's highly classified information. But I can tell you we have little prospect of getting much more out of our in-country agent at this time. Or of getting any more agents in."

"Where do we go from here?" Gardner was stumped.

At first, the only answer was silence, broken by a few sighs. Finally, the Deputy SG stated firmly, "we do what we've always done in such crises. Local health departments will continue their investigations, report new cases to the CDC, and get known contacts started on prophylactic antibiotics. U.S. Customs will continue to search and detain suspicious foreign travelers. And the FBI and CIA will try to get more information on those six Iraqis. Until we know more, what else can we do?"

"Right," Gardner said. "We fall back on the basics." He stood, looked around the table. "Unless someone's got something else, I think we can adjourn. But let's stay in touch by phone and e-mail."

As Gil and Tara headed for the exit, Dave Gardner held them back. "Hold on a minute, Tara," he whispered, "Oscar wants a word with you."

Oscar joined the trio with another man unknown to them. When the room had cleared he said, "The White House wants to know what's going on. They've been getting enquiries from the press about this. It's time we let them in on it. They've laid on a briefing for 8:00 a.m. tomorrow." He nodded at Tara. "I want you to be there."

She accepted immediately.

"Where's Agent Reed?" Gardner asked, looking at the new man Oscar had brought with him.

"Chip is a technical specialist. He's been reassigned to photo analysis, his real love. Meet my new partner, Jean-Claude Metier."

"*Parlez vous francais?*" Gardner asked.

"*Oui. Certainment.*"

At six feet four inches in height and 225 pounds in weight, the man looked fit and strong.

Highly fit himself, Gardner was impressed. "What do you bench press?"

He shrugged. "300 or so."

Gardner persisted. "I'll bet you run that three mile CIA course in under 18 minutes."

Another shrug. Then a hint of a smile.

"I'll meet you at the car," Oscar said to his partner.

Jean-Claude left with a wave to the others.

Tara watched him go. She had been sizing this new guy up as well: olive-complexioned and strong-jawed, with a semitic nose; dark, darting eyes which missed nothing; and a thick but closely-trimmed beard. He had the lean and hungry look of someone who was no stranger to trouble. But her eyes had been drawn irresistibly to an almost star-shaped scar below his right eye. An old wound poorly healed, she guessed.

Dave Gardner cocked a quizzical eye at his old friend. "A Frenchman in the CIA, Bullethead?"

"He's Algerian actually, the son of a mid-level career French diplomat. His specialty is security systems, a trade he learned in a brief career as a cat burglar in Paris before his father and the *gendarmes* persuaded him there were better ways to make a living."

"How did he get that scar?" Tara asked.

"Barbed wire. As in crawling under it. In addition to French, English and Italian, he's fluent in Arabic and most Middle Eastern dialects, including Kurdish. And he's a practising Shiite Muslim."

"What have you got planned for him?" Gardner asked.

Oscar smiled. "Oh, we'll think of something…"

Tara drove her ex-husband to the airport. They got his travel bag out and stared at each other, wanting to talk but not finding the words. They stayed with medicine, safe ground.

"You did well today, Gil."

"Thanks. Not my usual work but very exciting. We'll lick this thing, Tara. Some of those people in the meeting were a little scratchy. But it was a talented group."

"What did you think of the Deputy Surgeon General?"

"Your boss? She looked good in white. But given those rows of medals I wouldn't fool with her." He paused. "She thinks well of you, Tara. I could tell. This could be big for you. Promotions, that kind of stuff."

"Let's just get this epidemic killed off."

Gil nodded. "You're right there, of course, but…"

"But what?"

"I'm spoiling it, Tara, I—"

"But what?" An edge of anger now.

"Well, our problems came with your move to Atlanta. We could've—"

"Our problem. Is that what it was?"

"We should have stayed together, worked it out."

"We could have worked it out if you'd supported my move!" Gil's hand came up. "Sorry."

"Goodnight, Gil. Call me soon."

"Give my love to Cassie."

"Tell her yourself, you've got the number."

"Tara, remember *Serendipity*? You leaning out, laughing, face all suntan lotion and seaspray? Sometimes…" He hung there on his torment, then abruptly walked away.

Tara watched him go.

"Something more than a microbe is needed to make us ill, since we so often find the organism, and so rarely the disease."

Louis Pasteur

In downtown Los Angeles, Jerry Essminger, the EIS agent, looked harried. He felt the Sword of Damocles poised over his head. Its name was Dr. Michelle Goad. He had been up since dawn, had forgone his usual morning run. He grabbed some coffee instead of a proper breakfast and was the first one to the office. He was just hanging up the phone when a good-looking, young man dressed in a suit and pony tail knocked, then entered his office. It was 8:00 a.m. sharp.

"I'm Nathanial Windsong—Nathan," the pony tail announced, "one of the contact investigators. I'm yours for this project, and I'm up to speed on what's going on."

Essminger sipped his coffee and studied the man. "Can I call you Nate?"

"I'd rather you didn't."

Essminger nodded. "Fair enough." He stared at the man's string tie and the exquisite turquoise and silver clasp. "Indian?"

"I'm a half-blooded Dakota Sioux. Grew up near Missoula, Montana. My father was a Methodist minister. When he died, I came to Los Angeles. My uncle raised me and helped put me through school."

"How'd you get interested in this line of work?"

"I've always been curious, wanting to dig things up. Discover things. I considered police work for a time but thought this would be more interesting." He shrugged. "Maybe it's part of my heritage."

Essminger wasn't sure whether he was kidding or not. He motioned him to a chair. "Just before you got here I was on the phone to Air France. They pulled all the 747's assigned to their Paris-LA run off line yesterday and inspected them from stem to stern, even behind the bulkheads and up into the ventilation compartments where someone might have deliberately hidden a source of anthrax spores."

"Anything?"

"Nope. I also talked with U.S. Customs. They're compulsive now about checking foreign luggage for accidental—or deliberate—sources of spores. But, again, *nada*. And every foreigner who sneezes twice or coughs once is screened by medical personnel. I think we've got a rope around this thing."

"Where do you want me to start?"

"This should be a straight-forward contact investigation. Phone calls and knocking on doors. But it will be different from your usual job of tracking down contacts of infectious diseases. Inhalation anthrax is only transmitted by spores, so the population at risk is limited to just the passengers and crew on that airplane."

"Like the food-borne outbreak from bad cole slaw that we learned about in school, huh?"

Essminger laughed. The reference to this classic scenario told him the man knew about point-source epidemics. Every epidemiologist and contact investigator-in-training studied the 'company picnic,' the textbook example of a food-borne epidemic.

"Right," Essminger agreed. "Or the 'Great Ham Scam' we had last year."

Windsong was puzzled. "What in the world was that?"

"You didn't hear about it? Happened at a state prison up north. The inmates were all fed a breakfast of sliced ham and eggs. Within hours, half of them developed vomiting and diarrhea.

Since the eggs were powdered, the warden assumed the problem was the canned ham. He called an impromptu press conference, held one of the hams up to the camera, and made an impolite reference about fecal material. The food company which processed the ham was incensed. It held its own press conference and threatened a huge lawsuit for slander. What a mess! I was asked to investigate."

"What did you find?"

"I started with the basics—just like you learned in training. First, I got the menus, then took a tour of the kitchen and scullery and talked with the cooks—even lined them up for brief on-the-spot exams. Then I checked the temperature logs on the walk-in refrigerator."

"Was that the problem?"

"Yup. It was most embarrassing. Turned out that the night before, 2,000 slices of hot ham with pineapple sauce were served for dinner. So far so good. Another 1,000—the left overs—were placed, still warm, in the refrigerator for the next-day's breakfast. But later that night, 3,500 portions of hot jello were also placed in the same reefer, and the old thing was just not up to the challenge. The temperature logs faithfully recorded temperatures higher than 50 degrees for several hours as the refrigerator struggled to cool down the hot jello."

"So everything in that refrigerator should have been discarded. I'll just bet it wasn't."

"You're right, it should've been; it's the law: any perishables kept at temperatures greater than 40 degrees for longer than four hours must be treated as garbage and thrown out. But no one paid attention to the temperature log the next morning. So the left-over ham—which had been infected with a staph bacteria—had all night to incubate and grow. By the next morning, it was thoroughly tainted."

"But the inmates didn't have a clue, so they piled it in?"

"Correct. They were soon puking and crapping their guts out.

"I bet the warden was red-faced when you told him."

"He didn't have just egg on his face; he had ham and eggs on his face! He was not a happy guy. Not only did he have to publicly retract his previous accusation, but he also had to find funds for a new refrigerator. He's still pissed at me!"

"If you don't like the message, shoot the messenger."

Essminger remembered he had been quite a hero, at least in his own circles. It had been a great time to be an epidemiologist. Maybe this was another.

"Alright, Nathan, here's where you start."

He handed the investigator the master list of names, addresses and phone numbers for the passengers on Flight 62. "I don't have to tell you how urgent this is. Anthrax is a bad actor. But if we can get these people onto prophylactic antibiotics, we may be able to save their lives. It's their only chance."

"What should I tell them if they want to know what's going on?"

"Keep it simple and direct. Explain that they were exposed to an infectious disease and should contact their doctor at once, if they have one. Go to the nearest ER or urgent care clinic if they don't. We should be dealing with a small enough group that it won't overwhelm the local health care system."

Windsong rose to go.

"Meet me back here this afternoon. But call me if any questions come up you can't handle."

"What about the press? This is already an item for them. It's going to get bigger."

"That's one of Dr. Goad's jobs. She gets paid big bucks for it. And she's damn good at it, thank God."

* * *

While Tara Martin, Oscar Bentley and Dave Gardner struggled with the 'macro' view of the epidemic in that D.C. conference room, Nathan Windsong's focus was infinitely smaller: the 285 passengers and crew of Air France flight 62 which had landed at

LAX five days ago. Nor was his 'work environment' as global as Tara Martin's group. His was confined to the freeways and streets of Los Angeles.

By early afternoon Windsong had processed most of the names on his list. He scanned the passenger flight manifest one more time as he crossed the hall to Jerry Essminger's office.

"I called Air France again," Essminger told him. "They'll contact the rest of the flight crew and have them report to a company doctor immediately, either in L.A. or in Paris, for a medical exam and to begin prophylactic antibiotics."

"Good. That's one less job for us." Windsong checked the names off his list. "By the way, are any of them ill?"

"No. Except for that one flight attendant—Suzette Kelly—none of the crew has reported in sick. That's the good news."

"What's the bad?"

"The company has five other flights from which anthrax cases have been reported, all to U.S. cities."

"Five more! What the hell is going on?"

"I don't know. But let's stay focused on our own assignment, let CDC take the big picture. What have you turned up so far?"

"There are 276 passenger names on this list. I'm about ninety per cent done. The hardest part was contacting passengers who had changed planes in L.A. on their way to other airports, like San Diego, San Francisco, and a few places in between. But I reached most of them and left phone messages for the others. Hopefully, they'll get back to me by the end of the day. And there's a couple of passengers I want to interview face to face. But unless something unexpected turns up, I should be able to wrap it up by late this afternoon."

"How many sick ones have you uncovered so far?"

"Twenty-eight, a little more than ten percent."

"Since about 2-5% of the population is ill at any one time, that's more than expected."

"Right."

"What do you know about those 28?"

"Seven are children with ear infections, one a man with appendicitis, another a man with a heart attack, and another a woman with a kidney infection."

"That leaves 18."

"Correct. And nine of them appear to have colds or allergies." Essminger raised his eyebrows.

"I know, I know," Windsong answered quickly. "You warned me to be suspicious of anyone with a cold. That this strain of anthrax starts out with URI symptoms. But those nine have been sick for several days already, none has had fever, and all of them told me they were feeling well enough to return to work today or tomorrow. I think they really do have regular, old-fashioned colds or hay fever."

"O.K. What about the remaining nine?"

"Here's where it gets interesting. All were taken to local hospitals. Six were diagnosed with septic shock—two with meningitis as well—and are critical. Another is already dead of sepsis, and another was pronounced D.O.A. at a local ER. Most of the doctors I spoke to hadn't even considered a diagnosis of anthrax."

"You've got to be kidding!" Essminger slammed his pencil down on the desk, breaking it in half. A first sign of strain etched his features. "Even after those mail related cases in New York and New Jersey?"

"Are you really that surprised?" Windsong, not a physician himself, was more understanding. "None of them has ever actually seen a case of anthrax. To most, their patients just had sepsis, something they see occasionally."

This explanation for these human failings was both reasoned and reasonable. Essminger's anger subsided. "You're right. I remember a measles outbreak at a military boot camp I investigated a few years ago. Since none had personally seen a case before, it took days to convince the doctors that the rashes they were seeing were measles. If it weren't for an older physician who had treated measles prior to the vaccine, it would have taken twice as long to get the others on track."

"So they finally got it right?"

"Yes, but then the pendulum swung back the other way. They over-diagnosed, claimed that *every* recruit with the slightest fever or the faintest rash had measles. Even those with proof of prior vaccinations."

Windsong wanted to get back to his own report. "Let me tell you about my last case. This one is different, a patient named Van Der Hooven, Nils Van Der Hooven, a Dutchman here on business. He was taken to the same hospital near the airport which reported two of the original cases—Dr. Martin's hospital. They were on top of it. Suspected anthrax right away from the guy's clinical findings and blood stain. They stabilized him and transferred him to UCLA immediately. A positive ELISA confirmed their suspicions. It looks like Mr. Van Der Hooven is going to pull through."

Essminger summed up on his fingers. "So, you've probably got nine cases of anthrax: two already dead; six others who probably will die; and one, who was diagnosed early, who might make it. One out of nine. Shit!"

"We need to get the word out to the medical community."

Essminger selected another pencil from a cup filled with them. "I'll fax our passenger list to all the local hospitals and physician groups, alerting them to be on the look out for these people. And to consider anthrax if any of them is really sick. Hopefully, they'll make the diagnosis earlier and get these passengers on treatment sooner."

"What about right-of-privacy? Won't we be legally liable by revealing those names?"

"I don't think so. This is a public health emergency. Privacy takes second place here."

Windsong got up. "I have one or two names I couldn't get through to on the phone." He scrolled his finger down the list. "A Saundra Williams, out in the Valley. And another one out there. I'll swing by and see if they're home."

Essminger sifted through a stack of phone messages on his desk, selected one, and handed it over. "And call L. A. County Hospital, will you? Talk to this doctor in Infectious Disease. He's the one who took care of Suzette Kelly. See if there's anything he would like to add to our case definition of anthrax."

"Right."

"Oh, and one more thing."

"Yeah?"

"Where can I get one of those ties?"

Windsong headed west on the Hollywood Freeway, his destination the San Fernando Valley and the city of Encino, about an hour's drive from downtown. L.A. was in the clutches of a heat wave. The inversion layer which accompanied it covered the basin in a brown-yellow veil of smog. The San Gabriel Mountains, one of the few ranges in North America running east-to-west, was invisible barely twenty miles away, though somewhere above the 4,000-foot level, where the smog ended, Mounts Wilson and Baldy still sparkled in the alpine air.

Windsong thumbed his cellular phone for L.A. County Hospital's Infectious Disease Unit. "We're developing a new case definition for anthrax," he explained to the staff physician, "and we wanted your input."

The doctor was suspicious. "Why do you need a new case definition? Are you expecting more of them?"

"I didn't say that." Windsong tried not to sound too defensive. "We simply want to prevent a delay in diagnosis if there should happen to be other cases."

"So you do think we might get more?"

Windsong knew a trap when he saw one and didn't answer.

"Listen," the physician persisted, "I have a limited number of beds in this Unit. I need to know whether I should set some aside for future anthrax cases or not."

Windsong was cornered. There was only one way out: punt. "Listen, doctor, you should talk with Dr. Goad about this. My job is just to get your input for the case definition."

"Very well. I'll draft one up and send it to you." Then, as an afterthought, he asked, "By the way, how is the boyfriend doing?"

"What do you mean?"

"You know, Mr. McCarthy, or rather Captain McCarthy, the pilot. He came with Suzette and stayed at her bedside right to the end, though he was looking pretty ill himself by then. I offered to check him out personally, but he insisted on returning home to his family physician."

Windsong wrote it down. "Captain McCarthy, you said?"

"Yes. It's probably nothing, but you may want to check on him as well."

Windsong looked down his passenger list. No Dennis McCarthy. "So, this guy was part of the flight crew?"

"No, no. Just a personal acquaintance—hell, a boyfriend. Apparently the two of them were having a *liaison.*"

Windsong started to ask what this McCarthy guy had to do with his investigation. But instinct told him at least to check it out. He took the pilot's address and phone number in San Diego. And the number of the airline he flew for as well.

⎯⎯

While Nathan Windsong was swinging north onto the San Diego Freeway for the short jaunt over Mulholland into the Valley, Dr. Michelle Goad, his boss, was awash in phone calls from physicians and nurses wanting to know what the hell was going on. Patients were flooding their facilities asking for antibiotics to prevent what they were told was a deadly disease. What was it all about?

Worse, she now had a *Times* reporter waiting outside her office. Manny Reyes, who had broken what he thought was just a little fart of a story the day before, had followed it up today with

113

a callback to his brother-in-law Fergus, the ER technician. He had discovered there had now been a third case of anthrax. This prompted him to expand his snooping. He called every ER and urgent care clinic in the metropolitan L.A. area. Though he uncovered no additional cases—at least none the medical personnel knew about—he had gotten reports about droves of patients demanding prophylactic antibiotics. And all were from the same international flight, Air France Flight 62. Manny smelled a story.

Dr. Goad stared through the blinds on the door separating her office from the reception area. Manny was standing in front of the secretary's desk, declaiming in a loud voice his First Ammendment Right to information. There would soon be others in that room when more of the sharks smelled the blood and started circling. She could stall for a while, at least until Jerry Essminger and his team finished their investigation. But sooner or later she would have to deal with the press. She wished she still had her pipe.

Nathan Windsong pulled into the driveway of a home with the name 'Williams' stencilled in black letters on the mailbox. No one answered the doorbell. He rang again. Still no answer.

"They're all at the hospital."

He turned to see a neighbor approaching, gardening tools and a flower basket in hand.

"It's terrible, just terrible," the woman said, shaking her head.

"What is?"

"Why poor Saundra, of course. And her husband. And those children. All in the hospital."

Windsong pulled out his notepad again. "Which hospital?"

The woman became hesitant. "You should know that. Aren't you a family member?"

He identified himself and the purpose for his visit.

The woman's suspicion turned to alarm. "Do they have something contagious? Is my own family in danger?" She started backing away.

Windsong reassured her then hurried on to the nearby community hospital. His ID got him ushered into a small conference room where he was introduced to the Chief Nurse, the Chief of the Medical Staff, the Hospital Administrator and a gray-haired matronly woman with red eyes. She was weeping softly into a handkerchief. He discovered she was Saundra Williams's mother. Next to her was a teenage boy with a tight-clamped jaw and an angry scowl on his face. He looked straight ahead and barely acknowledged Windsong's greeting. The eldest son.

Windsong explained who he was and why he was there. In turn, he was informed that Saundra had died two days ago, followed by her husband yesterday, and her youngest child, a six-year old girl, today. Another child, a boy, was still alive but in critical condition. Only the eldest child, the one sitting here today with his grandmother—he had been on a camping trip when his family became ill—remained well. The rest of them, both the living and the dead, had been diagnosed with septic shock, one with meningitis as well.

Windsong offered his condolences. He had only one or two questions, then he would be on his way. Pointing to Saundra's name on the passenger list, he asked, "why do you suppose Mr. Williams and the two children are missing from the manifest?" He assumed the family must have all been traveling together.

The grandmother looked puzzled. "Because only Saundra made the trip to France. Her company sent her to Paris on business."

"You mean the others weren't on that flight?"

The woman looked at him like he was either deaf or stupid. "Isn't that what I just said?"

"And they were all well until Saundra returned?"

"Yes. Her husband Fred took sick about the time she was hospitalized. Same for the children."

Windsong was stunned. The implication of this discovery sickened him. In one moment of time, the dogma that anthrax never spread from person to person was swept from his mind. The conclusion was inescapable. Dear God.

He asked if he could have a word with the Chief of Staff out in the hall. "What do you think caused the infection?" he asked when they were alone. He controlled his agitation.

"Some type of bacteria," the doctor answered matter-of-factly. "Probably a staph. My bacteriologist hasn't identified it yet."

The man had not considered anthrax. Windsong followed up with another question. "Did you order any other tests to confirm the diagnosis?"

"What for? They cost a bundle and won't tell me any more than I'll know when the cultures grow out in a day or so."

"Could this be anthrax?" Windsong posed it as a question, but he was certain he already knew the answer.

"Anthrax?" The physician was incredulous. "Where would they get anthrax? Isn't that a disease of sheep farmers and wool workers? Or have there been more of those anthrax-by-mail cases?"

Windsong hurried back to his car. He dialed Jerry Essminger's number. Busy.

He tried again a few minutes later. Still busy.

Taking every shortcut he knew, he headed back to the office. He had big news: the first evidence of the human transmission of anthrax. He had no idea how such a thing was possible, but the evidence was staring him in the face. Anthrax, at least in his cases, was now a contagious disease.

As he was nearing the downtown area, about as excited as he'd ever been, he suddenly remembered the one remaining lead he had not yet investigated: Dennis McCarthy, Suzette's boyfriend. He dialed the man's home phone number. No answer. Next he called Continental Airlines. He was told Captain McCarthy had called in ill three days ago and was now in University Hospital in San Diego, very sick.

He called the hospital and got through to the ICU charge nurse. She was reluctant at first to give him any information. But when he convinced her he was legitimate, she told him the Captain had meningitis and septic shock. His prognosis was grave.

"Is there a positive blood culture yet?"

"No. They're still pending."

He had her transfer him to the lab. When he got through to the microbiologist, he came straight to the point. "Could it be anthrax?"

"Anthrax?" Then, with a snap of fingers, the man exclaimed, "why yes, it could be. It definitely could be. I've been staring at those bacteria under the microscope for hours, wondering what the hell they were, trying to convince myself they were an unusual form of strep I've never seen before."

Windsong heard a book flipped open and pages being turned.

"Yeah. There it is. Exactly like my own specimen. Anthrax."

The man was so eager to call the attending physician with his big news that Windsong had to shout at him to stop him from hanging up. He wrung a promise out of him to send specimens to CDC for confirmatory diagnosis. Then he accelerated the car.

He was almost at his office now. He had decided to tell Jerry Essminger face to face that he had uncovered two—count em, two!—secondary cases of anthrax. That wasn't supposed to happen even once. And one of them in a city sixty-five miles away!

When he pulled into his usual parking spot he saw a cluster of people milling around in front of the building: the press. They had found the story. Reporters with microphones were pushing and shoving to get in the front door, restrained by security guards. Windsong, unrecognized, slipped through the crowd, flipped open his ID to one of the guards, and bounded up the stairs and through the door.

Later, at home, Windsong cracked open a beer and watched the story unfold on the evening news, first on the local channels, then nationally. Talking heads pontificated about anthrax and speculated that the source of the infection—the spores—would ultimately be shown to be connected to the original six cases. Dark hints of bioterrorism were offered up.

"They don't know!" Nathan swigged his beer. "They don't know about my two secondary cases. They don't know this anthrax germ is contagious; Goad and Essminger are keeping them in the dark…"

Probably to prevent panic, he figured. But how long could that last?

Head down, shoulders hunched against the early morning cold, Ramazzan Fahrs walked through the dirt streets of Nabi Yunus. He had chosen a sunrise meeting for three reasons: first, to avoid the mid-day heat; second, so he would not draw suspicion to himself by missing work at the laboratory; and, third, because his boss Mohammed only visited the ruins himself during lunch hour or at the end of the day.

The village was just coming to life, the streets still largely empty despite the muezzin's call to prayer from the minaret. A haunting refrain from the Koran, it lingered in the air like a blythe spirit before wafting away. Next to the minaret stood a conical-shaped building. It had once housed a sect of Satan worshipers in earlier times but was now used as office space by the mullahs. Remembering the macabre stories he had heard as a boy about the rituals performed there, Ramazzan shuddered and scurried past.

When he entered the ruins of Nineveh itself, shadows from the rising sun stirred up ancient ghosts. His fear of being detected imbued them with fearsome human shapes. He could feel them all around, watching, silently guarding. The very path he now trod had been the Processional Way, a broad, straight road paved with bricks leading to the palace. King Sennacherib had posted a warning that no man was to walk this Royal Road except at the King's express pleasure. Violators were to be slain and impaled on stakes for all to see.

Ramazzan turned at a sudden sound. A shadow flickered briefly, then nothing. He reproached himself for his fear. "A jackrabbit," he muttered. "Nothing more." But he quickened his pace.

Passing the site of Sennacherib's mighty palace, he recalled that the King's only serious setback—until he was bludgeoned to death by his sons—was at the siege of Jerusalem. He was driven back, King Hezekiah claimed, by an angel with a flaming sword. But it had, in fact, been something less divine which caused his defeat. A plague ravaging his troops had forced him to call off the assault. Ironic, Ramazzan thought, that Sennacherib's descendents— Mohammed and men like him—were once again on the march. This time with anthrax.

Another sound. Footsteps. He stopped and listened over his shoulder, his heart pounding. Again, nothing. He hustled along to the meeting place near the ruins of Assurbanipal's temple.

"Bon jour," Jacques waved in greeting. He and his partner Henri were awaiting Ramazzan at their make-shift little camp. Two other men were with them, both members of the French Affairs Section who had driven up from Baghdad during the night. The archeologists brewed tea on a propane stove and served it to their guests, who seated themselves on wooden camp stools around a small fire.

"This is your meeting," the young man named Louis said. Ramazzan soon discovered he was the French *Charges d' Affaires.* "What's on your mind?"

"You have seen the news reports about the epidemic which is—how you say it—breaking out in America?"

"Oui."

"What does your French intelligence service say to you about this?"

"Not much more than we get on CNN. The Americans are certain the disease is anthrax, though they haven't found the source of the spores yet. They are suspicious that terrorism is involved but uncertain who it might be." Louis stared unblinking at Ramazzan, looking for any sign of complicity.

Ramazzan just sipped his drink. "Chinese tea?" he asked Jacques.

"English. Earl Gray."

The men drank in silence as the sun climbed over the Kurdish hills.

"Did you bring the equipment I asked for?" the Iraqi asked.

"A VCR and monitor? Yes. They're set up in the tent next to the generator."

"Then—what do they say in Hollywood—'let us get on with the show.'" He handed Louis a copy of part of the videotape he had stolen from Mohammed's laboratory.

Thirty minutes later, when the videotape had finished and the generator was silent again, the four Frenchmen continued to stare at the blank screen.

"Well?" Ramazzan asked.

Louis was visibly shaken. "What exactly did we see?"

"What did it look like?"

"It looked like germ warfare experiments on human subjects."

"You are correct. That is what it was."

"Are you not aware that such experimentation is in direct violation of the 1925 Geneva Protocol on the use of biological weapons? And of the Nuremberg Code prohibiting such experimentation?"

Ramazzan was irritated. He had brought them proof of Iraqi bioterrorism and, by implication, its role in the blossoming U.S. epidemic. Yet all they wanted to talk about were Western notions of morality.

"What you have seen," he said sharply, "is a copy of one-half of a videotaped record from a laboratory no more than ten miles from here. The other half is even more revealing. It shows a direct connection to the American problem. Are you interested in it or not?"

"We are interested, absolutely," the diplomat answered quickly. "We assume you will want something in return."

"Of course. Money: five million English pounds deposited in a numbered Swiss bank account. New identity papers: a French passport and driver's license. And a way out of here."

Louis sipped his tea and crossed his legs. "You ask for much."

"What I have is worth much."

"I must discuss your proposal with my Foreign Office."

"Do not take long. There are many others who would pay even more for what I have. Certain countries to the east of here, for example."

The men stood, shook hands and agreed to meet again in a few days, this time at a different location within the ruins. Ramazzan turned to go, but Louis was still curious.

"Why are you really doing this? It's not just for the money, is it?"

Ramazzan bowed his head and touched his fingertips first to his lips then to his forehead in the muslim sign of respect. "Allah akhbar."

Driving back across the river to Mosul, Ramazzan checked and re-checked his rearview mirrow. He sensed he was being followed but could not detect anything definite. The ancient ghosts again.

"Guilt," he muttered. "You are so paranoid."

When he finally turned into the parking lot of the old chicken processing building with the rusting red sign, he took one last look around before entering. Still nothing.

A few seconds later a second car pulled up, just short of the building. Unobserved, the driver circled the location on a map, made some marginal notes in French, then sped off.

11

Gil Martin's return flight from Washington D.C. touched down at LAX at 8:00 p.m. He had dozed fitfully, unsettling thoughts of Tara fading as his sleep was disturbed by that dream again. In it, for some unclear reason, he was forced to repeat medical school. Images of himself walking the same grounds he had trod twenty years earlier. Shame. Humiliation. The dream had started about five years ago and recurred regularly. Always the same. He didn't know what it meant. Was it connected to the divorce?

He collected his luggage and headed for the parking lot. It was a crisp, starry evening. The light breeze cleared the remaining cobwebs of the dream from his mind.

He wanted to see how Achmed, his first anthrax patient, was fairing. He drove straight to the hospital. The waiting area outside the ICU was deserted except for one person: a husky young man of average height with a goatee and a shaved head. He was reading quietly but looked up as Gil passed through on his way to the Unit.

Gil nodded to him. The man just stared back.

When he entered the ICU, Gil found Achmed sitting up in bed watching television. But when he approached him, he looked away.

"Hello. I'm Dr. Martin. I took care of you in the ER. How do you feel?" He held out his hand.

The man continued to ignore him and stared straight ahead.

Gil asked a few more questions but met with no more success. He finally gave up.

"Have you gotten anything out of that guy yet?" he asked the nurse.

"Not a peep. But we know he understands English. He follows our orders to roll over, or move, or hold out his arm for a BP check. He just clams up when we try to talk to him. Not a word."

"How's he doing medically?"

"Great. He's eating, up and walking to the bathroom. He'll be transferred to a regular ward bed in about an hour."

"Has he had any visitors?" Gil thought about that stranger in the waiting room.

"None."

"Phone calls? Either in or out?"

"Zippo."

"What's with this guy?"

"I dunno," she said wearily. "And I couldn't care less. We think he's just an asshole."

Gil headed back through the waiting room, surprising the same man he had seen before. He jumped back as Gil came through the door. Had he been listening? Gil tried to approach him but didn't get any closer than a couple of yards before he turned and hurried off.

"Hey! I just want to ask you a couple of questions. Are you a friend of Achmed's? Hey, what's the deal?"

The guy didn't stop or turn around, and Gil was too tired to give chase or follow him. He headed for his car in the parking lot.

The next morning, Gil started his ER stint with the usual stack of 'nickel and dime' cases. Kathy Roberts nudged him while he was writing a medical note.

"Did you hear about that guy, Achmed, the one with anthrax?"

Gil kept writing. "I saw him last night. He's doing well. Looks like he's going to pull through."

"He's dead."

"What!" Gil dropped his pen.

"Yup. Heard about it in morning report. It's all over the hospital."

"What the hell happened?"

"He was moved to a regular ward bed. And since he was taking fluids well, his IV was pulled and he was started on a regular diet."

"Yeah, yeah." Gil was impatient.

"At the change of shift, the LVN went in to take his vitals and found him unresponsive. She called a Code and they ran the full drill on him. But no luck, he never came out of it."

Gil just stared.

"Listen, doc, can anthrax do that? Cause sudden death like that in the middle of recovery?"

Gil ignored the question and asked one of his own. "Did anyone come for the body?"

"Nope. It was picked up by the Coroner's Office in the wee hours of the morning. The ME's ordered a full autopsy."

When he could break free from his patient load—about an hour into the shift—he phoned the ME's office and was put through to the pathologist who had done the autopsy. Her southern voice dripped with honey, but her language was all business.

"Dr. Martin, I read your progress notes before I began the post. Do you still think your patient had anthrax? Have you any additional lab results to confirm it?"

He sighed. "We've got positive blood cultures now. It's anthrax. What did you find?"

"I had to do some homework first, but my findings agree with your diagnosis. And they're identical to those in the cases from the Russian epidemic in 1979. Are you familiar with that study?"

He had read about it briefly. "Isn't it the largest single study we have of the pathology of anthrax in humans?"

"Yes. Ninety-six patients in the Siberian city of Sverdlovsk were hospitalized with anthrax…"

"By spores accidentally released from a nearby military bioweapons facility."

"Correct. Seventy-six cases were of purely inhalation origin, eleven purely cutaneous. And eight cutaneous cases which became systemic."

"Was it sixty who died?"

"Sixty-six. Forty-two of them were autopsied." She hesitated. "But your patient didn't die of anthrax."

Gil wasn't sure he'd heard correctly. "What do you mean?"

"He had petechial hemorrhages in both eyes. He was suffocated."

"Suffocated…"

"Right. Murdered."

Gil said nothing for a long time. She thought they had been disconnected. "Dr. Martin?"

"I'm still here." Gil's head was reeling. "Any idea how it happened?"

"A pillow, maybe. Or a towel. We'll look for fibers in his teeth and up his nose. If we find any, they might pinpoint what it was and where it came from."

"What happens now?"

"The case has been turned over to the police. To the homocide detectives."

"Will they want to talk with me?"

"I don't know. Do you know anything more?"

"No. The ICU nursing staff probably has the best feel for this guy."

"Right. I'll tell the detectives to be sure and check with them."

"What will you do with the body?"

"Hold it for 72 hours. If no one calls for it, we'll dispose of it."

In Mosul, it was dusk. Mohammed had locked the laboratory and was heading for his car when Rashid bin Yegal pulled into the parking lot.

"Achmed is with Allah and his 72 virgins," the *al-Qaeda* agent said matter-of-factly.

Mohammed recoiled a step from the man's tobacco breath. "He finally died?"

"He was sent."

Mohammed's cold eyes stared at him. "By your 'sleeper?'"

Rashid nodded.

The two men leaned against Mohammed's car, watching the sky.

Stroking his beard, Rashid confided, "there may be another difficulty."

"What is it now?"

"The 'sleeper' thinks Achmed may have revealed information to his American doctor, information which could threaten our purpose. He visited Achmed often, even once just before he..."

"What do you propose?"

"To send the American doctor to Allah as well."

Mohammed thought about it. He rubbed the stumps of his missing fingers. Finally, he said simply, "Do it."

"Allah Akhbar."

12

Two days later.

Dave Gardner had gotten a call from his sister last night. She had invited him down for a long weekend on her farm near Culpeper, Virginia. He was tempted. Mint juleps and good bourbon. The croaking of bull frogs in the rushes. His nephews and nieces playing under the gnarled oak tree.

He was considering the invitation when the phone rang. The call was from Atlanta, put through to his USAMRIID office. It was Tara Martin.

"Good morning, Miss Tara."

"Case reports are coming in faster now, Dave."

"How bad is it?" He put down his paper and began taking notes as she gave him the latest update

"As of an hour ago, I had forty-eight confirmed cases. Twenty-five are already dead, ten more in critical condition and not expected to live."

"The others?"

"Still alive. Some may pull through, though it's touch and go for most. And the course of the disease has been depressingly similar in all the cases. Typically a mild URI at first, then rapid progression to septic shock and respiratory failure. Only the ones who are diagnosed early and started on antibiotics immediately have any chance of surviving."

"Are the new cases all from the same original six cities?"

"No, a smattering have come in from other places as well: San Diego, Joliet, Indianapolis and Atlanta have each reported one case. This is not surprising. These were the final destinations for some of the passengers on the original six flights."

"I understand."

"Look, Dave. Last night I got some shocking news."

"What?"

"From Los Angeles, reports of two secondary cases. And this morning, another from Washington D.C."

"Let me get this straight, you have anthrax cases in people who were *not* on those airplanes? That's what you mean by 'secondary cases?'"

"It appears that way."

"How would that be possible?"

"They must have caught it from someone who was."

"Jesus Christ. You know what that means?"

"God, yes."

"Could your people be mistaken in this?"

"No. I checked with the epidemiologist and the contact investigator in L.A. And I reviewed all their laboratory data. They got it right."

"Jesus Christ."

"I get the feeling, Dave, that you're not all that surprised at this."

"It shows, huh? Ever since your ex told us he found adenovirus in his two patients, I've been bothered by it. It had to be purely coincidental, or…"

"Or the adenovirus was deliberately linked to the anthrax."

"You got it."

"Then you're really going to love this. Our lab here at CDC has found four more anthrax cases with adenovirus. DNA testing—mostly PCR's—shows that all six adenoviruses were of the same type."

Gardner's breath left him. "What type?"

"Type 35."

"That's a very unusual human type."

"But it would be perfect for a bioterrorist. Most of the population hasn't any resistance to it."

Gardner could see it all now. "Somebody's found a way to combine the DNA of a common cold virus with an anthrax bacterium or spore. The victim first gets a typical cold, with all its sneezing, coughing, red eyes and runny nose. This spreads the virus, along with the anthrax, to others through airborne droplets. And we know what the result is: forty-eight infected so far."

"And the choice of air travel to start the epidemic is fiendish," Tara added. "One good sneeze in a house, an office, or the closed environment of an airplane will produce enough airborne droplets to infect scores of people."

"That must be it. Customs and Air France tore those six airplanes apart looking for a source of the spores and found nothing. And nothing in the luggage or hotel rooms of those six men. Those fellers were the vectors themselves, probably infected before they boarded the planes."

"Any idea how they did it."

"I can guess. It was basic microbiology. Basic but very well-done. Recombinant DNA. First, you grow a batch of *adenovirus type 35*. Easy enough to do in any well-equipped lab. Then you dissolve the cell walls..."

"Leaving just the strands of viral DNA you want."

"Right. Next you innoculate your anthrax colonies with this DNA. When the anthrax incorporates it, you have an anthrax-adenovirus hybrid. Still deadly but now highly contagious as well."

"But Dave, I thought viruses were very host-specific. An adenovirus is a human virus. It wouldn't infect a bacteria like anthrax, would it?"

"Not in nature, no. But there are ways to get DNA into cells which normally don't accept it."

"Like what?"

"Well, one technique uses an electric current to force the foreign DNA across the host cell wall. Another is the so-called DNA gun."

"DNA gun!" What the hell is that?"

He chuckled. "Sounds far out, doesn't it? You coat the DNA onto microscopic pellets then fire them into the target cells."

"Christ! Then it is possible to make something like this."

"It is. Theoretically, at least, it is."

"So, you infect six fanatics with your new germ, put them on airplanes and *Voila!* You have your epidemic. No suicide bombers. Just coughers and sneezers." She could see clearly how the rest of it went. "The toxic effects of anthrax kill..." she started to say.

"But not before it's been spread to others." Gardner finished.

"They've created a monster," Tara whispered.

"More insidious: a Medusa."

"What?"

"Greek Mythology. Medusa, the lady with snakes for hair. Men turned to stone if they looked at her."

"What else?"

"What else? 'Medusa' means 'the cunning one.'"

"Then that's it, that's what we'll call this new biological weapon. The *Medusa Strain.*"

Gil put the last touches on his housecleaning, dusting off the dresser. There was a fresh smell of polish. When the phone rang, he grabbed it.

"Good morning," she said.

"Hi, Tara."

"Good trip back?"

He hesitated. "Restless. All the stuff that's going on."

"I understand."

Silence flowed down the line as they searched for common ground.

"After you got on that plane, Gil, I thought about sailing."

"It was special, Tara. You were special."

"*Serendipity* was, was—what did Kathryn Hepburn call it in that movie—yar? A New England sailing term. *Serendipity* was yar. She sailed with spirit and a touch of mystery."

"I like that."

"Cassie appreciated your call."

"She's a good girl, Tara. I'll try harder to be there for her."

"Thanks. And I'll try not to get in the way."

"You were never in the way. I stepped away. Into the vodka bottle."

"But those days are gone."

"Yes, they are. In fact, I just cleaned up the place. Found a sandwich I'd forgotten about."

Tara laughed.

Silence again. Then, "How can I help today, Tara?"

"It's my turn to ask for advice, Gil."

"What can I do?"

"I'm preparing a list of public health recommendations for the Surgeon General. Since you're a 'real' doctor—a clinician—I wanted your input."

"What have you come up with so far?"

"The usual. Continued investigation of case contacts by local health departments. Initiation of prophylactic antibiotics for any contacts. And immediate transfer to an Infectious Disease Unit of anyone sick with the infection."

"Physicians must have an adequate supply of antibiotics. My own hospital's running low on Cipro. I've heard the same thing from other ERs."

"The Deputy SG has authorized Cipro release from the National Stockpiles whenever requested by a local health department or physician group. FEMA has been charged with seeing they get delivered."

"What about the anthrax vaccine?"

"We don't have very much of it, certainly not enough for a large population. And even if we did, it takes too long for immunity to develop to do any good for someone who's already been exposed."

Gil looked at some ideas he'd been jotting down on a scratch pad. "I'm speaking as a clinician now, Tara, but I think you should approach the problem from another direction as well."

"Like how?"

"By not focusing just on the anthrax infection."

"What are you getting at?"

"Concentrate on the organism which *spreads* the infection."

"The adenovirus?"

"Exactly."

"How?"

"By preventing its airborne spread."

"Face masks?"

"Right. They're low tech, inexpensive, and readily available at hospitals, clinics, pharmacies and other places. This alone would reduce droplet spread by ninety percent."

"Do you think everyone should wear one, like they did during the 1918 Influenza Pandemic?"

"Heavens no! Not like that. Not everyone. Just those with URI's. A small percentage of the population."

"I'm not certain how well that idea will go over. Women won't want to wear them for beauty reasons, men because they look 'wimpy.'"

Gil persisted. "Some will. Many will, if properly instructed by health authorities."

"I'll put it on my list. It'll be up to the SG to accept it or not. Anything else?"

"For anyone who won't wear a mask—or can't because of lung or heart disease—they should impose on themselves a few days of self-quarantine if they become ill. Stay home. Postpone that shopping trip to the mall or the upcoming concert. That's not a lot to ask of a citizen."

"You're right. But again, I'm not sure. Freedom of movement in our country is almost as precious as freedom of speech. Few will voluntarily restrict their movements if they don't have to. Sure, they'll take sick days off work at the first sign of a snotty nose. Then go to a movie! And we sure as hell can't quarantine the 15-20 million people who have URIs at any given time."

"I still say, if government and health officers present these recommendations the right way, the public will comply with them."

"What do you mean, 'the right way?'"

"Posted notices, newspaper and radio announcements. Television interviews. Every way possible."

"I don't know if…"

"And if our political leaders stepped up with their support…"

"You want a mayor or a governor—or even the President—to wear one of these on television?"

"It might take a little political courage, but it would be effective. He would be a hero."

"Forget it Gil, there are few heroes in politics. But I'll pass the idea along with the others. Anything more?"

"There's always aggressive use of medication to reduce URI symptoms. That could reduce droplet spread significantly."

"Right. Oral and nasal decongestants and antihistamines. Those are all cheap, over-the-counter-remedies, readily available."

"There's one more."

"What is it?"

"Zinc."

"Zinc?"

"Zinc. Taken in the early stages of a cold it reduces both the severity and duration of URI symptoms, particularly the coughing, sneezing and runny nose. Both tablets and a new nasal gel preparation are available over the counter. They are very, very safe, even for children."

"I've heard of it. It just sounds like…"

"Quackery?"

"Yeah. Like leeches."

"Well it's not. I use it and it works. Read the scientific literature on it."

"I'm writing all these things down, Gil. I'll include them with the others. Anything else?"

"That's it. I've shot my wad."

There was an awkward silence as they grappled with the double-entendre. In the old days, there would have been bawdy laughter and ribald jokes. Now there was just silence…

"Sorry Gil," Tara said. "Got another call coming in that I have to take. Call me at home tonight."

Gil headed down the street to a nearby convenience store, his mind preoccupied with Tara's call. The sunshine was blinding. When he put on sunglasses, he caught the reflection in a store window across the street of a man with a glistening shaved head walking behind him. Following him. Wasn't it the same guy he'd seen in the hospital just before Achmed died?

He turned around. No one there. Cautiously, he retraced his steps. Still no one. Was he just being paranoid? Not good. Not good.

At home later, he pawed through some boxes on the shelf of a closet, pulled one down, and there it was. An old snub-nose .38 caliber revolver and a box of cartridges. He hadn't had it out since he moved from the Bay area.

He dug around in his desk and found the gun permit, still valid. It reminded him why he'd purchased the weapon in the first place: he'd been accosted in the hospital parking lot one night by two men looking for drugs.

He turned the gun over in his hands, released the cylinder. Chambers loaded, an empty under the hammer for safety. How quick things came back. Maybe it was time to clean it up and pop off a few loads at a firing range.

13

"Turning and turning in the widening gyre,
The falcon cannot hear the falconer.
Things fall apart; the center cannot hold;
Mere anarchy is loosed upon the world."

W.B. Yeats
The Second Coming

The rats were everywhere. Five or six of them were clustered in a corner of the laboratory fighting over a crust of bread from someone's sack lunch. Others scurried across the formica counter tops. They bypassed the cold bunsen burners for the sweet, sticky liquid coating a plate in the chrome sink. *Rattus rattus.* Thirty of them. Maybe even forty, roaming the room at will, the wrought iron doors to their cages gaping open.

Charlie, lead custodian for the Life Sciences Department of the University of Illinois's campus at Urbana, peered through the window into the freshman biology lab.

"Fuck!" he yelled, watching rats tear at lettuce, rat shit littering the floor around them.

His partner Al shook his head in disbelief. "Will you look at that!" He slapped the door with the palm of his hand, sending rats fleeing.

"Fuckin' little shits!" Charlie yelled, kicking at the mess. But he didn't mean the rats. He meant the human pranksters who had let them out of their cages.

It was the second week of October. Classes had been in session barely three weeks, just enough time for the new students to scope out the territory and hatch their little joke.

"Couldn't they stick to panty raids," Charlie complained, as he, Al, and two veterinary technicians began the clean-up.

"I don't think they do those sorts of things anymore," Al observed. "Now they just live together."

"Damn!" Charlie yelped. "I got bit."

Al looked at the drop of blood oozing from his partner's finger. "Better get a tetanus shot," he recommended gravely. "You never know what sorts of germs those things are carryin'."

When Charlie arrived at the campus medical clinic, two hundred or more students were milling around in front. This was exceptionally heavy patient traffic for the clinic, more than it usually saw in a week. A campus policeman stood guard at the entrance, allowing only a few in at a time.

Charlie slipped around to the rear entrance and used his master key to let himself in.

"It's been like this all day," groused a harried Katie McGraw, R.N. through her surgical mask. "Ever since that student died from anthrax yesterday at University Hospital they've been clamoring for medicine. Anyone with a fever or runny nose thinks he's terminal. And now we're running out of antibiotics."

She took off her gown and poured Charlie a cup of coffee. That's when he noticed that all the other staff—the doctor and two aides—were also wearing gowns, as well as gloves, masks and eye protection of some sort, mostly wrap-around safety glasses.

"Is it really that bad?" Charlie asked, thinking he ought to read a newspaper, or at least watch the evening news now and then.

"It's bad," the nurse said. "Sixty cases have been reported in the Chicago area alone in just the past week. More than two-thirds of them are already dead. See for yourself."

She laid open a copy of the morning's *Chicago Sun Times* on her desk.

The headlines read:

DEADLY EPIDEMIC SWEEPS COUNTRY:
STARTS OUT LIKE COMMON COLD
Terrorism Suspected

Charlie was half-way through the article when the sound of a crash and breaking glass startled him. He looked up just in time to see a rock explode through one of the front doors, followed by the crowd of students surging past the guard into the building. The clinic staff peeled off their gloves, tore off their gowns and, along with Charlie, beat a hasty retreat out the back, abandoning the building to the rioters.

In Los Angeles, it was Monday, October 11, and Michelle Goad, the County Epidemiologist, was under siege as well. But in her case it was from the press. She had tucked her father's pen into her pocket for good luck. Now she faced them.

"One at a time, please. One at a time," she ordered, glaring at the audience. She pointed to an upraised hand.

"How many cases in L.A. so far?"

She signalled to an assistant who put a posterboard chart onto an easel. Pointing to a column of numbers, she continued. "We've documented 12 cases from the Air France flight, 11 passengers and 1 crew member. But there were 25 cases total by the end of the first week, up to 75 by the end of this, the second week. The epidemic is gaining momentum."

A reporter in the back of the room gestured for attention. She recognized him next.

"There's a lot of e-mail traffic claiming the epidemic was started by tainted Mexican meat. Supermarkets are being picketed. And a City Councilman wants the border patrol to interdict all out-of-state meat. What do you say about that?"

"Nonsense." She snorted and slapped the podium with her hand. "Gastrointestinal anthrax has a completely different set of symptoms. Nausea, vomiting, bloody diarrhea, and severe stomach cramps. Totally different from inhalation anthrax. Which is what all our cases have been."

"How many dead so far?" was the next question.

"Sixty."

Someone whistled. "My God, that's higher than AIDS. Seventy-five percent. Is that true?"

"Actually, it's closer to 80 percent. It shows how lethal this disease is. Three out of every four persons who've contracted it are already dead. Usually within five or six days from the onset of their illnesses."

There was a palpable quieting of the listeners. Even the veteran reporters were stunned. It took some time before a new hand went up.

"There are rumors that terrorists have poisoned the water supply. What do you…"

Michelle cut him off with a chop of her hand. She had expected this question and wanted to nip it in the bud quickly. "Listen up." Her eyes swept the room. "Water-borne diseases are characterized by the same gastrointestinal symptoms as food-borne ones. And I've already told you, there have been no such symptoms reported. Got it?"

"A local civil rights leader claims minorities are being turned away from medical facilities because of racial prejudice." The questioner was an African-American man standing in a side aisle. "What's your answer to that?"

Michelle considered this politically-loaded question a full ten seconds before answering. "There may be bigotted doctors and nurses out there. I can't say for sure. I certainly hope not. But one thing I am certain about is that the *germ* causing this epidemic is not racist. Look here and I'll show you why."

She called for a new chart, this one pie shaped, and pointed to the individual 'wedges' as she spoke. "Ten cases have been reported in persons of color, twenty-four more in those with Latin American surnames. These 34 cases exactly match the percentage of the County's population made up by those same minorities. In other words, on a *per capita* basis, there is no increased rate of cases in these ethnic groups. Furthermore…"

She fingered her father's pen as she walked over to a second easel. This one held a map of the County. She pointed to a bunch of red dots scattered about on it. "These mark the locations of our sixty-two cases. There has been no more of them in affluent communities like Palos Verdes, the San Fernando Valley, Santa Monica, Hollywood and Malibu than in Watts, Inglewood or East Los Angeles, where most of our African-Americans and Latinos live." She slapped the map with her wooden pointer. "Draw your own conclusions about racial bias."

"Follow-up question, please," the same man insisted. "What about the charge that minorities aren't getting prophylactic antibiotics as rapidly as whites?"

"There has been a drawdown of our antibiotic supplies," Michelle admitted. "But it's been the same in all neighborhoods: black, brown, or white. Some physicians are over-prescribing them, handing out prescriptions to anyone who asks. Regardless of his or her symptoms. This has severely lowered our reserves. I've asked the Federal Government to release extra doses from the West Coast Stockpile. This should ease the problem soon."

She next called on a local television reporter. "A research biologist at Cal Poly claims the epidemic was caused by secret government experiments gone awry. Like the Soviet outbreak in Siberia years ago. What do you think?"

Michelle smiled. The conspiracy demon was bound to raise its head sooner or later. "The Sverdlovsk epidemic was confined to just one city. It was a true point-source outbreak. Ours is nationwide. It started in six separate cities thousands of miles apart. If you think our government is deliberately using its citizens as guinea pigs for some nightmarish biological experiments, there must have been not one but *six* government 'accidents' around the country. Pretty unlikely, I think." She shook her head. "But I suppose it was only a matter of time before extra-terrestrials or some conspiracy plot was blamed for the epidemic."

She fielded questions for another thirty minutes before holding up her hands. "That's enough. You've been given a written *Press Briefing Statement.* Please publish our recommendations about the use of disposable surgical masks, decongestants and self-quarantine. Thank you."

As she stepped down from the podium and headed for her office, Jerry Essminger caught up with her and tugged on her arm. "Boss, about those antibiotics from the government stockpiles…" he began.

In Philadelphia, a news conference similar to the one in Los Angeles took place the next day. But this one had a twist. The Health Director ended with a strong recommendation for anyone with symptoms of a URI to wear a disposable face mask in public, unless there were medical reasons against it. He held up a blue-green mask—the kind available in most medical clinics—for all to see, then demonstrated its proper use.

The Mayor, to show his support, strode up to the podium wearing a three-layer cotton face mask given him by some surgical nurse. A short, dapper man, the Mayor bore a striking resemblance to Hercule Poirot, Agatha Christie's debonair detective. Someone had painted a moustache identical to Poirot's famous one on the outside of the Mayor's mask. 'Hizzoner' hammed it up, something Poirot would never have approved. He modeled his new face wear for the audience, turning right, then left in profile, finally spinning around to show how it tied in the back. The press loved it and applauded him loudly. The story was carried on the national news shows that evening.

The next night, at a Black Tie charity concert in a venerable old hall on the banks of the Schuylkill River, the city's elite, beautiful and wealthy showed up wearing. . .face masks! But not the three-for-a-dollar hardware store kind, nor even the plain cotton surgical type. Theirs were designer masks. Some were painted with floral print patterns, others crafted into sensuously seductive shapes with silk ties and bows. Still others were embroidered with jewel-encrusted roses and chrysanthemums.

For the men, black—jet black—was the color of choice, with hard-leather ties. 'Black Mask' had replaced 'Black Tie' as the required dress code for formal wear. The shapes of the masks ran from a batman style knock-off which fitted over the nose and mouth, to a 'Phantom of the Opera' look alike with a solid gold overlay for the nose piece.

Everyone thought the whole thing a big hoot. "City's Funny Bone Remains Un-Fractured by Deadly Plague," blared the newspaper headline.

Unfortunately, the real purpose for the masks—to reduce the droplet spread of the *Medusa Strain* by persons with URI symptoms—was missed. Only the healthy and wealthy wore them. Those who were ill or poor felt excluded and didn't. The city eventually paid for its prank with a steep increase in fatal cases of anthrax in the ensuing months, especially among the poor.

In the Bronx, a mob attacked a pharmacy. Not in search of narcotics, but of antibiotics. The Police Commissioner (the 'Comish') ordered beefed-up patrols near such stores. Armed, private security guards were also hired by the drugstore companies to stand round-the-clock vigil outside their establishments.

The Mayor went a step further. He issued an executive order that anyone with URI symptoms caught in public without a face mask was guilty of a misdemeanor and would be cited.

"This is nothing to sneeze at," an ACLU lawyer responded. "The idea of 'cough police' patrolling the city, waiting to haul off a cigarette smoker, asthmatic, or allergy sufferer who lets out an uncontrolled rasp, bark or snort, is not only ludicrous but probably a violation of the privacy protection guaranteed by the U.S. Constitution."

In Denver, which had been especially hard hit by the epidemic, with seventy-five cases and fifty-eight deaths, the City Council carried the quarantine mentality almost to its logical conclusion. Almost. It didn't *order* everyone with URI symptoms to remain indoors. But it strongly recommended it. Then, by way of taking the first step, it ordered all sporting events and concerts cancelled, schools, movie theaters and churches closed. The merchants, bankers, businessmen and clergy howled about lost profits and wept into their silk handkerchiefs, predicting economic and spiritual doom for the city. But the Council held firm, threatening to use the police to enforce its order if it was not complied with voluntarily.

Web-based businesses and e-commerce start-ups saw a real opportunity here. They increased their advertising revenues, pointed out the safety of on-line shopping from home, and soon witnessed a dramatic rise in sales revenues.

In Lexington, Kentucky, which had yet to feel the epidemic's bite, one man sued another for sneezing in his direction in an elevator and not covering his nose and mouth.

'Snot is now a lethal weapon,' the brief filed with the Clerk of Courts charged. 'Just like blood.'

When a reporter pointed out that the city had yet to report a single case of the deadly new disease, the plaintiff's lawyer answered. "If someone points a gun at you, you can't tell whether it's loaded or not. If someone bleeds on you, you don't know whether you're in real danger from AIDS or not. The same is now true for snot."

Unexpectedly, the judge did not throw the case out of court. Instead, he set a trial date.

In Mystic, Connecticut, which also had yet to report its first case, a mailman with a long history of ragweed allergy was shot to death by an elderly man as he came to the door to deliver a package, then sneezed.

14

Gil Martin had been busy, as busy as he had been since his residency training years ago, working six, sometimes seven days a week. But for a change it was a good kind of busy, not just toil and 'scut work.' He wasn't just a 'doc-in-a-box' any longer. He was needed now, sought after. Life and work had purpose again. He began to like the face he saw in the mirror each morning. Even his fingernails had begun to grow.

And his phone calls to Tara and Cassie were going well, with tension slipping away on a first laugh, a first joke. He could trace when it changed, the benchmark:

"So, Tara. How about you?"

"How about me what?"

"You seeing any one? Is there a man in your life?"

She could have said she was totally caught up in her work. Instead, she let the truth carry itself. "No, Gil. I'm not seeing anyone."

His first task on returning from Washington nearly three weeks ago had been to evaluate the 'Case Definition' for the epidemic. A universally-accepted definition for the disease was essential. Both to stop over-diagnosis—and needless antibiotic prescribing—and to prevent under-diagnosis and delays in treatment. He had read virtually every piece of literature on both anthrax and adenovirus. And he now had six actual cases of *Medusa* under his belt. He was L.A.'s acknowledged clinical expert. He even took several phone calls a day from physicians who wanted to discuss their own cases with him.

Jerry Essminger had sent him the Health Department's working 'Case Definition' for his review and comment. Gil's rewrite had been so precise and clinically relevant it was immediately accepted without change as the Department's official one. It was then sent to all physicians, physician assistants, nurse practitioners, nurses and health care facilities in Southern California. The result, Jerry informed him, had been a gratifying reduction in over-diagnosing. Health care practitioners were beginning to use the 'rifle'—that is, the specific criteria of the 'Case Definition' for diagnosis and treatment—instead of the 'shotgun'—treat every cough, sneeze, or runny nose with antibiotics and hope you 'hit' a few actual cases of *Medusa*. In addition, Jerry told him, true cases of anthrax were now being recognized and diagnosed earlier. This gave the patient a slim but definitely improved chance for recovery.

On this particular morning, Gil was standing at the counter in front of the nurse's desk. He was writing up a minor trauma case he had just treated when Essminger called to thank him for his efforts on the 'Case Definition' project.

"How are the antibiotic supplies holding up?" Gil asked. His own hospital pharmacy had hit bottom. Others were depleting their stores at an alarming rate as well.

"Not good, but at least the massive over-prescribing we saw last week is tapering off. The big problem now is laboratory capability. Since we've asked physicians to be more certain of their diagnosis before ordering antibiotics, labs have been inundated with requests for PCR's and ELISA's. Even standard micro labs are having a hard time keeping up with demands for blood stains and blood cultures."

"Sounds like defensive medicine."

"Probably. Nobody wants to be sued for missing a case of anthrax or failing to begin antibiotics soon enough."

That evening, Gil phoned Tara. His pretext for the call was to complain about the dwindling antibiotic supplies and to ask for her help. But the truth was, he simply wanted to hear her voice. He looked forward eagerly to their conversations, now nighttime regulars.

"It took us a week to figure out how to submit a proper request to FEMA," he griped. "Then we were told the request had been approved but there were no vehicles to pick up and deliver the medications. When that was supposedly corrected, and we still hadn't received any drugs, we called again. This time we were told they had no record of our original request; would we please re-submit it. Can you light a fire under them?"

Tara promised to do what she could at the federal level.

After the business part of their conversation was over, there were questions and stories about Cassie, about other family members Gil had lost contact with after the divorce, and about mutual friends he had forgotten about.

"What's the latest buzz about that new French exchange student at Cassie's school?" he asked. "What was his name?"

"Alain. He's gone."

"What happened?"

"He got sick almost immediately. Within a few days of his arrival. The school nurse became alarmed when he showed up for his first day of class with a high fever.

"*Medusa?*"

"'fraid so. He was one of our first Atlanta cases. But he survived. As soon as he could travel, he returned to France."

"What about the family he was staying with?"

"Not so lucky. Their 8-year old daughter caught it. Despite prophylactic antibiotics, she died."

Gil stopped his doodling. "Oh, Christ, Tara. I'm so sorry."

"But that was all, Gil. Cassie and her friends are fine. And there have been no other school cases."

"Thank God."

Their conversation brightened after this, with personal banter. He hadn't had a drink in three weeks.

Shortly after lunch the next day, Miguel, the hospital's radio dispatcher, came rushing into the ER from his office down the hall. He was red-faced, wild-eyed, and breathing rapidly.

"It's the Junior High School around the corner! *El epidemico* has hit there! The kids are all…"

"Calm down!" Kathy Roberts ordered. "Take a breath. What's going on?"

The young Latino did as ordered. "The school nurse, she's sending us four eighth-graders. Says they all have the anthrax. Two of them are having fits."

The color drained from Kathy's pretty face, leaving it pale and tense.

"It'll be alright," Gil assured her. "We'll manage." He put a hand on the dispatcher's shoulder. "Now, slowly, Miguel. What else did the nurse tell you?"

"The kids are all from the same class, three girls and a boy. Two fainted and started having the fits. Another, a *muchacha*, is in a coma. And the fourth one, a *muchacho*, is holding his head and moaning. She couldn't get anything else out of him."

Gil looked at Kathy. "Have there been any other cases from that school?"

"Yes. A week ago we had Ella. You remember, the daughter of one of the original Flight 62 passengers. We transferred her to County Hospital, but she died there. A local television station went to the school and interviewed the teachers and students. They did a whole show on it yesterday."

"I remember watching it last night myself. That was the same school?"

"The very one."

"Why do you suppose the nurse is sending all four kids here?"

"I guess we're the closest," Kathy answered. "Why else?"

"No, no," Miguel interrupted. He pointed at Gil. "It's because of you, *senior* doc. You're famous. The nurse wants all the students to be seen by you. She screamed at me."

"Looks like fame is a mixed blessing," Kathy said, points of color back in her cheeks. She hurried off to get everything ready.

Gil stood well out of the way when the four students were brought in, undressed, gotten into gowns, and their vital signs recorded. But he could see right off that two of the girls were indeed intermittantly twitching. But not with the full, generalized motor seizures of epilepsy. Rather with spasmodic jerks, first of an arm, then a leg, then back to the arm again. The third girl was unconscious, or appeared to be. Totally limp, she was dead weight when they moved her from the ambulance gurney onto the exam table. The fourth student, the boy, was sitting on the table holding his head and moaning. Kathy Roberts tried but got no more information out of him than had the school nurse.

Gil was handed four clipboards. The first thing he noticed was a significant 'negative,' the absence of fever. There was not even the slightest temperature rise above normal in any of them. The rest of their vital signs were equally unremarkable: stone-cold normal heart rates, blood pressures, and respiratory rates.

When he glanced in the direction of the exam booths, he was suddenly struck by how quiet it was, deafeningly so. There was none of the sneezing, coughing, snorting and hacking he'd come to expect from *Medusa* patients. Except for the groans from the boy with the headache, these kids barely made a sound.

Gil had a pretty good hunch about what was going on. But he examined each of the children carefully to be certain he wasn't missing something. In the first booth, a little girl with dark hair tied up in a bun appeared to be unconscious. Her lids were so tightly shut he could see the muscles tensed around her eyes. When he picked up her hand and let it drop, it fell lifelessly down to her side. No resistance at all. He checked her neck. Completely supple. No sign of the nuchal rigidity characteristic of meningitis.

Abruptly, he clapped his hands near her ear. She stiffened, opened her eyes for a moment, and let out a small cry. Then lapsed back into her pseudo-coma. Gil wrote his diagnosis on the record: 'Hysterical Conversion Reaction.'

He went quickly from booth to booth, examining the other children in turn. The so-called convulsions, on closer examination, didn't match any seizure disorder he was familiar with. And neither child showed any typical post-seizure phenomena, like soiling or wetting the pants. Again, he wrote 'hysteria' on their records.

When he examined the boy holding his head, he found no objective physical findings to explain his distress. No sore throat or fever, no swollen lymph glands or ear infection. Not even a toothache!

"What's going on?" Kathy asked suspiciously. "None of these kids has *Medusa*, do they?"

"'Epidemic hysteria,'" Gil said. "Probably triggered by all the media attention at their school yesterday."

"You mean they're just faking it?" Fergus Robinson, the ER technician, was disgusted.

"No, not at all," Gil answered quickly. "The boy holding his head really has a headache. The others are truly convinced they are sick with anthrax. Their symptoms—pseudo-seizures, pseudo-coma—are the physical expressions of those beliefs."

"What should we do with them?" Kathy asked, relieved but annoyed. "I can't afford to have four of my examination beds occupied if it's not necessary."

"Keep them here until their parents arrive, explain what's going on to mom and dad, and reassure them. Then send them home. They can follow-up with their family physicians tomorrow. They'll be fine."

••

That evening, he called Tara to tell her about the four kids with hysteria.

"We've had reports of epidemic hysteria from all over the country," she said. "Usually in ones or twos, sometimes more. I'm keeping a record of them."

"What other kinds have you heard about?"

"Well, let's see: there were the four laundry workers from Cook County Hospital in Chicago who were brought to the ER complaining of breathing problems. They were not wheezing or breathing hard, their lungs were clear and the chest x-rays were normal in all of them."

"Hyperventilation?" Gil guessed.

"Exactly. The ER staff had them breathe into brown paper bags. Their symptoms all disappeared within minutes."

"What triggered it?"

"They discovered they had been handling the bed clothes of a patient who died of *Medusa* the day before. One of them was convinced she could smell the infection on the sheets."

"What else?"

"You name it. Dizziness. Nausea and vomiting. Headaches and weakness. Coughing. Numbness and tingling of the legs. They've all been reported. And my favorite: hysterical dancing."

"Dancing?"

"Yup. Twirling 'round and 'round for hours. Another good one was a case of hysterical laughing which went on for hours and hours. Then there was the patient who suddenly started screaming obscenities, like someone with Tourette's syndrome. There was even the case of a teenage boy found wandering around in a park in the middle of the night dressed in bathrobe and slippers."

"Like an Alzhiemer's patient."

151

"Except this boy was thirteen years old. It turned out his grandfather, who would wander off periodically to the same park, had died the day before."

"Of anthrax?"

"Of a heart attack."

During the next two weeks Gil saw four more cases of epidemic hysteria. Two were men brought in with chest tightness and coughing. They worked at the County Landfill and claimed they smelled some sort of toxic gas there. They were convinced it was loaded with *Medusa* spores and they were going to die. The other two were women employees of a beauty parlor who complained of numbness and tingling in their hands and feet brought on by some unusual smell in the building. The brown paper bag treatment promptly cured them.

By the end of the third week of October, international consequences from the American outbreak were being felt. Canada closed its borders to the U.S. And, in a stunning reversal of the normal state of affairs, so did Mexico. The government of Turkey, stung by accusations that the epidemic had originated there, cancelled all U.S. flights, both inbound and outbound, from its airports in Istanbul, Ankara and Izmir.

The stock market initially had no reaction to the epidemic, watching it warily like someone on the sidelines of a cat fight; there was a lot of scratching and hissing, but no apparent damage. But as a plague mentality spread throughout the country, stores began to close when employees became too ill—or too frightened— to staff them. Or customers too frightened to patronize them. People shunned shops, malls, theatres, and even their neighbors' backyard barbecues. The only businesses which remained brisk were those selling motorhomes, travel trailers, and camping supplies. Campgrounds filled up, and it became commonplace to see families tenting or RV'ing in remote parks or on stretches of desert or seashore.

Wall Street finally realized that while the total number of anthrax cases was relatively small, the plague mentalilty had multiplied its economic effects many times. The market dropped five hundred points in a single day. Not a crash, but enough to get the White House's attention. Gold shot up to $350 per ounce. Demands for the President to do something were heard from all corners of the land and from both sides of the political spectrum.

15

The Persian Gulf, the third week of October.

The *Ticonderoga*-class guided missile cruiser U.S.S. *Cowpens* (CG-63), on direct orders from the National Command Authority, took up her lonely station off the Kuwaiti coast. But even by herself *Cowpens* was a formidable threat. With her Advanced Weapons Fire Control System she could detect, track, and kill multiple attacks from the air, and both on and under the sea. And that was only on defense.

On offense, her chief strategic punch was the Tomahawk Ballistic Guided Missile. Tipped with either conventional explosives or a tactical nuclear weapon, and with a reach of 1000 statute miles, *Cowpens* could, if so ordered, spray most of the Middle East countryside with missiles almost as fast as you could say "gezundheit." Virtually every Iraqi target could be brought into her crosshairs within minutes.

Tomahawk's guidance system was designed to fly the missile through a one meter square opening at a precisely designated time, a space about the size of the average American bedroom window. And these claims of accuracy had been borne out again and again in the ten years that the missile has been in operational use: eighty-five percent or better strike rates have been well documented.

From the same station *Cowpens* was on now, Tomahawks were launched on August 20, 1998 against anti-terrorist targets in

Sudan and Afghanistan. And later that same year *Cowpens's* sister ship, U.S.S. *Gettysburg (CG 64),* launched Tomahawks from both her fore and aft missile compartments against military sites in Iraq.

At the U.S. Air Force Base at Diyarbakir in southeastern Turkey two F-15 Eagles spun up to 'ready' status. Normally part of routine no-fly zone patrols, these particular Eagles had been briefed on a possible special mission against a target in the northern Iraqi city of Mosul. After months of boring patrols, the pilots were itching for some real action.

In Washington, D.C., Gil Martin craned his neck for a better view of the Ionic capitols on the columns of the White House South Portico. Tara looked at the magnificent magnolia trees shading the porch. They had been planted originally by President Andrew Jackson. No doubt so he could sip his Kentucky whiskey in comfort.

Tara was awed. "I'll bet this place has seen some history," she whispered.

"Ya think?" Gil whispered back.

This was the seat of world power, this one 'house' on Pennsylvania Avenue. Only Buckingham Palace and the Kremlin rivalled it in their heydays. Originally built in 1792, the President's House, as it is now called, burned to the ground during the War of 1812. President James Madison and his wife Dolly had to flee for their lives. It was rebuilt five years later. But porticoes, rooms— even entire stories—were added to it regularly since.

The ghosts of history were everywhere in this building. Lincoln, head bowed, pacing the dark halls in search of an Army commander who would fight. Franklin Roosevelt, cigarette holder clenched between its teeth, rallying the nation against the Axis powers with fireside chats. And Kennedy, staring down Khruschev during the Cuban Missile Crisis.

One of the most popular tourist sites in the country, the White House normally saw a million and a half visitors annually. But tours had been abruptly cancelled after September 11, 2001. Even now, security remained tight. Tara and Gil had undergone both hands-on and electronic searches when they arrived and would have to endure still more. The mood was somber, the faces on the staff long. A smile was hard to find.

Gil looked around the room. They had been escorted to the White House Situation Room. This was the Inner Sanctum, the Holy of Holies. No one got admitted here unless you had a lot of stars on your shoulders, had an impressive title after your name—Cabinet Secretary or Agency Head—or there was a national emergency and you had something your country needed. Like Gil and Tara had now. The room had been party to all the great post-WWII events: Truman's decision to drop The Bomb; Kennedy's to launch an invasion of Cuba at the Bay of Pigs; and Lyndon Johnson's to dip his toe into a place called the Gulf of Tonkin off the coast of Vietnam. He would end up drowning his political future there.

"When was the last time we were here?" Tara asked, looking crisp in a beige suit with a print scarf and the faintest hint of a new perfume.

"About twelve years ago," Gil recalled. "We were on vacation, doing all the usual things, including the White House tour. Cassie was still a toddler and hadn't quite got the toilet training thing down yet."

They took their seats at an enormous mahogany table, so polished the overhead light gleamed in its luster.

"Thanks for coming, Gil," Tara said. "Dave Gardner specifically asked for you. And I'm glad you're here as well." She gave his arm one last squeeze before letting go.

In addition to the two Doctor Martins, the President's Chief of Staff was there: Thomas O'Malley. 'Tommy' to his friends, a crusty veteran pol from Massachusetts. Also present was the White House Director of Communications, Janelle Burke Hyde, or JB.

When the Chief of Staff greeted him with a perfunctory handshake, Gil was hit by the unmistakeable breath of a long-time tobacco user.

"Whew!" he whispered to Tara.

"Cigars," Tara whispered back. "The man loves cigars. It's rumored the President selected him to be COS as much for his well-stocked humidor as for his political savvy."

"They allow cigar smoking in the White House?"

"Shh! Everyone knows but nobody talks. It's considered one of the perks. There's a long tradition of cigar smoking here, especially among the senior staff. Pierre Salinger, Kennedy's Press Secretary, and Marlin Fitzwater—President Bush's—loved their stogies."

Tara and Gil Martin, along with the other members of the Anthrax Task Force, were seated around the perimeter of the room. Today, they were but soldiers in the fight. The leaders of their agencies took center stage at the main table itself. They included the heads of the FBI, CIA, FEMA, NSA and the State Department. The military was represented by the Chairman of the Joint Chiefs of Staff (CJCS), the Service Chiefs, and SECDEF himself. The nation's top non-military doctor, the Surgeon General, who wore rank insignia equivalent to a three-star general, took his place at the table next to the White House Chief of Staff.

Dave Gardner and Oscar Bentley slipped in just as an aide was closing the door.

When the President arrived, everyone jumped to his feet. The military men and women came to full attention.

"Good morning, Mr. President" rang out, practically in unison.

"Good morning, good morning."

Cautious by nature, the President followed the dictum, make haste slowly. He had watched the epidemic's beginnings with practiced detachment, resisting the cries for him to do something. He saw the crisis as principally a local public health problem. There was adequate governmental machinery to handle it, albeit with predictable bureaucratic snags and snafus. But the foreign threat could not be ignored. He was the Commander-in-Chief. The entire world looked to him for leadership. It was time to get into the game.

He looked around the table. "Who's up first?"

"That would be the Surgeon General," the Chief of Staff said.

"Good morning, Mr. President," the SG began. "CDC now has reports of over a thousand *Medusa* cases. Most are from large cities. But scattered ones have come in from suburban and rural locations, and from just about every state in the Union. The fatality rate remains near 65%. Worse, physicians and health facilities are running out of antibiotics. Supplies from the National Stockpiles just aren't getting to them, despite their urgent requests."

The Head of FEMA, stung by mounting criticism of his agency's poor performance, responded quickly. "We'll take the hit on that one, Mr. President. It's our fault. We've had delays getting transport. But Reserve Army Units have been activated. With their Motor 'T' capabilities the situation should soon improve."

"We certainly hope so," the President said with a frown. He turned next to the Director of the Central Intelligence Agency. "What do we know about where this damned thing, this *Medusa Strain*, came from?"

"I have two videotapes for you to view, Mr. President. You'll see, in a very graphic way, the answer to your question."

Oscar Bentley, who was standing by a VCR, switched it on.

"The images you are about to see," the CIA chief warned, "show human biological experimentation not unlike what the Nazis and Japanese did during WWII. They are very disturbing."

All heads turned toward the monitor as it played Ramazzan Fahr's secret tapes...

Abdullah, weak and frightened, looked around the small room. Then Serina lay on her bed, life draining from her. Her hand draped down to touch the floor. The foulness of what was happening projected from the screen into the lustrous paneled and polished Situation Room. Tara stiffened, watching Serina. Gil's hand found hers in the dark and closed over it. Then he released it...

"Those bastards," someone muttered when the show was over and the lights were back up.

"Where did you get those?" the President asked.

"They were purchased by the French from someone who witnessed the experiments first-hand. Our anthrax expert, Dr. Gardner, says they prove beyond any doubt the Iraqis have found a way to make anthrax contagious by linking it to a common cold virus."

"Do we know where the experiments were carried out?"

"We do now, thanks to the French. They had someone follow the informer back to his laboratory in Mosul. We know exactly where it is."

"So, what are we going to do about this new biological weapon?" the President asked. "This *Medusa Strain*."

"I have a one-word answer to that, Mr. President." The Chairman of the Joint Chiefs of Staff banged his fist down on the table. "T-LAM! I have a T-LAM shooter in the Gulf right now. U.S.S. *Cowpens*. And the GPS coordinates of that lab are loaded into her weapons computer. You give the word, Mr. President, and *Cowpens* will turn that building and everything in it into just another patch of Iraqi desert."

Tara Martin nudged Dave Gardner. "T-LAM?"

"Tomahawk-Land-Attack-Missile," he whispered. "Our biggest and best spear."

"With all due respect to the general, Mr. President," Gardner said from his seat on the side of the room, "but y'all can't do that."

"And why not?" the nation's top military man shot back. "We've conducted surgical Tomahawk strikes before. Hell, we've been doing it for almost ten years in the Gulf against a variety of Iraqi targets. We can take out that lab and its germs, and all its equipment—maybe even some of the bad guys—with one missile. And with little collateral damage."

Gardner was firm. "You can't do that, suh, precisely *because* of those germs. Some quantity of *Medusa* may already be in spore form."

"So?" CJCS demanded. "We'll vaporize them too!"

"No suh, it's not that easy. Anthrax spores can survive the most severe conditions you could imagine. I oughta know. We froze 'em, boiled 'em, dried 'em out, dumped strong acids and bleaches on 'em. Even tried blowin' 'em up. They survived all our efforts, still intact, still highly infectious. Once that spore's formed, it's practically in-de-struct-ible. Besides, your T-LAM shot would scatter the damned things across Mosul and most of northern Iraq. There would be many innocent deaths."

CIA quickly added, "prevailing wind patterns in that area are east-to-west. Spores liberated by such an explosion would be blown into Syria, Lebanon, Israel and Turkey. Some of these nations are our friends and allies. And we wouldn't want to deliberately antagonize any of the others either. The international consequences would be too terrible to contemplate."

The President was frustrated. "So," he asked, "what exactly can we do to eliminate this threat?"

"Whatever you decide, sir, you better do it quickly." The warning came from the Director of the NSA. Started by a bunch of code breakers during WWII, this premier spy agency developed hi-tech surveillance methods for snooping on the Reds during the Cold War. With that threat behind it, its glory days were fading fast. Until the War on Terrorism began after the WTC attack. NSA was now infused with new funding and a new purpose.

"SIGINT—Signal Intelligence," the NSA General continued, "intercepted a satellite phone conversation between Baghdad and Mosul. We're pretty certain it was Saddam Hussein himself on one end of the line and the Director of the lab in Mosul on the other."

When the man paused to check his notes, the President grumbled. "Get on with it, General. What did you hear?"

"Yessir. Saddam wanted to know when the next batch would be ready."

"Those were his exact words? The 'next batch.'"

"Yessir. But we're not certain whether he meant a new group of agents they've recruited or a new batch of germs. Or both."

"What was the answer?"

"'Within ten days.'"

The President was shaken. "Ten days. Are you certain?"

"Yessir."

"Six more vectors," Dave Gardner said to Tara Martin. "Headin' to six more American cities."

"But how would they get in?" the Chief of Staff asked. "Now that we know about those first six, shouldn't we be able to stop them from gaining entrance to the country?"

The Secretary of State had been silent until now. "I'm afraid, Mr. President, that our 3,000-mile border with Canada and our 1,000-mile one with Mexico are as porous as a sieve."

"Because of the North American Free Trade Agreement—NAFTA?"

"Partly. And we're just a short speed boat ride from Cuba. I can imagine any number of ways one or more of these 'vectors,' as Dr. Gardner calls them, could be slipped in."

Grim-faced, the President summed up. "This is not good news. We can't blow up the lab because we may spread spores all over hell's half acre. But we've only got ten days before we get hit with a new group of disease carrying agents." He searched the faces at the table. "Is there nothing we can do?"

The room was so quiet the scratchings and scribblings of pencils and pens could be heard.

Finally, Dave Gardner stood up beside his chair. "Yessuh. There is something we can do. We must inactivate *Medusa*. Then we can destroy that lab with impunity."

The President looked at him, his face ugly with tension. "And just how do we do that?"

"I have a plan."

"What plan?"

"It has two parts. And it will be risky. But it might work."

"Let's hear it. There's nothing else on the table."

Gardner cleared his throat. "I've been able to duplicate the Iraqi process at my lab and produce a few *Medusa* colonies. And I've discovered a weak link in their procedure. Once *Medusa* is converted into spores, it must be used right away. Otherwise, the part of it which causes disease becomes inactive. *Medusa's* then completely harmless. I suspect the Iraqis save this final part of the process—making the spore forms—until their human 'vectors' are fully trained and their mission plans finalized. So, most of the bacteria is still sitting in culture flasks and agar plates, still vulnerable."

"How do we inactivate them?" The President was leaning forward now. "Dump acid or something like that into the vats?"

"We could do that. But it would be difficult and risky. And it would completely destroy the cultures. The bacterial colonies would disappear. The flasks and agar plates would be totally empty. The Iraqis would instantly know we were onto them. They could simply shut down and go underground for a while. Then relocate to a different site and start up again. We would have to go through this whole nightmare again."

"What's your idea?"

"I want 'em to think *Medusa* has changed, has mutated into somethin' harmless. Mutation is common in biology. Living organisms change, adapt and mutate. There's no way to predict it. Too bad, the Iraqis will think. It's happened to *Medusa*. Then, perhaps, they'll abandon their bioweapons research altogether."

The President was impressed. "But can we do it?"

"Yes. Yessuh! But this is where the second part of my plan comes in. I've developed an agent against *Medusa*. It infects it, grows and reproduces inside it, and renders it harmless."

The President's face softened. "You can do that?"

"I've done it."

"How does it work, doc," the Chief of Staff asked.

Here goes, Gardner said to himself. He launched into his explanation...

Gil Martin's was the first hand up when Gardner was done. "What did you test it on?"

"Rabbits. First, I infected some *Medusa* colonies with my new agent. Then I sprayed 'em on the rabbits. The furry critters remained perfectly healthy. Not even a rabbit cold! But a control group exposed to *Medusa not* inactivated by my agent all died."

"Christ, that's good, that's good," the President said. "To the Iraqis, this new *Medusa*, infected with your agent, will look the same. Just like an evil twin. But it will be completely inert."

CJCS brightened, following the President's lead. "And before they can figure out what went wrong, we'll zap 'em with our missiles."

"We hope so," Gardner cautioned. "It should work. Let's hope it works."

"But rabbits aren't people," Gil Martin pointed out. "How do you know it will work on humans?"

Gardner hesitated, then turned and looked at his old poker-playing friend, Oscar Bentley. "Well, Bullethead...?"

Oscar had been fiddling with the videotape machine. When he felt all eyes focused on him, he looked up. "Because it worked on me."

The President jumped to his feet. "What! You've carried out experiments on humans, Dr. Gardner? Who the hell..."

"I volunteered," Oscar said, interrupting the most powerful man in the world.

"Better hear him out," Gardner said.

"This could mean jail, Dr. Gardner," the Chief of Staff warned.

"Rusty Gardner saved my life in Vietnam," Oscar said. He looked around, his calm presence quieting the room. "I owe him. And I trust him completely. He confided to me that he wished to use himself as a test subject. To see if his agent really worked on people. Self-testing is not unprecedented in the medical research community. Jonas Salk tried out his new polio vaccine on himself. Rusty's plan was to do the same. But that wouldn't work, of course, because he's fully immunized against anthrax. As are all USAMRIID researchers. He was frustrated and told me he really needed a human test subject to be certain his agent worked. The stakes were too high to go ahead without it.

"I'm a widower, with no children," Oscar continued. "My own physician says my heart won't last but a couple of years. All I can do is play out the hand I've been dealt. I have little to lose, and we all, our country, in fact, has everything to gain. So I volunteered."

"I tried to talk him out of it," Gardner said quietly. "He wouldn't listen."

"We got me admitted to USAMRIID's research ward. Rusty explained the risks. I told him to get on with it."

Gardner took over. "I followed the same protocol for Oscar I did for the rabbits. That was six days ago, almost to the hour."

"I got a little cough and a runny nose," Oscar reported. "I took some decongestants and drank plenty of fluids. But that was it. Nothing more. By the time I was released, I felt as fit as a fiddle. Still had a bummed out ticker. But fit nonetheless."

The President offered Oscar a small smile. It faded as he looked at Dr. Gardner. "And this doesn't violate our own ban on the development of offensive biological weapons?"

"No suh," Gardner answered. "My new agent is only dangerous to *Medusa*."

"Questions?" the Chief of Staff asked, looking around the table.

"How do we get your new agent into that Iraqi lab?" someone asked. "I assume we can't just drop it from the air?"

"No," Gardner admitted. "We can't. It will have to be secreted into the lab somehow, then injected into the *Medusa* cultures. And it must be done before *Medusa* is turned into spores. I estimate we have about six or seven days at most to accomplish this."

CIA raised his hand. "That may be possible, Mr. President. We have a new ground-based operative in Iraq right now, near Mosul in fact. If Dr. Gardner can get us his new agent soon enough, and in enough quantity to do the job, there's a good chance our man can get it into the laboratory undetected."

"He will have to know where *Medusa* is kept," Gardner insisted. "And he must be protected. I won't be part of any suicide mission."

"Trust me," CIA assured him. "This agent is fully trained in biological research techniques. He's even had experience in Biosafety Level 4 labs, where only the most dangerous bacteria are kept."

"What about that Iraqi informer, the one who smuggled out the videotape?" the Chief of Staff asked. "Can we use him?"

"He will be of some use," CIA answered. He smiled mysteriously. "Of this you can be certain."

"How can you be so positive?"

"Because we've uncovered some very interesting personal information about him. It should, shall we say, motivate him highly. But he's only an administrative assistant. He knows the way around the lab and where *Medusa* is stored. But he cannot carry out the mission himself. That will be up to our man in place."

"What do you call this new biological agent of yours, this thing which infects *Medusa* and knocks the stuffing out of it?" the President asked. "Have you given it a name."

"Yessuh. In keeping with our Greek mythology theme, I've called it the '*Perseus Factor.*'"

"Ha!" the President chortled. "Perseus was the Greek hero who destroyed the Medusa, right?"

"You are correct, Mr. President. By looking at the monster's image indirectly in a highly polished bronze shield, he avoided *Medusa's* direct gaze and was able to cut off her head."

The President looked around the room; there were no other questions or comments. "Dr. Gardner's plan seems to be our only chance. Unless there are any other questions, I'm prepared to authorize the mission. As soon as you have your process completed, Dr. Gardner, you will make *Perseus* available to CIA. They will do the rest."

The President stood. Everyone else jumped to his feet. He looked from face to face but said nothing. The tension mounted. Finally, he said, "Let's get on with it," and departed.

"Thank you, Mr. President."

Dave Gardner headed for the exit. He had a lot of work to do and not much time left in which to do it.

But the Chief of Staff stopped him on the way out. "Before you head back to your lab, there's a very special patient I would like you to see. The White House physician asked for you. The President himself has approved it. What do you say? It would be a great personal favor to me."

"Of course," Gardner said, his curiosity piqued. "But you understand I'm a lab researcher. I haven't actually treated any patients with *Medusa*."

"They still want your opinion, doc."

"Then lead on."

On her way out, Tara Martin nudged Oscar Bentley. "I think you're a genuine hero."

He winced. "Or just an old fool."

"If you had died, they would have given you a medal. Now, it's likely no one outside this room will ever remember what you did."

Oscar shrugged. "I'll be in a file somewhere. And Rusty Gardner will always have a good word for me."

"By the way," Tara said, heading for the door. "Where's your new partner? What was his name? Jean-Claude?"

"Let's just say he's on a special mission and leave it at that." Oscar looked at the pin on Tara's new beige suit and at the scarf nestled at her throat. "That's a lovely brooch."

"Thank you. From the old country. It was my mother's. I thought this was a rather special occasion. But after those videos…"

Oscar looked from Tara to Gil, who had been standing quietly. "You two belong together," he said.

16

The small convoy—three vehicles in all, a jeep in the lead—crept out of Mosul in the early morning hours and headed for the Kurdish hills. By midday the platoon of Iraqi soldiers had reached its destination and disembarked. They continued up the gravel road on foot to the small Kurd encampment just ahead. Their orders had come directly from Saddam Hussein: capture two more Kurds. Do not harm them. Blindfold them and escort them back to Mohammed's laboratory in Mosul. They must be young, well-fed, and appear free of obvious infirmities. Anyone in the clan who resists or tries to help the captives is to be shot.

The soldiers had little moral reluctance about their mission. Kurds were stiff-necked outsiders, as different from themselves as the Dakota Sioux were from Custer's 7th Cavalry troopers. A proud, ancient people, Kurds didn't even speak the same Arabic dialect the soldiers did, but rather a distant cousin of the Iranian family of languages. They also dressed differently, distinctively so, ate different types of foods, and to most Iraqis were *l'etrangers,* strangers.

Devout Sunni Muslims, even their religion separates the Kurds from the majority of Iraqis who are Shiites. And while Islam is in principal a gentle religion (the word itself means 'surrender to God' in Arabic), it is as familiar with hatred and violence as its Christian counterpart.

Two days after the Iraqi patrol had completed its assignment, on a cold, clear, moonless night as still as well water, three men huddled together around the hood of a Land Rover. The sky in this remote area along the bench of the Kurdish Hills was free of city light pollution and offered a cascade of stars.

There was Polaris in the north, the Pole Star, and its circumpolar constellations: the distinctive 'W' of Cassiopeia; Ursa Major, the Great Bear, which we call the 'Big Dipper;' and Ursa Minor, the Little Bear or 'Little Dipper,' whose handle is nailed into the sky by the Pole star itself. All the stars of the 'Little Dipper' were visible tonight, not just one or two in the bowl, the usual case for city dwellers.

In the east, rising over the hilltops, was the first of those glorious winter constellations: mighty Orion, the hunter with his three distinctive belt stars; the v-shaped face of Taurus the bull; and the seven sisters—the Pleides—sometimes mistaken as the 'Little Dipper.'

In the west, another point of light appeared to the three watchers. But this one was not in the sky. It was on the ground, a single luminescense which finally resolved itself into twin automobile headlights. The three men around the Land Rover watched in silence as the vehicle climbed up the dirt road towards them.

When he arrived at the meeting place, Ramazzan Fahrs was visibly agitated. "Why have you asked for another meeting? You put my life in great danger." He could make out the face of Louis, the French Diplomat, whom he'd met with twice before. But only the silhouettes of the other two men were visible. In his paranoia, they were menacing.

"We know the risks," Louis said gently. "Be assured, you were not followed. Your secret is safe."

"What do you want?" Ramazzan demanded. "You've had the two videotapes I gave you for more than a week. That is all there is. I have no more."

"We are grateful for them. The money you asked for has been safely deposited into a Swiss bank account. And your new identity papers are almost ready."

This had a noticeable calming effect on the fearful Iraqi. "Very well. My bags are packed. When do I leave?"

"Soon. The plans to smuggle you out are nearly ready. But it will not be easy. You will be notified."

Ramazzan was irritated. "Did you have me come all the way out here just to tell me that?"

"We have…" Louis searched for words…"how shall I say it…another proposition for you."

"No! No, no." Ramazzan stamped his foot. "I have risked much already. You have what you wanted. A bargain is—how is it you say?—a bargain. I expect you to carry out your part of it."

"Hear us out," Louis insisted, then stepped aside. One of the hooded shapes moved out of the shadows and introduced himself.

"My name is Jean-Claude," the man said in perfect Arabic.

Ramazzan recoiled. Here was a tall, rangy, powerful-looking, man. His voice was husky and his stance confident, like a boxer's. Bathed in celestial light, a star-shaped scar glistened on his right cheek.

"What we ask is simple," Jean-Claude said softly. "And what we offer is much. Double the five million pounds you've already been paid."

Ramazzan hesitated. Another ten million! A fortune. There was much he could do with it. Political goals. Revenge against Saddam. Humanitarian ends. And still have enough for a comfortable life himself. But wait! For that kind of money the risk must be equally great.

He steeled his resolve. "I don't need the extra money. Whatever it is you want, I will not do it. I expect you to honor your contract with me just as it is."

He turned to go. But, like a deer in the headlights, he was frozen in his tracks by the next words from the big American CIA agent, this time in Kurdish.

"Wait, Little Fox," Jean-Claude ordered. "Wait!"

Ramazzan had not heard that name applied to him since his childhood, when he had to run and hide from Saddam's helicopter gunships in these very hills.

Louis's tone was more conciliatory. "We know you are not helping us just for the money."

The third man of the group moved forward but remained silent, his face still partly in shadow. Ramazzan searched his memory. There was something familiar about him. What was it?

"We know you were born Ali Hassan," Louis continued, quickly unravelling the details of Ramazzan's life. "An illegitimate child of a Kurdish hill woman whom your father—an Iraqi bureaucrat, wasn't he?—took a fancy to one day in a village marketplace. When he tired of her, he abandoned her along with you, her infant. Fearing his transgression would be revealed and his career, if not his very life, terminated, he sought to rid himself of you both. Saddam's brutal suppression of the Kurds in 1988 provided him the perfect opportunity. Many of your friends and family were killed, including your mother and two brothers. But, like your nickname, Little Fox, you knew where to hide and escaped the killings."

Jean-Claude picked up the story, telling the truth under the stars. "You fled into the hills with the survivors of your clan. There you bided your time and plotted revenge. Word was passed to your father that you were still alive and would publicly denounce him if he did not live up to his paternal obligations. He gave in to your threat and provided you a basic education in Mosul. He also supported you with enough money to live on. When he died two years ago, you were recruited by Mohammed Ali Ossman as a low-level clerk for his new laboratory. You worked hard and rose to become his chief administrative assistant. He has never suspected your background."

Ramazzan was trembling. He had to sit down. "No more," he muttered.

Jean-Claude smiled. "There's just a bit more. 'Little Fox' was the nickname given you by your mother when you were very young. Because you were so much craftier than the others."

"How do you know this?" Ramazzan ran dirt through his fingers. It was as cold as the night.

Jean-Claude shrugged. "That is not important. It only matters that we do know."

Louis was more sympathetic. "It must have pained you greatly to watch your kinsmen die in those first experiments Mohammed carried out in the laboratory. You must have wanted to shout and scream and beat your chest. But you suppressed it. You kept the hatred alive inside until the time was ripe for vengeance."

Ramazzan's eyes were misty. "One of those who died in the experiments was from my clan. Some of the others were known to me from long ago. I had to bite my fist to keep from crying out. But there was nothing I could do. And I knew my own death would not have prevented theirs."

Jean-Claude's next words were more conciliatory. "We know Mohammed has almost completed production of the second batch of his hybrid anthrax germ. And that he has recruited six new agents and is already indoctrinating them about their missions. Soon, he will infect them with the spores and send them to America to start a new round of the disease."

Ramazzan spat into the dust. "America! What do I care about you Americans? When we put our trust in you and rose up against the Dictator Saddam you abandoned us, just stood by while we were slaughtered, our villages gassed."

Jean-Claude's scar darkened in a rush of blood. "That is past history. This is now. Did you know Mohammed plans to retest his new batch of germs before giving it to his agents?"

Ramazzan nodded. "Of course. That is our standard protocol, to be certain it has not lost potency. Six rabbits will be selected for the testing."

"He means to follow the rabbit tests with more human testing."

Ramazzan jumped to his feet. "No! There is no reason for that. It is not necessary."

"Just two humans this time. So as not to waste any of his precious supply. The subjects were captured two days ago. They are Kurds, your clansmen."

Ramazzan looked up into Jean Claude's eyes. "No. You are lying."

"It is true," Louis said gently. "They were captured yesterday by a patrol of Saddam's secret police. They were taken at their camp in the hills about a hundred kilometers north of Mosul."

The third man in Louis's trio, who had remained silent and shadowed until now, stepped forward and threw back his hood to reveal himself.

Recognition spread across Ramazzan's face. "Uncle Achmed?" He moved closer to the man. "It is you!" They kissed on both cheeks. He turned to the others, his eyes wet. "He sheltered me after my mother was killed."

"What the American says is true, Little Fox," the uncle said. "One of the women they took is Fatima, your cousin."

Ramazzan stared at the stars. "We played hide and seek as children."

"I remember. Look, Ramazzan. The money would be helpful," the uncle said. "For Fatima's family. For Kalashnikov rifles and explosives. For our one-day liberation."

Ramazzan was quiet for some time. The Land Rover's heat bled off in the cold. Finally, he turned to Jean-Claude. "What do you want me to do?"

"Tell me about the late-night sentry," the CIA agent asked quickly. "When does he come on duty and what time is he relieved? Is he right or left-handed? When does he eat? And what weapons does he carry?"

Before he could answer, Louis fired other demands at him. "And a floor plan of the building. We want you to draw us a detailed map. Where the alarms are located. Which labs hold the hybrid cultures."

Ramazzan nodded. "I will do as you ask. But what are you going to do about rescuing my cousin Fatima and the other captive?"

"A fair question," Jean-Claude said. "If all goes well, they will be brought out after this is over."

Mohammed was in his office early the next morning, engrossed, as usual, with newspapers and wire service reports. He barely noticed his weary and anxious administrative assistant slip past him into his own cubbyhole of an office. He grunted a "good morning" as Ramazzan went past, not even looking up from his computer monitor and the Associated Press story he was devouring with great relish:

> Chicago, October 23. A confirmed case of *Medusa* has been reported from the U.S. Navy Training Center at Great Lakes, Illinois. The patient is a recent graduate from boot camp at the Recruit Training Center. He was in his first week of instruction to become a cook when he became ill. He was seen at the medical clinic then transferred to the base hospital, where the diagnosis was confirmed. He is in critical condition and on life support. His prognosis is 'guarded'. Since the Seaman worked in the Enlisted Dining Facility and could have exposed the entire Training Center to *Medusa*, Navy officials have canceled further training and confined all personnel to their barracks, where they will be regularly monitored by base medical staff.

Mohammed was amazed at how just one case could have such far-reaching effects. Then he chided himself and remembered the social disruption and economic aftermath from those few anthrax-by- mail cases in the U.S. in 2001. He had not concerned himself with this aspect of the epidemic. His focus had been primarily on producing the maximum number of deaths. The maximum amount of terror. And he assumed there would have to be tens of thousands of cases to make a real difference.

But in one month, with just a little over a thousand American cases, he had seen evidence of widespread effects: mob violence, economic upheaval, growing isolation of the citizenry and now a significant slowdown in vital military training.

He continued scanning the wire service reports until he came to one which made him shake his fists and shout for joy.

> U.S. Submarine Base, Groton, Connecticut. Navy sources report that the Fast Attack Submarine U.S.S. *Dallas* was unable to begin its regularly-scheduled patrol cycle today because of concerns of *Medusa* in her crew. Three sonar technicians with severe URI symptoms were admitted to the base hospital for further diagnostic tests and treatment. Until *Medusa* is ruled out, all other members of *Dallas's* crew are being confined to quarters. Navy officials stressed that the three sick crewmen may only have 'colds'. But no chance will be taken since, in the closed environment of a submarine, the disease could spread like wildfire throughout the entire boat. *Dallas's* patrol start date has been delayed indefinitely; another submarine will remain on patrol until *Dallas* is able to relieve her.

The psychology and sociology of terror from *Medusa*, it seemed, were out of all proportion to the small number of actual cases. And many times more devastating to the population than the disease itself.

Mohammed next turned to the editorial page of *U.S.A. Today*, where the lead commentary made his eyes light up:

U.S. MILITARY READINESS AFFECTED BY EPIDEMIC?
More and more U.S. warships are unable to meet their
deployment dates because of fear of *Medusa* in crew
members. Even when the illnesses turn out to be
nothing but colds, the sailing delays are forcing other
ships to remain at sea for days or weeks past the end of
their normal deployments, resulting in a drop in the
morale and readiness of their home-sick crews. The
situation became so acute at the Pacific Fleet Base in
San Diego that an entire Amphibious Ready Group,
consisting of two amphibious ships filled with Marines
and a helicopter carrier, were kept out of port for three
weeks because of several cases of *Medusa* in shore-based
personnel there. This is becoming an all-too-familiar
story: ships can't sail due to fear of the disease, which
often proves groundless; entire Army brigades quarantined
because of single cases of *Medusa*; and Air Force flight
crews not able to meet their ready status because of
medical quarantine of crew members. Contributing to
the crisis has been the unavailability of anthrax vaccine
for several years due to ceased production by its only
supplier. The Military had better get its house in order.
Already, formerly cool spots in the world are heating
up again: the Persian Gulf, the Balkans, the Caribbean,
to name but a few. Troublemakers there see the U.S.
military weakness as an opportunity to raise hell again!"

Mohammed clapped his hands in delight. "Allah Akhbar!"
He knew Saddam himself was aware of these developments. In
fact, he had seen a Republican Guard Unit normally garrisoned
just outside Mosul, heading south. And he had heard whispers of
new military plans in the wind. With the U.S. preoccupied and
militarily weakened, might not this be a good time to re-assert
Iraqi claims to Kuwait and its oil fields?

Mohammed pushed back from his monitor and yelled for Ramazzan to bring him tea.

When he arrived a few minutes later carrying a tray with cups, sugar and a pot of tea, Ramazzan hoped the Director wouldn't notice the cups shaking. He placed the tray on the desk and turned to go.

"Wait. Have you seen these?" Mohammed held up a handful of newspapers and wire service reports. "Our success is even greater than our wildest expectations. What do you think of that?"

Ramazzan stammered. "I am pleased that you are pleased, Director." Sweat appeared on his forehead.

"Come on, man," Mohammed demanded. "Isn't your breast filled with pride at what we have done? Look, it's in all the newspapers. Aren't you overjoyed at our revenge on the Americans?" He waved the sheaf of press clippings in his assistant's face.

Ramazzan muttered a few words.

"What? Yes, well, that will be all." Mohammed dismissed him with a wave of his hand. The man was great for filing papers, getting tea, ordering supplies and performing other clerical work. Other than that, he was as bright as a fence post. Which was exactly what Mohammed had been looking for when he hired him. Ramazzan knew nothing about—nor seemed at all interested in—the real purpose of the laboratory. No curiosity, no independent thought—no security risk.

When he finished his tea, Mohammed began his morning rounds. He paused first at the room containing the pure anthrax cultures. He watched with satisfaction as the technicians used a DNA gun to inject the bacteria with DNA from *adenovirus type 35*. When finished, they would store the new adenovirus-anthrax hybrid in shiny thermos-sized flasks. *Medusa*, the American newspapers called it. He liked the name. It sounded menacing. A small portion of it would be kept on agar plates for testing the rabbits. And the two Kurds.

Mohammed continued his rounds, stopping at the room with the six cots and their overhead monitors. He studied the

Kurdish women captives. They had been bathed, dressed in scrub suits, and carefully examined and tested for evidence of current infectious diseases. After seventy-two hours of observation to be sure they were healthy, they would be cleared for the experiment. If the rabbit tests were successful, another portion of *Medusa* would be tested on these two women.

Farther down the hallway, in a small conference room secure from the rest of the laboratory, Rashid Bin Yegal was briefing the six new 'vectors' he had recruited on the dos and don'ts of their missions.

Mohammed paused at the doorway to listen.

"After two days in a special room for observation," Rashid explained (Mohammed had to smile at the oblique reference to the room with the two-way mirror and videocamera) "you will be taken out under cover of darkness. Half of you will go to Mexico, where 'coyotes' will smuggle you across the frontier into one of the U.S. border towns. The others will go to Canada and be taken across the U. S. border at separate points."

"Aren't the Americans more vigilant now, since the glorious attack in New York?" one of them asked.

Rashid reassured them. "Trust me, you will get through."

What Rashid didn't tell them was that the rest of this batch of *Medusa* was reserved for them. After the two Kurdish women were dead, they would get their doses while they slept.

Back in his office, Mohammed leaned back in his chair, his hands behind his head. He was immensely pleased with himself. His project, and the funding which came with it, was proving to be a huge success. And when the next group of agents carried out their missions, the result would be even more glorious. Even more American deaths. Even more terror.

But after these six agents had completed their missions, he would turn the production of *Medusa* over to others. To one of his scientist friends. His own thoughts had turned instead to future projects. Plague, for example, had always appealed to him as a biological weapon. Because the victims died such horrible, painful deaths. With his recombinant DNA technology he would develop a highly virulent plague bacterium, as infectious as *Medusa,* and also spread by airborne droplets. Then he would send it to America in the bodies of other human vectors.

He rubbed the stumps of his missing fingers and began diagraming the research steps of his new project.

The end of October finally brought the Los Angeles basin a breath of relief from its early-fall, smog-filled heat wave. Public Health officials, however, feared the cooler weather might have a worsening effect on the spread of *Medusa*. People now were more likely to spend less time out of doors in the parks and at the beaches and more time indoors at theaters, malls, concert halls and other enclosed places where the droplet-borne infection could be easily spread.

But the good news, Gil Martin noticed, on the rare occasion he went to one of these places himself, was that the number of people wearing face masks as they strolled and shopped had risen sharply in the past few weeks. Some with URI's wore the masks out of a sense of civic duty. And some of the still-healthy donned them to ward off germs and prevent contracting the infection from others. It didn't exactly match the picture he had in his mind of a Beijing winter street scene, where all citizens wore masks. But it was a step in the right direction at stopping the epidemic's spread.

Gil also noted that his ER's patient traffic had decreased noticeably, both in the numbers and the types of cases. There were fewer worried-well now. Fewer with just mild URIs. And there was less anxiety on the faces of his patients now than in the early days. It had been at least a week since a drove of them had shown up at the ER's door demanding antibiotics for some minor symptoms, or as prophylaxis because they *knew* someone who *knew* someone who *might* have been exposed to *Medusa*. And since the pharmacies had been desperately low on their antibiotics, this let-up in demand had given them time to restock. There had been a much-awaited delivery of medication by FEMA trucks from one of the National Stockpiles.

And Gil noted a small but definite decrease in the rate of rise of *Medusa* cases. The epidemic, if not yet abating, appeared to be leveling off. Jerry Essminger at the Health Department said this was true for other health care facilities in the County as well. Business-as-usual was returning. Public health measures appeared finally to be having an effect.

It was just before lunchtime on a quiet morning when Gil received an urgent message from the hospital administrator: would he come to the front office as soon as possible? In other words, immediately. Walter Burke, the hospital's Chief Operating Officer, had been evasive when Gil asked what it was all about.

As he headed for the front office, 'Mahogany Row'—his name for the suite of business offices near the front entrance— was waiting for him. Most of the staff had turned out to greet him as he was ushered into Burke's office by the receptionist. Such courtesy was very unusual. Before he had become famous, he, like most of the clinical staff, had been treated like hired help by the lawyers, accountants, and other medical bureaucrats on the 'Row.' Now they used his name in advertisements.

"What's up, Walter?"

"Dr. Martin, we have a call for you from the White House operator. I had it put through to our secure phone line here. They said it was urgent. They specifically requested you."

Gil picked up the phone. But before he punched the flashing white button he looked at the administrator. He had moved away from the desk but was still there.

Gil cradled the phone on his shoulder. "Please Walter, a little privacy, huh?"

When he was alone, Gil identified himself to the operator and was told to stand by.

The next voice he heard was southern and warm. "Good mornin'. This is Dave Gardner."

"Hello, Dave. How are you? What's with all the cloak and dagger stuff?"

"I've been asked to consult with the White House medical staff on a patient here. But I'm mostly a lab researcher, and this is clinical. I'm runnin' the lab tests at USAMRIID, and I wanted your advice on the patient's course so far. But I must ask you to keep it private. Just between the two of us. Can I count on you?"

"Absolutely. Is it the President?"

"Sorry, Gil. This really is confidential. I'd rather not identify the patient."

"Alright. Tell me about it."

"Symptoms began 'bout three days ago, startin' out like a simple URI with coughin', sneezin', a runny nose and red eyes. But then it progressed to a sinus infection and bronchitis. Now, the patient's sick as hell, with fever of 103 degrees and a wet cough."

"What did you find on your physical?"

"Bilateral pneumonia."

"Any sign of meningitis?"

"Nope. The neck was supple, the mental status alert. And the spinal fluid clear."

"Do you think it's septic shock?"

"Nope. Not yet. The BP's up, the pulses are strong. And the skin color's as pink as my own."

"What have you done so far?"

"Started IV fluids, cultured and stained blood, sputum and nose specimens, and begun antibiotics."

"Any growth on the cultures yet?"

"No, still too early."

"What about the ELISA and PCR tests?"

"They're still pendin'. Maybe tomorrow."

"Sounds like *Medusa*."

"Maybe. Very large lymph nodes on the chest x-ray. That's got me worried. And the nasal stain shows blue bacteria in two's, three's, and longer chains."

"Anthrax?"

"Possibly."

"What do you want from me?"

"I'd like to send you the chest x-rays and stains by phone modem. You've seen way more cases of *Medusa* than I have."

"Send them out. I'll look at them later today and get back with you first thing tomorrow morning."

Gardner didn't respond. "What else, Dave?"

"Gil, this particular person has had recent contact with virtually every senior government official here in the White House. From the President and Vice President, to the Cabinet Secretaries, on down to the Agency Heads. If this truly is *Medusa*, it would really bollix up our government. Everyone exposed would have to be quarantined. A lot of 'em would get very sick, some would die. None would be able to do his or her job. And this at a time when we have both a domestic and an international crisis. I need to make my recommendations to the medical staff here ASAP."

Gil thought about it. "Are you certain this person was exposed to *Medusa*? If there's been no real exposure, there's no contagious problem. Just the medical one of getting your patient better. No exposure, no risk."

"I asked the EIS agent here in Washington to conduct the contact investigation himself. By working backwards, he found a chain of contacts from the patient to a proven *Medusa* case."

"Okay. So we move fast. Send the x-rays to our radiology department. I'll view them as soon as we hang up. And e-mail the stain photos to this number. I'll look at them on the monitor here. Cover up any identifying information to protect your patient's privacy. I'll get back to you within the hour."

"Attaboy!"

"Is it the Vice President?"

Gardner chuckled. "I'll be awaitin' your call."

Gardner gave instructions to an assistant to send the material Gil Martin requested. Then he turned to face the group of men and women who had gathered with him in the West Wing conference room: the Speaker of the House; the Majority and Minority Leaders of the Senate; and the Chairmen and Ranking Minority members of the House and Senate Foreign Affairs Committees. In other words, the senior members of the Legislative Branch of Government.

"Well?" the Speaker demanded.

"Within the hour. Dr. Martin has promised to give me his opinion within the hour. I will then give mine to the White House Physician. Any decision to quarantine the President, Vice-President, and other senior staff will be his call."

The Speaker nodded his approval. "Very well. I'm sorry for the urgency. But since the entire top rung of the Executive Branch of government could be declared unfit for duty, I, we"—he indicated his colleagues around the table—"may have to assume some of their duties. To keep the government running."

"Gil Martin won't let us down."

"Very well. In the meantime, I'd like to hear more about this thing you've developed, this *Perseus Factor*. What is it? How does it work? And what's the status of the mission to use it?"

"Yessuh. *Perseus* is a bacteriophage." He looked hopefully at the faces. "Does anyone here know what that is?"

His question drew nothing but blank stares. "Sorry, doc," the Senate Majority Leader, a Tennessean, drawled. "Most of us are lawyers. Biology is not one of our strong suits."

"Very well. I'll make it as basic as I can. A phage is a virus. But it infects bacteria instead of humans or animals. I discovered a phage which infects anthrax bacteria. I used it to infect *Medusa*."

"Is that what *Perseus* does," someone asked, "destroys *Medusa* by infecting and killing it?"

"Sort of. Mostly, it inactivates the anthrax toxin."

"How?"

"I injected a piece of protein called a 'repressor' into the phage. This is *Perseus*. When *Medusa* takes up the phage, this repressor protein inactivates the anthrax toxin. *Medusa* is then completely innocuous. It will continue to live and reproduce itself like any other bacteria. But its fangs are gone, its disease-producin' days over. The body's natural defenses can then make short work of it. Kill it like they do other bacteria all the time."

"So the patient won't even get a cold?"

"That comes from the adenovirus part of *Medusa*. *Perseus* has no effect on it. The patient will have to endure the URI symptoms. But it will be mild. He'll get over it in a few days."

"Won't the Iraqis detect the presence of your *Perseus*," the Tennessean drawled, "when they see *Medusa's* no longer harmful?"

"Maybe. If they look for it. And if they have the time. But I think they'll just figure it's simply mutated into an innocuous form."

Someone else asked, "Won't the Iraqis try to fix this mutation with genetic engineering of their own?"

"They won't get the chance."

"Why not?"

"Because, as soon as *Perseus* has been deployed, a follow-up mission will be triggered." He started to explain, then thought better of it. "You'll have to ask the Pentagon about that. It's a strictly military operation."

"What is the current status of the *Perseus* mission?" the Speaker asked.

"It's underway now, even as we speak. This mornin' four vials of *Perseus* were placed into portable incubators along with all the syringes and needles necessary to deploy it. They were taken from my lab to Andrews Air Force Base and loaded onto an Air Force C-17 cargo plane for a flight to Mildenhall RAF Base, England."

He looked down at his watch. "The C-17's ETA is about an hour from now. From Mildenhall, *Perseus* will fly via a C-130 Hercules transport to Paris. A French diplomat is waitin' for it there. He will personally escort *Perseus* on a chartered French aircraft to Baghdad, where our CIA man is standin' by. If all goes accordin' to plan, the *Perseus* mission should commence tomorrow night, Iraqi time."

"And we will know immediately if it's been successful?" the Speaker asked hopefully.

"Soon after, yessuh. When the Iraqi's run the tests on their new captives, then we'll know."

"How?"

"We have an informer in the laboratory. He'll alert us. That will also be the go-signal for the next mission, the military one."

Gardner noticed a flashing light on the phone by his elbow. "Excuse me. This oughta be Gil Martin now."

***

"Hello again, Dave."

"Forty-five minutes, Gil. You outdid yourself."

"This must set a speed record for medical consultations."

Gardner laughed. "I'm puttin' you on a speaker phone. If that's okay?"

"It's your patient."

"Right. What do you think?"

"I don't think it's *Medusa*."

"Really?" Gardner looked at the faces around the table. Some were beginning to smile. And he heard a few sighs of relief, including one of his own. "That's good news. Tell me why you don't think so."

"Let's start with the blood stains. I compared your patient's with stains from some of my own. They just don't match. I'm betting your patient's cultures will grow out some type of a streptococcus species."

"What about the chest x-rays?"

"Once again, I matched your patient's chest films side by side with x-rays of my own patients. They don't compare either."

"In what way?"

"First, your patient has bilateral pneumonia. This is uncommon in *Medusa* infections."

"What about the large lymph nodes? They fit the picture of *Medusa*, don't they?"

"Maybe. Maybe not. It's true, they are a little larger than normal in your patient. But in real *Medusa* cases they're massively enlarged, much bigger than your patient's."

"But why should they be enlarged at all?" Gardner persisted.

"Do you have any previous x-rays for comparison?"

"No. The patient's been very healthy for years. No reason for 'em. Why do you ask?"

"I'm guessing you would have seen the same enlarged lymph nodes on previous films. I think they are old findings, maybe ten or twenty years old. Unrelated to this present illness. And I bet they're still there when the pneumonia clears."

"You've convinced me. But I'm still gonna recommend that all high-level government contacts be continued on prophylactic antibiotics until the cultures come back negative for anthrax. Just to be safe."

"That's what I would do."

"You've made a lot of people around here very relieved."

"Are you going to tell me who it is?"

"You'll find out soon enough. Send us your bill!"

***

"No Presidential quarantine," the Speaker said, leaning back in his chair with a sigh. "Pity. I was looking forward to having a go at that job myself for a while."

Gardner gathered his papers and was preparing to leave. "I want your patient to do me a favor when she's feelin' better," he said to the White House physician.

"Absolutely. She'll be happy to oblige, if she can. What is it?"

Twenty-four hours later, at a regularly-scheduled Presidential press conference, the President was asked, "where's the First Lady. She hasn't been seen in public for over a week. And all her appointments have been cancelled. There are rumors she's been very sick. Maybe even with *Medusa.*"

The President ran his hand through a shock of gray hair. "She was hurt it took you so long to notice her absence. It's true, she's been ill. But not with *Medusa.* It was a bad cold, which turned into pneumonia. She's under treatment and is feeling much better. In fact"—he gestured to an aide—"she's here today. See for yourself."

A few minutes later the First Lady was rolled into the room in a wheel chair. Though wan, she waved vigorously to everyone. She was wearing a face mask.

"How do you feel?" a reporter asked.

Before she could reply, the President answered. "The doctor says she'll be back to normal in no time. She's got a positive 'lipstick' sign now."

"'Lipstick' sign?"

The President grinned. "I'm told that a reliable indication that a woman's getting better is when she asks for her lipstick and a mirror."

As if on cue, the First Lady pulled off her mask and showed her make-up, lipstick and all. "I don't need this," she said, pointing to the mask. "I only wore it to set an example for all women. And to do a favor for someone who helped take care of me."

Public Health officials were delighted. Soon the Mall in Washington, D.C. began to look like Gil Martin's image of a Beijing winter street scene. Face masks were everywhere.

In Baghdad, Jean-Claude was on hand to greet the French Diplomat and his precious cargo: *Perseus* had arrived safely in the Middle East. Later that afternoon, Jean-Claude, Louis, and *Perseus* headed north.

In Mosul, Mohammed's cold black eyes stared through the two-way mirror at the Kurdish women. The six rabbits he had tested with *Medusa* had died and been dissected, their lungs filled with frothy, bloody effusions. The predictable ravages of anthrax. Tomorrow, these two Kurds would get their own doses. He had debated with himself whether to cancel their tests. It would conserve his small *Medusa* supply. But he finally decided to stick to the protocol. It had worked before. There was no reason to tempt fate by changing it now. In a few days, when these women had also perished, his six new 'holy warriors' would get their own exposures and begin their deadly missions to America.

He loaded a blank videotape into the VCR and adjusted the focus.

In his small office, Ramazzan Fahrs tried to look busy, poring over supply requests for culture tubes, swabs, and petri dishes. He maintained his outward composure, but inside his heart was pounding. He periodically caught himself breathing heavily. Too much of this and he'd be discovered.

From his house in the Frederick foothills, close enough to his office at USAMRIID to ride his bike to work, Dave Gardner strolled out onto his backyard patio to look at the stars. The night was clear, the weather balmy. There it was, twinkling in the western sky, the constellation 'Perseus,' easily recognizable by its 'K'-like shape. Through his binoculars he saw two thumb-sized greenish smudges side by side in the heart of the constellation. This was the 'double cluster' of stars for which Perseus was famous. Did it look the same over his boyhood home in the Shanendoah, he wondered?

He put down his binoculars and searched the southeastern sky. The constellation 'Pegasus' was also visible high overhead. The four bright stars of its body formed a great square, while a few others above it outlined the stallion's massive head. Pegasus, in Greek myth, was Perseus's noble steed. He rode it through the heavens to rescue the maiden Andromeda from a sea monster. According to the ancient Greek legend, her salvation had been up to Perseus.

Gardner sipped his bourbon and considered: it was as true today as it was twenty-five hundred years ago. It was all up to *Perseus* now.

It was a cold, moonless night at his campsite in the Kurdish Hills east of Mosul. From the information Ramazzan had supplied, Jean-Claude had put together a plan to distribute his priceless supply of *Perseus*. He prepared for the dangerous mission by loading a backpack with four 50-milliliter sterile syringes full of *Perseus*, one for each of the four large flasks of *Medusa* in the laboratory. He then drew up the rest into 10-milliliter syringes. They were for the individual petri dishes full of *Medusa*. According to Ramazzan, there were about seventy-five of these. To keep *Perseus* active, he kept the pre-filled syringes in a small battery-powered incubator at a constant temperature of 37 degrees centigrade.

In addition to the syringes, Jean-Claude added to his pack two sets of sterile surgical gloves, a surgical gown, a full-face respirator mask with a viral filter, and safety eyewear to protect him from accidental splashes. The last item into the pack—night vision goggles—would be the first one out. The pack now weighed nearly sixty pounds. But it was still an easy heft for the big man.

His gear stowed in the Land Rover, Jean-Claude's next task was to re-sight his tranquilizer gun. He did this by focusing on an object he had hung from a tree exactly fifty yards away. Fitted with a powerful night vision scope, the rifle was a standard veterinary stun weapon, the kind used to disable large animals at zoos and open air animal parks all over the world. To get the weapon's feel, he had fire-tested it with small doses of a tranquilizer mixture on animals weighing up to one hundred-fifty pounds, mostly large dogs and goats. (None of the animals was permanently harmed.) The hypodermic dart was a 6 milliliter syringe tipped with a sterile 18-gauge needle. Four small, tapered, plastic vanes fitted to the dart's plunger end caused it to spin. This prevented it from tumbling in flight.

Before he left Baghdad, Jean-Claude had carefully pre-filled the tranquilizer dart's syringe with three milliliters of midazolam—almost twice the normal adult dose—and three milliliters of pentobarbital, again, almost twice the normal adult dose. He then tested this mix on a large goat. The animal became unsteady on its feet within sixty seconds of impact, was asleep within three minutes, and remained unconscious for three hours. One of the drugs, midazolam, had a side effect which would be especially useful for this mission: it produced amnesia. This was why, in its everyday use, it was given as a pre-anesthetic sedative to patients being prepped for surgery, so they wouldn't remember the experience. It was also why Jean-Claude had specifically included it in his tranquilizer mixture.

Ramazzan was waiting exactly as planned at 0130 hours at a small, unlit park on the western edge of Mosul. His tension had been building through the day so that now he was nervous almost to the point of incoherence. It took ten minutes before Jean-Claude got him calmed down; he had even considered using a little midazolam on him. But he opted against it. Ramazzan was the get-away driver. He wanted him sharp-eyed and clear-headed, even if anxious.

The two men drove through the city's deserted streets to the drop-off point near Mohammed's laboratory. Its location proved to be of great benefit for their mission. For Mohammed had originally chosen the old building with the rusty red sign because of its location. On the western edge of the city, it backed up onto the desert at the dead-end of a quiet residential street. And that street was the only way into it, except through the desert itself. Also, the building's low profile and absence of high walls, electric fences, or other imposing barriers let it blend into the neighborhood. A single floodlight over the entrance was its only nighttime illumination. To its neighbors, the building was just a smelly chicken processing plant.

The lab's security was of two types: simple deadbolts on the door into the building (there were no windows) and a coded electronic lock at the entrance to the lab complex itself. Each of the culture rooms was separately and electronically locked, and the bacteriological part of the lab was rigged with both movement and light sensors. If these were triggered, outside alarms would sound, interior lights would come on, and a nearby detachment of military police would come running.

But Mohammed had not placed all his faith in electro-mechanical locks and alarms. He also relied on guards. From dusk to dawn, an AK 47-toting sentry patrolled the building's perimeter. These men were regular Iraqi soldiers from a garrison north of the city. Mohammed had personally recruited them for this 'moonlighting' assignment. Each of their watches was four hours long. Their principal job was to keep looters and vandals away.

The sentry for the last watch was Corporal Farrad. Beginning at 0200 hours, he would be on patrol until he was picked up by someone from the barracks at 0600 hours, about an hour before Mohammed himself arrived to open up the building. Mohammed paid the men well, an excellent supplement to their paltry army income. And the work was easy, if boring.

About an hour into his watch—exactly six revolutions around the building by Jean-Claude's count—Corporal Farrad would take a ten minute break, lean or squat against the wall, and eat a snack of cheese, bread and olives, washed down with tepid, sugary tea. He rarely deviated from this routine. Jean-Claude had timed it to the minute the night before with a portable telescope from the cover of a nearby abandoned oil derrick.

Ramazzan drove the Land Rover to the edge of the desert. At the end of a street about half a mile north of the lab, he started to whine.

"When will you be back?"

"Two hours," Jean-Claude said, unloading his gear.

"Why so long?"

"We've gone over this again and again," Jean-Claude said through clenched teeth. "You be here"—he looked at his watch—"at exactly 0400 hours."

"What if someone sees me?"

"At this time of the morning? Who would be looking? This is a residential neighborhood. Everyone is asleep."

Ten more minutes of this whining was all Jean-Claude could take. He strapped on his pack, slung the tranquilizer rifle over his shoulder, and flipped the night vision goggles down over his eyes.

Grasping Ramazzan firmly by the collar, he stared down at him. "If you fail me in this…if you're not back here…there will be no place you can hide. This is a good plan. If we stick to it, we'll both come out alive. And you'll be rich beyond your wildest dreams."

Ramazzan was barely able to nod.

Jean-Claude watched the Land Rover's taillights disappear, then hitched the pack's shoulder straps higher onto his back and headed off. In this dark of the desert, it took him fifteen minutes to make his way to the laboratory. He detoured around two barking dogs. From fifty yards out, hidden by a small dune, he watched the greenish glowing figure through his night vision goggles: Corporal Farrad, right on time. This should be his fourth circuit. Two more and he would stop to eat.

The Corporal was on the desert side of the building, still in darkness and thinking of his meal break, when the tranquilizer dart hit him in the back. The two inch long needle buried itself into the bulky mass of muscles between his shoulder blades. Activated by impact, the spring-triggered plunger drove the six milliliters of drug mixture through the big needle into Farrad's flesh. The syringe emptied in three seconds.

When it struck, Farrad gasped from the shock of it, straightening up and squaring his shoulders against the pain. He dropped his weapon and clawed at his back. Thoughts of a hornet sting, a spider bite, or even a snake bite faded as his brain began to fog. Seconds later, as the full effect of the drugs hit him, he slumped against the wall.

Jean-Claude waited another five minutes to be certain the drug was in full effect. Then he crept from cover. The Corporal was out cold. Jean-Claude pulled free the tranquilizer dart, capped the needle, and slipped it into his pocket.

Ramazzan's hand-drawn blueprints of the building were accurate. Jean-Claude located the circuit box for the alarm system, picked the lock and, using two alligator clamps, bypassed the light and motion sensor systems. At the front entrance, the big man first hugged the shadows, then flipped up his night vision goggles when he reached the flood-lit area. He easily handled the lock on the front door. The pass codes Ramazzan had stolen from Mohammed's office got him into the laboratory itself. He clicked on a red flashlight—fastened by a strap above his right ear—donned his gloves, gown, mask and protective eyewear and headed for the incubation rooms. Locked doors yielded to Ramazzan's stolen pass codes.

Jean-Claude parcelled out his supply of *Perseus* exactly as planned. It was injected first into the large flasks of *Medusa*. He agitated them for maximum dispersal of the liquid, then he squirted one milliliter into each of the individual petri dishes. Again he swirled it around for maximum contact with the growing colonies. There were seventy of these, and they ate up most of his time. But he had practiced the technique during several dry runs and was finished and back outside again seventy-five minutes later. All doors were re-secured, his emptied syringes and protective clothing were re-packed. He removed the alligator clamps from the security circuit box, re-locked it, and retraced his steps through the desert. He arrived at the pick-up point ten minutes ahead of schedule.

When 0400 hours came and went, he silently swore at Ramazzan and reviewed in his mind the fall-back plan. He would hike into the desert to an agreed-upon map grid point. There he would wait for his friend Louis who would pick him up later that evening. But Ramazzan finally showed up, and by 0600 hours Jean-Claude was back at his camp. Ramazzan was soon back in his apartment, exhausted beyond endurance. He vomited twice, then got ready for work.

Jean-Claude punched a number on his cellular phone and gave the simple code phrase, "Pegasus has flown." His friend Louis, waiting in the rising dawn at the French Affairs Office in Baghdad, acknowledged the code and alerted the French Ambassador in Washington, D.C. Just before midnight the National Security Advisor awakened the President.

"It's done, Mr. President. *Perseus* has been deployed."

The President grunted, fighting sleep. "Now we wait. Four days, Dr. Gardner said. I hope I can keep the military at bay that long. They want action now."

As the President of the United States tried to get back to sleep, a military jeep pulled into the parking lot of Mohammed's laboratory in Mosul. When Corporal Farrad didn't immediately appear, the driver honked twice. Still no corporal. The driver walked around the building and discovered his comrade still leaning against the wall, sound asleep.

"Farrad! Farrad!" he shouted, shaking the man roughly. "Wake up! Wake up! The Director will be here soon. You'll be punished."

Like a drunk after a binge, the Corporal finally aroused himself, stared blankly at his friend, then rose shakily to his feet.

"What's that on your back?" his friend asked. He turned him around and pulled on his shirt. "Is that blood? What happened to you?"

Farrad felt like he was swimming to the surface through a pool of molasses. He shook his head to clear it. Something extraordinary had happened last night. But for the life of him he couldn't remember what it was. He was just glad it was over. He picked up his weapon, stared dumbly at his uneaten meal, and stumbled to the jeep. As they headed back to the barracks, they saluted Mohammed coming down the street to start his day.

When Ramazzan arrived for work his edginess was noticeable: he spilled the tea when serving it, and jumped when Mohammed asked him to locate a file folder. But when he realized the covert mission remained undetected, his nerves quieted. No one had noticed anything out of the ordinary. All work stations in the laboratory were exactly as they had been the night before. And the two Kurdish women captives had heard nothing. Ramazzan managed a smile.

Eager to begin today's project, Mohammed called his technical staff together and gave them their orders.

"Our first task," he began, "is to turn another small sample of the *Medusa* colonies into spores so we can continue our testing."

"Director," one of the technicians asked, "why can't we just spray the bacteria into the room with the two women? Why first convert them into spores?"

Mohammed was patient. "Because the sprayer disrupts the fragile bacteria; only the spore forms can withstand the high pressures."

"Thank you, Director," the technician said with a slight bow.

In the soil, sporulation happens over a period of days or weeks. But Mohammed knew how to drive the process much faster than mother nature ever could. He used pure oxygen to mist a very weak dilution of hydrochloric acid. He gently sprayed this over the exposed culture plates. At the same time he slowly lowered the temperature. Rapid sporulation was triggered. By dusk, Mohammed had more than enough of them for his two test subjects. He made a watery slurry of the spores. This he poured into a specially adapted air-driven sprayer, similar to the kind used for crop dusting.

One of the two Kurdish women, Irena, was then led away and locked in another room. When Fatima, the remaining captive, nodded off from the sleeping pills Mohammed had crushed into her food, he sprayed the spore slurry into her room through a ventilation duct. Fans circulated the air for thirty minutes. As Fatima peacefully slept, her mouth slightly open, thousands of spores found their way into her respiratory tract.

Four hours later, an exhaust fan sucked the air out of the room along with any spores still in it, replacing it with fresh air. Three full volumes of room air were exhausted and replaced, eliminating all spores from the atmosphere. The entire room—walls, furniture, fixtures—was then decontaminted.

Just before midnight, Irena was led back to the testing room and Mohammed finally sent his staff home. He took one last look at the two women: Fatima, who would prove that this batch of

Medusa could kill. And Irena, who would prove it was still contagious. Then he returned to his office and pulled out a folding bed. Until this experiment was completed, he would not leave the building.

At Fort Detrick, Dave Gardner received a phone call from his friend Oscar Bentley.

"Rusty, I've just heard from Jean-Claude. He's deployed *Perseus*."

"Any problems, Bullethead?"

"None. Now we just have to wait."

"Right, my friend. There's nothin' more we can do now. It's all up to *Perseus.*"

While she slept, the smallest of *Medusa's* spores were deposited in Fatima's nose and throat. There, her body's warmth instantly reversed the sporulation process. *Medusa* was revitalized back into its bacterial form. *Perseus* had no effect here. It could not prevent this step.

Then the adenovirus within *Medusa* went to work, causing Fatima's nose and throat to swell and produce copious mucous. Some of the virus worked its way up her eustachian tubes into the middle ear spaces, causing infection. Others did likewise in her nasal sinuses. This was not where *Perseus* worked either. Soon Fatima would have all the symptoms of a full-blown URI: sore throat, sneezing, coughing, and hacking. She would then be contagious by droplet spread to her roommate Irena.

It was in the lungs that *Perseus* protected. If the adenovirus part of *Medusa* was the *spreader* of the disease, the *killing* part was supposed to be in the bigger spores, the ones about the size of a red blood cell. These bypassed the upper respiratory tract completely and were inhaled deep into the lung sacs themselves. Then they were carried by scavenger cells to the lymph nodes in the chest. Here they should have regerminated and released their anthrax toxins. These would have killed Fatima rapidly.

But they didn't. Thanks to inactivation by *Perseus*, there were no toxins to be released. And the few anthrax bacteria still alive were soon killed by the body's immune system and other natural defenses.

So much for *Medusa*, the once lethal lady.

19

Gil Martin had finished an exhausting but satisfying ER shift and stepped out into a star-studded evening. An aircraft, its landing lights almost blinding, zoomed overhead toward the airfield. He took a deep breath, tasted the salty air blown in on the gentle sea-breeze, and headed for his car across the parking lot. He stopped at a local market, picked up a steak, some salad greens and rolls, and continued on to his apartment.

Half-way there, his old Porsche 911 sputtered, coughed and slowed down. Finally, it caught again. This wasn't the first time it had done that.

"Damn!" He said. "Must be the fuel pump. Or maybe the carburetors." There was no fuel injection on these old models. He shook his head. "Better get it into the shop. Before it gets worse."

He lived on the top floor of a duplex in a development along a quiet street. The four buildings were all lined up like soldiers on parade ground formation. Parking for the residents was provided in two poorly-lit covered carports which flanked a long driveway behind the buildings.

He parked and locked the car. With the bag of groceries in one hand, his briefcase in the other, he headed down the driveway to the rear entrance of his building.

When a darkened car's lights came on to a high revving engine, and the car came at him like a leaping cat, he couldn't make himself move. His brain couldn't grasp it. Only at the last moment did some atavistic instinct galvanize him. He dropped his bags and threw himself behind one of the metal poles holding up the carport's roof. The car veered, sideswiped the pole, then fishtailed into the night.

He watched it go, his heart thumping, then checked himself. He was already in aftershock, shaking uncontrollably. A shredded shirt moved under his hands. His elbows were skinned. Blood ran down his face and blurred his vision. An exploring finger found the gaping, two-inch laceration in the hairline above his right eye.

Later, in his own ER, a colleague stitching up his head, he gave his report to a police detective.

"You didn't get a good look at the driver?"

"It was all headlights and darkness. But I know who it was."

The sergeant held up a photograph. "Is this the guy?"

Gill studied the picture. "Looks like him." It was the man with the goatee and shaved head. "Where'd you get this?"

"Your ICU nurses. They sat with a police artist. We ran it through our own files. Nothing. Then we cross-referenced the big FBI computer. Bingo! He's an Egyptian national, name of Marwan Hanjoun. Has strong ties to *al-Qaeda*."

"This is the same guy I saw in the ICU waiting room. Just before my patient Achmed was murdered."

"That's what we figured."

"Why is he out to get me?"

The detective shook his head. "I dunno, doc. He must think you're a danger to his cause. That you know something way too important."

"Like what?"

"I dunno. But maybe you should take a vacation. Leave town. Get outta here for a while."

"Can't you provide me some police protection?"

"Look, doc, this outbreak has stretched our resources thinner than a ten-dollar hairpiece. I can have a black-and-white unit take a few extra turns past your apartment. And the hospital security patrol can keep an eye on you until you leave the grounds. But that's about it."

"I'm not going to be driven out. There's an epidemic going on. I'm needed here." He could hardly believe he was saying this. Barely four weeks ago he was so fed up with medicine, with life, that he was almost physically sick from it.

"That's up to you," the detective said. "Just be careful, will ya?"

20

His calendar read October 31. EIS agent Jerry Essminger was wearing the new string tie Nathan Windsong had given him. The clasp was an oval, half-dollar size piece of turquoise fringed with silver. A few brightly colored beads decorated the strings themselves.

Essmiger sighed. He wished he was anywhere else but here. More than a month had passed since Achmed, L.A.'s first *Medusa* case. Michelle Goad had ordered him to compile a summary of the epidemic's statistics. He would rather take a beating than have to endure her disapproving stare again. Better get it right this time.

He hunched over his desk, studied some computer printouts, and made computations on a hand-held calculator. After about an hour's work, he leaned back, fingered his new tie, and glanced at a photograph on his desk. The beach at Santa Monica. A pretty blonde in a bikini, the bottom piece no bigger than a face mask. He grinned at that. What he wouldn't give to be there now. Reluctantly he turned back to his calculator.

By lunch time he was ready. His mouth dry, he made his way to Michelle Goad's office and knocked softly on her door.

"What have you got for me?" Dr. Goad looked up from her desk. She twirled her father's keepsake pen in her hand and studied

Essminger through owl-shaped glasses. They were the ugliest things he had ever seen.

He laid out his work on her desk. "First, here is the Epidemic Curve." He had plotted the weekly *Medusa* case totals on graph paper, then connected the dots. The result: a snapshot of the epidemic's course.

She ran her finger along the curve. "Two hundred and thirty-one cases so far, right?"

"Yes. That's the grand total. Twenty-five the first week. Eleven of them were direct contacts of Achmed Malabee aboard AF Flight 62."

Michelle's eyes opened wider as she followed the curve further along. "Sixty-three the second week. I remember that from my first press conference. What a jump!"

"Yes, ma'am. I figure these were caused by *Medusa's* spread to family and other immediate contacts of those original 12 cases."

"That makes sense."

Essminger pointed to a third dot. "Week three: 76 cases. Still climbing, but not as fast."

"Encouraging." She placed her father's pen back in the desk. "These cases must represent the widening circle of patient contacts from week two."

"Fellow employees, classmates at school?"

"Yup." She traced her finger further to the right on the curve, then stabbed at a point. "It's flattening! See here, the curve's flattening out..."

"Yes, ma'am. That's the fourth week, the one just past. Eighty cases came in."

"The epidemic's plateauing."

Essminger nodded. "An additional confirmation of this leveling off—an indirect measure—is the number of contacts I'm having to assign for Nathan Windsong to investigate. They've peaked at around 20 per day."

"Maybe all the preventive measures I've been nagging the public about are finally paying off."

Essminger was not about to argue.

She glanced at the old photo of her mounted on that pony next to her dad. A brief image of horseback rides across the Texas prairie passed before her eyes. Skin browned by the sun, ponytail flying, the smell of his pipe tobacco. She shook her head to clear it.

"What else you got?"

"The Case Fatality Rate. The percentage of people who've caught *Medusa* and died from it."

"How bad is it?"

"Bad. It started out at about 80 percent..."

"I remember that."

"It's down to 66 percent now, probably from earlier diagnosis and more aggressive treatment. But it's not getting any lower."

She looked at the map Jerry showed her, little red dots indicating real people who had passed away. There were 171 of them. She shook her head. "And some patients still on the critical list won't survive. They'll push the rate even higher."

"Yes, ma'am. *Medusa* is still very lethal. The key is to prevent the disease in the first place."

"Anthing else?"

"My last statistic, the Secondary Case Rate. As you know, this is a measure of *Medusa's* contagiousness."

"What is it?"

"Thirty percent."

"Thirty percent! Has it changed any from the first week?"

"No, ma'am. It's still 30 percent."

"Christ." She threw her pencil down and eyed Essminger. "Are you a gambler Jerry?"

"No, ma'am."

"Well, this 30 percent means that if you were exposed to someone with *Medusa* and weren't wearing a face mask or taking prophylactic antibiotics, you would stand a 3-in-10 chance of catching the disease yourself."

"Not good odds?"

"Bad odds, Jerry. Very bad odds."

He said nothing. It was sobering.

"Anything else?"

"No, ma'am."

"Please e-mail a copy of your statistics to CDC. Tara Martin is trying to get a nationwide picture of the epidemic's course. Your data will help."

"Yes ma'am." He started to leave.

"Jerry."

"Yes, ma'am?"

"Good job."

At USAMRIID, Dave Gardner was also thinking about the epidemic. Not in the narrow specifics of laboratory experimentation. But in that larger, blue-sky sort of way which considered all aspects of a problem. Some people did this brain work best in front of computer screens. Others in easy chairs listening to Bach or Mozart. But for Gardner, physical activity and the serenity of the out-of-doors had been his catalysts to thought for as long as he could remember. Ever since the days he and his father had wordlessly hiked the hills and valleys of the Old Dominion.

He just had to get away from the office. He loaded a daypack with sandwiches, fruit, water and insect repellant, plopped a floppy hat on his head, and headed for the mountains. From his lab in Frederick to the Catoctin National Park Visitor Center was less than thirty-minutes by car through dazzling fall foliage: russet-hued oaks, yellow and orange-yellow maples, dark green junipers, and pale green moss. By mid-morning he was well up the trail to Cunningham Falls, an 80-foot cascade where he would eat his lunch and gather his thoughts.

His principal concern was how to stop the epidemic, how to keep *Medusa* from spreading further. Even though *Perseus* had rendered *Medusa* useless for future terrorist attacks, there was still the ongoing U.S. epidemic. He had seen the statistics Jerry Essminger and others had compiled, which showed new cases leveling off. But he knew from long experience that all the public health and preventive measures in the world could never be completely successful. And the problem with case contact investigation was that only *known* contacts could be discovered and treated. Persons exposed through innocent, anonymous, and unknown encounters—shopping in a store, playing on a beach, or walking the dog through a park—guaranteed *Medusa* would have susceptible victims for a long time to come.

The sound of rushing water drew his ear. He looked up the trail and caught site of a plume of spray from the cataract. At the bottom of the falls, water boiled up in a rainbowed steamy mist.

Gardner was not a man to sit contentedly by and wait for the epidemic simply to peter out, at a cost of thousands more lives. He wanted something to stop the epidemic now. For all his southern folksiness and down-home humor, he was a methodical scientist. He ran through in his mind all the standard approaches to epidemic control...

Anthrax immunization was out of the question. For all the reasons he and Tara Martin had already discussed. But immunization against the adenovirus component of *Medusa* was another matter. If that could be achieved, it would gut it. While there was some natural immunity in the population—'herd' immunity—to a few adenovirus types, there was none to type 35, the very uncommon one used in *Medusa*. A separate vaccine would have to be developed. And that would take a long time and cost a lot of money.

He paused his thoughts to watch a woodpecker, a blur of color, flatten itself against a tree. Soon its insistent knocking echoed through the woods.

Another approach was 'passive' immunizations. First infect animals with anthrax. When they're immune, harvest their antibodies to give to people who've been exposed. Just like gamma globulin shots for hepatitis. But he shook his head. That wouldn't work. Anthrax killed so rapidly there was no time for the animal to develop protective antibodies before it died.

A scrub jay raced past, its shrill cry ricocheting off the trees. It landed on a branch and continued to scream at him.

"Hey!" he yelled. "These are my woods too."

A smile on his face, he turned his attention to anti-viral drugs. There were specific ones against influenza, herpes viruses, and AIDS. But none of these had been tested on *adenovirus 35*. That would take many months, even years.

By the time he opened his lunch, he had gone through his list of possibilities and discarded them all as impractical or impossible. He was more frustrated than ever. He threw his pack on the ground. Worry chewed on him.

While Jerry Essminger worked at his computer in Los Angeles, and Dave Gardner racked his brain in the Catoctin Mountains of Maryland, in Mosul forty-eight hours had passed since the Kurdish woman, Fatima, had been sprayed with Mohammed's new batch of *Medusa* spores.

Mohammed was joined bright and early at the test chamber by Rashid Bin Yegal. The *al-Qaeda* agent informed him that the six new recruits were now fully trained, completely briefed, and filled with a holy zeal to begin their missions. They were ready to be infected with *Medusa*.

The two men stared through the mirror at the Kurdish women. Fatima, as expected, had all the symptoms of the adenovirus infection: a full-blown URI. Further proof of this was the half-empty box of tissues she had used on her red, runny nose. The other woman, Irena, was also beginning to exhibit signs of a cold.

"This new batch is highly infectious," Rashid remarked. "It can still cause plenty of URI symptoms."

Mohammed winced at the man's tobacco breath. "And contagious as well. It has been passed from one woman to the other. See. Irena's got it now."

"The anthrax effects should start soon," Rashid said.

"Twenty-four hours for Fatima, a day or so later for Irena. Just like the first batch we tested." Mohammed stared at the women then refocused the videocamera.

Mohammed began the next day in front of that same test room. Rashid was already there, waiting. Three days—more than seventy-two hours—had now elapsed since Fatima had been exposed to *Medusa's* spores. Both men were shocked to find her sitting up, eating hungrily from her tray, and chatting with her roommate. They could hear her cough occasionally. But it was a loose cough. And she didn't clutch her chest as if it was painful. They could also see that her breathing was normal, neither labored nor rapid. The monitor above her bed showed the rest of her vital signs were normal too, as were Irena's.

Rashid's raised eyebrow was questioning and accusatory.

"Too soon," Mohammed muttered. "Different subjects react differently. It will just take a little longer for these two. There is nothing to be concerned about." His confidence sounded hollow.

"I suppose so," Rashid said, both doubt and tobacco on his breath.

This morning, Mohammed awoke with a start, his breathing rapid, his night shirt soaked with sweat. The old nightmare had returned: warplanes swooping in to bomb and strafe…he was running, dodging in and out of buildings…helicopters chasing him, weaving in and out…he couldn't escape them…sudden, stabbing pain and bleeding from his hand…

It took some time for his head to clear. It had been years since he'd had that nightmare. Not since the days of the Gulf War. Why had it recurred now, why last night? Dreams could be portents. Omens. All day yesterday he'd had a premonition that something wasn't quite right, something he couldn't get at. Like an itch he couldn't scratch. Only worse.

As he washed his face and dressed, he looked in the mirror and warned himself, "Today, it must be today. Fatima must have signs of anthrax infection today. It *will* happen today." No other subject—neither rabbit nor human—had ever gone four days with a *Medusa* infection without becoming toxic and going into shock. But his words sounded more like a prayer than a prediction.

Rashid, once again, was waiting at the mirror. Neither man spoke. They focused on the two women. Irena's URI was full-blown, Fatima's clearly better. Both women had eaten their food. Fatima was at the sink washing her hands. Her blood pressure, pulse, and respiration read-outs on the monitor were all normal. She didn't even have a slight fever.

Mohammed collapsed against the wall.

Rashid's silence was more damning than words.

Not willing to admit defeat, Mohammed said, "I will examine them myself. Prepare them," he ordered one of the nearby medical technicians.

When Mohammed emerged from the room, Rashid said drily, "I take it the monitors are correct. The women are not ill with anthrax."

Mohammed sighed. "The monitors are correct."

"What has gone wrong?"

"Come to the culture room with me. Let us see what is growing there."

A few colonies of normal nasal flora—the kinds of bacteria which grow in everyone's noses—were scattered about the culture plates from both women. But so were colonies of *Medusa*. Mohammed had seen them so often he had no doubt about their identification. But even they were thinly dispersed through the agar medium. They didn't crowd out the normal flora the way a genuine infection would.

"They look like benign nasal organisms," Rashid pointed out. "I think your killer has become harmless."

Mohammed considered this. What else could it be? His monster had become a pussycat, no more dangerous than the lumps a kid picked out of his nose.

"I will do some additional tests," Mohammed said, not willing to let it go.

Rashid watched him. "That will take time. What should I tell the new agents I've trained? They think they are about to embark on a holy jihad."

"Tell them whatever you want," Mohammed said, his thoughts elsewhere.

"And what about them?" Rashid pointed to the two women. "Shouldn't they be disposed of. They know too much."

Mohammed was horrified. "No, no more senseless killing of the Faithful. They were blindfolded when they were captured. They cannot identify our laboratory. Have them blindfolded again, driven into the hills where they came from, and set free."

Rashid reluctantly agreed. Then he added, "I must inform Sheik Ibn Fahdil of this new development. He may wish to re-evaluate his allocation of funds."

Mohammed saw his career, his future, burning out like a guttering candle. "Give me a little more time," he pleaded. "Just a few more weeks. I know I can find the problem and fix it."

Rashid's response was another raised eyebrow.

It was dark when the two Kurdish women were taken away by the same men in the same convoy which had captured them. Ramazzan watched from a distance as they were blindfolded and helped into the vehicles. Mohammed gave the officer-in-charge some last minute orders.

"Where are they taking them, Director?" Ramazzan asked hesitantly as the convoy departed. He recalled his meeting in the hills with his uncle, Louis, and Jean-Claude. How dark it was. How cold. He shuddered for the two women.

"Back to where they came from," was all Mohammed would say. He stormed into his office and slammed the door behind him.

Ramazzan breathed a sigh of relief. It wasn't long before he learned the whole truth: the experiment had failed; the new biological weapon—*Medusa*—was now useless; funding for the lab might be cut off. Worried looks on the faces of the technicians told of concern for their livelihoods.

Ramazzan himself left the building as soon as it was safe. He had arranged with Louis and Jean-Claude to stand on the corner of a quiet street near his apartment every night at a certain hour. Unless he wore a particular colored shirt, they were to pass him by. He recalled how the big man, Jean-Claude, had grasped his collar, lifted him off the ground, and threatened him. Maybe they wouldn't come at all. Maybe they would just leave him here.

But, full of hope tonight, he wore that shirt. When the Land Rover stopped, he jumped in, carrying the few transportable belongings he owned. Ninety minutes later they were at the now-familiar campsite in the Kurdish Hills. His uncle, already there and waiting, greeted him with a smile and an embrace.

"They are safe!" He waved his cell phone in the air. "I have just heard. Both women were dropped off unhurt. Our people have them now. You have succeeded."

Choked with tears, all Ramazzan could manage was, "Allah akhbar, Allah akhbar."

Jean-Claude left the two Kurds to celebrate. He thumbed his own cellular phone. Within minutes of his call, two Huey gunships lifted off from the U.S. Airbase at Diyarbakir, Turkey. They used night-vision goggles and hugged the ground at tree-top level to avoid radar detection. The helicopters covered the two hundred miles to the Kurdish Hills in about an hour, guided by the GPS coordinates Jean-Claude had given them. One Huey circled overhead while the other swept in to the Landing Zone, which Jean-Claude had illuminated with green chem-lites at the first sound of the choppers.

Ramazzan said goodby to his uncle and climbed aboard the aircraft. Jean-Claude and Louis embraced and kissed one another on both cheeks.

"Mon ami," was all the CIA agent was able to get out before his friend pushed him aboard the Huey.

"Bon voyage," Louis said as the helicopter lifted off.

The Hueys were back at the airbase by 0130 hours. Once on the ground, Ramazzan was taken to pre-arranged quarters while Jean-Claude headed to the base communications center. He was quickly patched through to the Director of Central Intelligence in Langley, Virginia. The CIA Director, in turn, passed his terse message on to Tom O'Malley, the White House Chief of Staff.

The President and First Lady—now completely recovered—were just sitting down to a State Dinner in honor of the President of Pakistan. Black ties and formal gowns decorated the State Dining room. A string quartet played background music. Mozart.

The President was enjoying himself. Until his Chief of Staff tapped him on the shoulder. "Mr. President, *Medusa* is now headless."

The President went stiff in his chair, looked at the ruddy face of his COS, and asked, "for sure?"

"Yessir, for certain."

The President excused himself. When the two men were in private, the COS added, "it's now time for the follow-on mission, Mr. President."

"Who gives that order, Tommy?"

"You do, sir."

The President stared at an oil painting of Washington during the Revolutionary War. "*Perseus* was completely successful, you say?"

"That is what CIA tells us. And the Director places the highest confidence in his source of information."

"Well," the President grunted, "it will be his ass if he's wrong! Issue the necessary orders. What are we calling this new mission?"

"*Operation Payback*, sir."

The President stared at George Washington. "I love it!"

21

The Commanding Officer of U.S.S. *Cowpens* (CG 63) was sound asleep in his sea cabin just off the bridge when he was awakened at 0530 hours by the Officer of the Deck.

"Sir," the nervous junior officer reported, "we've received Flash Radio Traffic from the National Command Authority."

The CO shook his head to clear it and reached for his reading glasses. He read the message once, then again.

"Has this been authenticated?" he asked the young officer.

"Yessir. Both the Executive Officer and the Communications Officer have confirmed its authenticity."

"Very well, Lieutenant, let's get to General Quarters."

Within minutes, the 1MC—the main ship-wide public address system—was blaring the bosun's call to 'GQ,' followed by the verbal order: "General Quarters, General Quarters. All hands man your battle stations. This is not a drill. Repeat, this is not a drill."

The command was repeated three times as the ship's 325 enlisted men, 33 Chief Petty Officers, and 33 Officers scrambled to their assigned battle stations.

Once on the bridge, the CO established communications with his CIC—Combat Intelligence Center—from where the ship would be maneuvered and fought. Until now, *Cowpens's* sea station had been to sail large donuts in the water of the northern Persian Gulf, cruising in circles at ten knots. Suddenly, her four General Electric gas turbine engines, connected to twin propeller shafts, roared to life with 80,000 horsepower as the command,

"All ahead full, make turns for 30 knots," was relayed from the bridge to the engine room.

With a bone in her teeth (the bow wave) and a rooster tail flying (the stern wake), *Cowpens* changed course to north-by-northwest and prepared to carry out the mission her CO shared now with the crew over the 1MC: "All hands, this is the Captain. Prepare for Missile Launch, Tomahawk. This is not a drill."

By 0645 hours the ship had reached its designated launch position, bearing and speed. The Captain gave the order,

"Launch Tomahawk. Repeat, launch Tomahawk."

With a roar of tail flame, the 20 foot long, two-ton metal spear exploded from its tube and climbed into the dawn on a pillar of fire. The missile fought for height, then steadied into its cruise altitude of fifty feet and its speed of 550 miles per hour.

Twenty minutes after the Tomahawk launch, as the missile was crossing to the east side of the Euphrates River near the ruins of Ancient Uruk—a Sumerian City four thousand years old—two F-15 Eagles charged down the runway at Diyarbakir Air Base in southeastern Turkey and lifted off into the sky. One plane, conventionally armed, would fly cover. The other was equipped not with weapons but with high-resolution photographic equipment. Its mission: to assess battle damage from the Tomahawk strike. The Eagles crossed the Turkish-Iraqi frontier heading for the chicken plant with the rusty red sign on the outskirts of Mosul.

The Tomahawk skirted the Iraqi city of An-Najaf and boomed across the empty desert toward its target. Its narrow silhouette offered little reflective surface to enemy radar.

At 0725 hours a traveler on the main Baghdad-to-Jordan Highway was startled by a silver streak flashing past no more than 500 yards away from his old Mercedes truck. He tried to focus on the apparition. But it was out of sight before he knew it, rising up and over a nearby hillock followed by a deafening roar.

At 0750 hours Mohammed was just arriving at his laboratory. He had finally left his office bedroom the night before and gone home to sleep. As he unlocked the door, he heard the familiar whine of jet engines and looked up. A low-flying F-15 Eagle was visible overhead. Then he caught sight of a second aircraft, much higher, this one a mere glint of reflected metal in the dazzling sunrise. He shrugged. It was unusual for warplanes to buzz the city itself. But not unheard of. Simply another insult to put up with.

He was turning the door knob when he heard another sound coming out of the southern desert. He could see nothing, but the sound increased to a roar. In that last moment, Mohammed saw only a winged monster plunging out of the sky.

The Tomahawk struck his laboratory with its 1000 pound high explosive warhead. Within seconds, the building and all its culture media, petri dishes full of bacteria, storage flasks, shiny chrome counters and incubators were smoking ruins.

The photography-equipped F-15 Eagle made three flaps-down passes over the area, then radioed a message to his base that the target was gone, obliterated. *Cowpens* was prepared to send another Tomahawk if needed. But the Eagle pilot made it clear that on visual inspection alone there was no longer a target. The F-15s headed for home.

At Diyarbakir, the Eagle's film canisters were loaded onto a waiting C-141 Transport aircraft. With Jean-Claude aboard, it headed for Andrews Air Force Base, Washington, D.C. Shortly after this, another aircraft, a 4-engine propeller driven EP-3 spy plane also lifted off from Diyarbakir. The surveillance aircraft made two north-south passes across the length of Iraq, its snooping gear scooping up electromagnetic signals like a Norwegian fisherman scoops up herring into his nets. These signals would be stored and later decoded and interpreted by the cryptographic experts at the NSA.

Finally, about mid-morning, a third aircraft took off from Diyarbakir. This one was a commercial Boeing 737 under contract to the CIA. Its lone passenger was Ramazzan Fahrs. His destination: Geneva, Switzerland and the 15 million pounds deposited in his name in a numbered bank account there. He would never return to Kurdistan. Instead, he would use his money and administrative skills in the service of the PKU, the Patriotic Union of Kurdistan, whose objective was nothing less than a free and independent nation for the Kurds, similar to the one the Jews carved out of British Palestine at the end of World War II.

Twenty-four hours later. The President of the United States and a group of his advisors huddled around a handful of photographs in the Oval Office. These were the BDA's—Battle Damage Assessment —photos, the processed and printed results of the F-15 Eagle flyby mission over Mosul after the missile strike.

"What about collateral damage?" the President asked.

"None to speak of, Mr. President," Oscar Bentley replied. "Except to the chickens."

"What?" The President's face showed a childlike innocence.

Oscar grinned impishly. "You all remember, sir, part of that laboratory building was a chicken processing plant. Apparently the surrounding neighborhood was showered with about a thousand pounds of very crisply-done chicken parts."

The President moved forward. "But no collateral damage to *people*?"

"None that we know of."

The President next turned to Jean Claude, looking up at the huge man. "And to you, sir, I say, well done, well done, indeed!"

Jean-Claude nodded. "Thank you, Mr. President."

"How are the Iraqi's playing it?" the President asked him.

"My friend Louis informs me that the Iraqis are taking the official position that it was a simple chemical explosion and fire. There's no mention about a military strike."

"That was predictable, Mr. President," the Secretary of State said, pointing to the photos. "If they admit that the building was the target of a military strike, they would have to acknowledge that there was something more going on there than just making chicken dinners. And that could be just the stimulus the U.N.

needs to screw up its courage and order an UNSCOM inspection team back in there."

Oscar Bentley agreed. "And the Iraqis wouldn't want that."

"So, it will be suppressed?"

"I think so," Oscar answered.

"Is it possible they don't know we hit them?"

The Head of the NSA took this question. "Iraqi communications are abuzz over this. Our EP-3 surveillance flights have picked up numerous transmissions between Baghdad and Mosul. Some Iraqi officials think it *was* an air strike. Others that it was simply an internal explosion. But one thing is for certain, they have no clue that *Medusa's* failure was due to our *Perseus* mission. From all the communications traffic we've heard and analyzed, they still believe *Medusa* simply mutated into a harmless form. Their entire biowarfare program has been thrown into a state of turmoil."

"And I have more good news, Mr. President," Oscar Bentley added. "My deep cover asset in Iraq has evidence that Rashid Bin Yegal is high-tailing it through the mountains, probably heading for *al-Qaeda* hideouts in Pakistan. He will not receive a warm welcome when he gets there. They don't tolerate failure well."

The President turned to his Press Secretary. "How do we play this to our own media?"

"If asked, we admit that a missile strike was carried out against an Iraqi military target. Nothing more."

"What about the *Cowpens* crew?" the Secretary of State asked. "When the ship returns to port and the crew goes on liberty, the secret is sure to get out."

"No, sir," CJCS responded quickly. "All *Cowpens* knows— from the Captain on down to the missile technician who pushed the trigger—is that she launched a Tomahawk missile against an Iraqi military target. And that it was at such and such GPS coordinates. And that it was a successful strike. The same for the two Eagle pilots. We've been attacking Iraqi military targets for years. Why, just last month, we hit a radar site near Mosul which had locked onto one of our patrol aircraft. To those sailors on

Cowpens and the airmen at Diyarbakir, this was just another mission. And professionally carried out, I might say."

The President seemed satisfied.

"One more thing, Mr. President," the Secretary of State said.

"What now?"

"We could not have pulled this off without help from the French. From the two archeologists who first made contact with the Iraqi informer, to the *Charge d'Affairs* in Baghdad who provided Jean-Claude so much assistance, right up to their Foreign Ministry. They played a critical role in the mission's success."

"You think we owe them?"

"Yessir."

"What did you have in mind?"

"Perhaps improved trade policies. Or our support at the U.N. for one of their initiatives. I'll draft a list of recommendations for you."

"Very well. They can't have the Statue of Liberty back. Other than that, I'll consider your suggestions."

He looked from face to face. "Anything else?"

Everyone shook his head, or answered, "No, Mr. President."

"Then thank you all. You are excused. Except for you, Dr. Gardner. Would you and the Chief of Staff remain?"

When the room cleared, the President held out his hand. "Dr. Gardner, let me congratulate you again on the success of your *Perseus*. It was a brilliant accomplishment. Your country owes you an enormous debt of gratitude."

Gardner was uncomfortable.

"But we're really only half-way finished, aren't we?" the President said. "We've eliminated the foreign threat but we still have a devastating epidemic to deal with here at home. Despite all our public health efforts, our citizens continue to die. Our hospitals are overwhelmed, our drug supplies dwindling."

Gardner chose his words carefully. "The most recent data from CDC indicates the epidemic has plateaued."

The President was not content with that. "But when will it end? Or at least begin to end?"

"I don't know, Mr. President. I've racked my brain—and lost a lot of sleep—over that very question. I don't have a good answer for you. Like most epidemics, it will just have to slowly fizzle out over time."

"But that could take weeks, maybe months. Meanwhile, many more will die. Even those not directly infected will suffer from the epidemic's effects on our economy."

"Which is worsening as we speak," the COS said. "Except the security business, which is going gangbusters."

The President agreed. "Dr. Gardner, you're our expert on this. Is there no magic left in that laboratory of yours—no other rabbit you could pull out of a hat?"

Gardner sighed. "I'm sorry, Mr. President. "I'm fresh outta rabbits at the present time."

Gil raised the snub nosed .38 and loosed off five rounds. It had been a while. He had to relearn to tuck his thumb down or get it chewed up by the cylinder catch. The ammunition was new, a precaution suggested by the gun range owner, who discarded the old ammunition for him. His shooting wasn't too bad, but he needed the practice. Meantime, high tech had moved forward, and others at the range were using Glocks and Berettas. Still, the snub was good and it fit into his pocket. His license was current, but it was not a carry permit. Given the attempt on his life by the Egyptian national, Marwan Hanjoun, he would carry anyway.

The beginning of this second week of November was a good time for Gil. The only thing dampening it was keeping from Tara and Cassie the attempt on his life. But he had been able to cut back on his ER shifts to only five twelve-hour stints per week. This had given him time to get some exercise, shop for some badly needed clothes and consider a new place to live. His shabby room, even with his cleaning, was still next to a porno shop, hardly a place to bring Tara and Cassie if that ever happened. Gil smiled as he reloaded the revolver. Oscar of all people. CIA tough guy. *'You two belong together…'* But neither Gil nor Tara had followed up on the observation. Things were still too raw. Yet they were changing. He could see it in Tara's eyes, the way she walked close to him. Old and good memories were shaking loose for both of them, a firmament of hope perhaps.

He trained the revolver twohanded and fired slow-fire. All five shots grouped well. With that, it was time to get to work on finding his new digs. He settled on Santa Monica, buying paintings and bric-a-brac and furniture. The cheap suitcase filled with bad dreams would need to be looked at. Maybe it was time to bring out the diplomas. The wedding ring and divorce decree would have to stay.

During the move, he found an old Blue Ribbon—1st Place—from some school race of Cassie's. Underneath was a forgotten photo of the three of them, when Tara had long hair tied in a pony tail. He bought a good frame and displayed it in the living area.

Gil's medical reputation continued to grow, enhanced by the publication of several interviews he gave to local newspapers about *Medusa*, appearances on television news programs, and the acceptance by the *New England Journal of Medicine* of an article he had written describing his first ten cases of the disease. He continued to be regularly consulted by other physicians. And he had received invitations to lecture at both UCLA and USC Schools of Medicine and at a local nursing college.

He hadn't had a drink in seven weeks. And he had fingernails now. Long enough to clean under.

"So how are things with Cassie's braces?" he asked during one of his nighttime phone calls to Tara. His head laceration was healing. And the sutures were out. But it still hurt.

"She knows she needs them. But they cut into her social life. You remember how that goes."

"Has she actually had a date yet?"

"Not really. I took her and the boy across the street to a Saturday afternoon movie. Then out for burgers and fries. She's too young for a real date. You agree, don't you?"

"Completely. And thanks for asking."

"Of course. You're her father. She's also mad that she doesn't have complete control of the phone in the evening anymore."

He laughed. "Next she'll be wanting her own line."

"She's wondering when she'll see you again. You remember she's got a birthday coming up." She paused. "Ditto for me, when are we going to see you?"

He hedged his answer. But he thought about it the rest of the evening.

During a quiet time at the ER, he and Kathy Roberts shared a coffee break. They had become good friends. Just friends.

"My daughter's birthday's coming up," he said. "Fourteen years."

"Bet you miss her."

"More than I realized."

"What about her mom? Anything still there between you two?"

"Maybe. I think so." He sipped his coffee. "Before Tara and I married—even before we became lovers—she was my best friend." He grunted. "At times, my only friend."

"And now?"

"She's still the only one I can really talk with. The only one I really trust—no offense, Kath."

"None taken." She refilled their coffee cups. When she sat down again, she said, "Friendship is as good a basis for marriage as anything else. Start with that and love will follow. 'Marry your best friend,' my mother always told me."

"But there must be some…"

"Physical attraction? Of course. Do you feel any for her?"

He thought of Tara's gorgeous body. "She's still got it." That warm feeling came over him. Was he blushing again?

She grinned. "Has she caught you looking? Here's a tip: let her catch you." Then seriously, "Look, Gil. In a good marriage you can't tell where friendship ends and love begins. They're seamless. Like a good weld."

He considered this. Perhaps that basic love-friendship for Tara was still there. Just under the surface. Waiting to re-emerge. "Things are still new."

"Give it time."

One late night he was on his way home from Oxnard. Thoughts of Tara and Cassie were on his mind. That's when it happened.

He had been invited to speak to a local medical society. After the meeting, he went to dinner with some of the physicians, then lingered over dessert and coffee. It was nearly midnight when he finished. When he finally headed for his car, he noticed a new Cadillac with a bashed-in right front fender in the parking lot. He thought nothing of it. He must have been tired, preoccupied. He left for home without his usual vigilance. His guard was down.

Patches of ground fog hovered heavily over the road. A gentle drizzle was falling, wetting the pavement and blurring the lane lines.

He was half-way down Pacific Coast Highway, mostly deserted at this time of night except for the occasional semi, when he noticed headlights approaching from behind. His vigilance at a low ebb, he paid them no attention. Until he was jolted—his head whip-lashed—by a rear-ender. When he became fully alert, he saw it was the Caddy with the dented fender. Silhouetted by headlights from behind him was Marwan Hanjoun.

Christ! Where had his mind been? His stomach knotted, his muscles tensed. He gripped the wheel tightly and swallowed hard. What was with this guy? Didn't he know it was all over for him? Apparently not! Or didn't he care?"

He dragged the revolver awkwardly from his pocket, the hammer catching on the fabric. "Shit!" He floored the car. But all he got from the old Porsche was another spasm of coughing and sputtering. He kicked himself for not taking care of the problem sooner. He could barely get the car up to 65 miles an hour down the dark road. The Egyptian terrorist couldn't be shaken. He hung right on his ass and rammed him again, almost forcing him off the road.

Think. Don't panic. If you do, he's got you.

He managed to keep the Porsche just ahead of the Cadillac. Each time he saw the other vehicle make a run at his rear bumper, he veered across the double line, or skidded onto the right shoulder, his tires spinning rubber before getting a grip on the highway again.

An idea slowly built in his brain as he skidded and turned his way down the road. It was incredibly dangerous. It would have to be timed to the split second. But it was all he could think of. It was that or he was a dead man.

The road was deserted. But when he hit a straight stretch, about mid-way between Malibu and Santa Monica, he saw what he wanted. A half mile ahead, its running lights a hazy orange through the mist, a big semi was coming right at him. One final check in his rearview: Hanjoun was having his own driving problems and had backed off a little.

Gil spun the wheel hard left, at the same time stomping on the brakes. The Porsche's real wheels broke traction with the road and started to slide, bringing the car's rear end across the front of the truck. Gil hung on; there was nothing else to do. Either he had judged correctly or he would be a corpse.

To the sounds of the semi's blaring airhorn and screeching brakes, the Porsche continued across the road to the opposite shoulder, completing its 180 degree turn and coming, finally, to a shuddering standstill.

Gil watched with both horror and satisfaction as the semi, swerving into oncoming traffic to avoid the Porsche, slammed square into the Cadillac. The car flipped completely onto its hood, skidding upside down like that for another hundred yards. Gil considered getting out to render medical assistance. But the Cadillac exploded into great gouts of flame when the gas tank went up. Huge tongues of fire licked at the fog like devil's breath. He could see the truck driver standing on the shoulder and shielding his face from the flames.

Gil made a u-turn and drove off. The trucker had seen the old Porsche. Better get it off the road. Rent a car for a while.

At home later, Gil sat fully dressed on the bed in the dark, staring at an unopened vodka bottle he had purchased at an all-night convenience store. Finally, he rose, opened the bottle and got out a small tumbler. But he didn't pour right away. Instead, he went back to his seat on the bed and stared at it again.

Body shakes came first, then he sobbed, bleeding off the fear. Once started, he wept for some time. Finally, he curled up on his bed. He was awakened at dawn by the telephone. It was the homicide detective.

"Did you hear, doc, your friend Marwan Hanjoun is dead? Burnt to toast in a misadventure with a semi last night."

"Yeah?"

"You wouldn't know anything about that, would you, doc?"

"Not a thing."

"Okay, doc. The trucker said a Porsche caused the accident. An old Porsche. But I bet it's long gone, right? We'll put out an APB, but it's in Canada by now—right?'

"Yeah, right."

"Have a good rest of your life, doc." The phone went dead.

Gil emptied the vodka bottle into the sink, showered, shaved, and crawled into bed. He was off work today. He could sleep til noon.

23

Gil had barely recovered from his encounter with Hanjoun the terrorist when he got a phone call from Atlanta. The timing of the call—the middle of the day—was in itself unusual. He and Tara had established a regular schedule for their chats: after dinner while Cassie was doing homework. He was instantly suspicious something was wrong.

But it was Tara's voice—quiet and restrained, fighting panic—which alarmed him most.

"Gil?"

"What is it, Tara? What's wrong?"

"It's Cassie. She's sick."

His stomach caved in. He was standing at the counter in front of the nurse's station and had to lean on his elbows. He needed to sit down, find a private place to take this call.

"I'm transferring you to my office," he told her. "In case we get cut off, I'll get right back to you. Where are you calling from?"

"Emory Hospital Emergency Room." She gave him the number.

When he picked up again in the seclusion of his office, he said as calmly as he could, "Tell me what's going on."

Her voice was shaky. "Cassie was perfectly well when she went to bed last night. I kissed her and tucked her in like I always do, even though she thinks she's too big for that now."

The tender image tore at him.

"But this morning she awoke complaining of vague aches and pains. She had a temperature of 101 and refused to eat. I

228

checked her out to be certain it wasn't something obvious. Appendicitis or tonsillitis. But everything was normal. No URI symptoms nor much of anything else. I assumed it was the start of a viral infection. I phoned the school and told them she wouldn't be in today. I told her to take some Tylenol, try and drink some fluids, and get some rest."

Gil could hear the sounds of the Emory ER going on around her. The same kind he heard every day in his own ER.

"I came home at lunch and found her much worse."

"How so?"

"Her temperature had spiked to 103 degrees and her breathing was fast, labored, and raspy. But what alarmed me most was when I couldn't arouse her. I called 911 immediately. They brought her here. The ER team is with her now."

She sounded desperate. "Oh God, Gil!"

He was trying to remain cool himself. "You told me she had no URI symptoms," he said slowly. "Just aches and pains, flu-like."

"That's right. She did have a mild URI several weeks ago. But she got over it within a few days. Nothing came of it. And she's been well ever since."

He was comforted by this. He had yet to see, hear, or read about a case of *Medusa* which had not been immediately preceded by typical URI symptoms. The adenovirus part of it. But he decided that any further clinical discussion could wait. He knew what he must do now.

"I'll get the first flight out of LAX. I'll be with you by morning. In the meantime, hang on. We both know Emory's top notch. Cassie will be well-cared for. I'll call you in a couple of hours. We should know more by then."

"Thanks Gil. See you soon."

Four hours later—ninety minutes after his shift ended—he was on an American Airlines direct, non- stop flight to Atlanta. He had paid for a first-class seat in the hopes of getting some privacy. Turned out he had the whole row to himself.

He called Tara inflight. "What's going on now?"

"I spoke with the ER physician."

"And it's anthrax?"

"Yes. He thinks it's *Medusa*."

Gil leaned his head against the seatback in front of him. "Oh, Christ," he said under his breath. "Not Cassie. Please, God, not my daughter." He remembered that when he had been at the bottom of the pit, a bitter drunk, despairing of both his personal and professional future, the one true constant, the one anchor to his life, had been his daughter's unquestioning love.

But wait. Something wasn't right here. "What about the absence of a URI prodrome? What did the ER doc think about that?"

Tara blew her nose. "He's as puzzled about it as we both are. But he says she's got all the classic signs of anthrax: enlarged lymph nodes on her chest x-ray and signs of septic shock. He's seen a lot of these cases. Maybe not as many as you. But a lot."

"What are they doing for her?"

"They've done a full work-up, cultured everything: blood, urine, and nasal swabs. And they did an LP."

"A spinal tap!" Now he was really scared.

"It was negative, Gil," she said quickly.

"That's a relief. Have they started treating her yet?"

"Yes. She's on IV antibiotics and a bolus of fluid for the low blood pressure. She's getting oxygen by face mask and they're getting ready to transfer her to an isolation bed in their ICU."

Gil waved away a flight attendant and grappled with the problem. It didn't make any sense for Cassie to get sick like this, a bolt out of the blue, without the typical URI symptoms to start with. This wasn't *Medusa's* usual behavior. What was he missing? What in Christ's name was he missing?

The sun was just rising when the American Airlines flight turned onto final approach and descended over the red Georgia clay toward landing. Gil purchased a few toiletries in an airport shop on his way to curbside—he had no luggage, not even a flight bag—and hailed the first taxi he saw. By breakfast time he was heading into Emory Hospital's main lobby. Tara was there waiting for him.

They hugged, clinging to one another.

He shrank back. "I must look awful. I haven't shaved, changed clothes or brushed my teeth."

She kissed the stubble on his cheek. "You look terrific to me. I'm glad you're here."

He gave her a quick look over. He had never seen her like this: face taut, eyes red.

"How's she doing?" he asked. They headed for the elevators.

"She's stabilized. Her BP's back up and she's breathing more easily.

"Has she shown any movement, any response at all?"

"Not yet."

When they reached the door to the ICU, the Infectious Disease specialist was just coming out. He shook hands with them both.

"Your reputation precedes you," he said to Gil. "You diagnosed one of the first cases, didn't you?"

Gil nodded. "How's my daughter? Her mother tells me you think it's *Medusa*."

"The cultures will take two or three days to grow out, as you know. We won't know for certain until then."

"The stains?"

The man hesitated.

"Come on, doc," Gil insisted. "What did they show?"

"I'm afraid it looks like anthrax. But," he hastened to add, "we're very optimistic. Your daughter's young, healthy, and strong. We've gotten her out of toxic shock, she's breathing on her own and she..."

"Doesn't have meningitis?"

"That's correct."

Gil extended his hand again. "Thank you. I—" he pulled Tara closer, "that is, her mother and I, appreciate everything you're doing for her."

"I'll be back in a few hours," the specialist promised. "But I'm available by cell phone and pager if there's any change. And if you can think of something yourself that might help, let me know."

Tara warned him as they entered the ICU. "This won't be easy. I almost didn't make it the first time I saw her."

Despite the warning, when he pulled aside the curtain surrounding his daughter's bed and got his first look at her, only years of medical training saved him. She was full of tubes: catheters, IV lines, oxygen lines. He'd seen these many times in many patients. But this was different. This was his daughter.

He gasped.

Tara walked around to the other side of the bed and sat in a chair. He remained motionless, checking out each of the catheters, intravenous lines, monitoring leads, and oxygen tubes. Satisfied he understood what was going on, he approached the bed. Cassie's nose and mouth were covered with a green oxygen mask, but he could see her cheeks. They were pink. He was encouraged by that. He bent down and placed his own cheek against hers. It was warm. Another good sign.

Over the hiss of flowing oxygen, he whispered into her ear, "Cassie, it's dad. I'm here, honey."

He watched her eyelids for any response, anything at all. Nothing.

On the chance she could still hear but could not respond, he added. "Daddy's here. I'm with you." He looked at Tara, who was staring at the carpet. She gripped a sodden tissue. "Mommy's here, too. We both love you. You're going to be better soon."

He sat down on a chair opposite Tara's. They joined hands across their daughter's body, as if they could somehow impart their own life forces to her.

When the ICU nurse asked them to step outside for a few minutes while she changed Cassie's catheter, they found a small waiting area down the hall. He bought some coffee from a vending machine.

"Are you hungry?" he asked. "Do you want some breakfast? I hear Emory's cafeteria is pretty good."

She shook her head. "Couldn't eat a thing."

"Me either."

They sat silent with their coffee until Gil asked, "Any idea where she might have caught it?"

Tara shook her head. "When we first knew *Medusa* was contagious, I grounded her from all the usual teen hangouts: malls, concerts, movie theaters."

"How about at school? Could she have been infected there?"

"Very unlikely."

"What about that boy you told me about? The one that got sick. What was his name?"

She had forgotten. "Alain. The French boy."

"Could he have been the source of Cassie's infection?"

Tara shook her head. "I don't see how. Alain was a senior, not even in the same classes as Cassie."

"But they did go to the same school. She could have been exposed during a chance encounter in the library, at lunch, or even standing in line at the cafeteria. You know how contagious *Medusa* is."

"It's possible. But that was seven weeks ago. And except for Cassie's mild URI—the one I told you about—she's been completely healthy ever since."

Gil played a hunch. "Did she get that URI around the same time as the French boy's illness?"

"Yes, yes, it was around the same time. The last week in September."

"Did you think about starting Cassie on prophylactic antibiotics?"

She looked at him wide-eyed, guilt-stricken.

He quickly squeezed her hand. "Why would you? The first case of *Medusa* hadn't even been diagnosed yet. It probably was just a common cold."

She searched his eyes for any hint of accusation but didn't find any.

"I guess she might have been exposed at that time," she admitted. "But from everything I've read, the average time for *Medusa* infections from the URI symptoms to the onset of toxic shock is about 48 to 72 hours. Certainly not more than a week. And it's now been seven weeks—seven—since the French boy got sick. I don't see how he could have been Cassie's source of infection."

He agreed with her. But he couldn't get it out of his head. He didn't believe in coincidence when it came to medical causation. The timing of the French boy's sickness and Cassie's own seemed too coincidental, despite the long interval between her URI symptoms seven weeks ago and her current illness.

For the next day-and-a-half there was little change. Cassie's vital signs remained stable. But she continued to be unresponsive, though Gil thought he saw her eyelids flicker once when he whispered to her. He and Tara settled into a routine. Sometimes, they were together at the bedside, then one of them would go to her house for a shower, a few hours sleep, and something to eat.

During his solitary bedside watches, Gil returned again and again to the puzzles of Cassie's illness: how had she caught it; why hadn't she developed the URI prodrome first; and was there any connection between her present illness and the long-past URI? And one more: if her original URI was *Medusa's* first symptoms, why hadn't Tara become ill herself? Just luck? Or had she been protected in some way she hadn't been aware of? Frustrated, he passed the time doing crossword puzzles. These, at least, he could answer.

Tara brought her work to the hospital and busied herself with pencil, calculator, and computer print-outs.

"What are you working on now?" Gil asked when they were sitting across from one another at Cassie's bedside.

She put down her papers, removed her reading glasses, and rubbed her eyes. "So far, I've gotten a little over 11,000 case reports of *Medusa*. I'm trying to make some sense out of all the data."

"Like how?"

"Like identifying groups with high-risk for *Medusa*. So we can target them for prophylactic antibiotics. Prevent the disease."

"The 'rifle', huh, rather than the 'shotgun'?"

She managed a smile through her fatigue. "Exactly. By focusing on high-risk groups—if I find any— we make the best use of our limited antibiotics."

"Found any?"

"Not so far. Certainly no particular age, sex or ethnic group stands out. I'm just beginning to look at occupations."

He put down his crossword puzzle. "How do you do that?"

"Well, first, I sort the cases into broad occupational categories, like this." She handed over her laptop. "Here, take a look."

He could see how she had set up the analysis. Down the left-hand side of the page was a list of work categories: *Professionals, Managers, Sales Workers,* etc. Down the right-hand side were columns of numbers: the number of workers in each category; each category's percent of the total workforce; and the actual and expected number of *Medusa* cases for each category.

He scrolled down page after page, scanned category after category. Finally, he gave up and looked at her. "Nothing stands out."

She sighed. "I didn't find anything either. I asked our statisticians to take a look as well. They wrote a computer program to identify any group with a significantly higher risk. But they didn't come up with any." She put her glasses back on. "I'll keep looking."

It was during one of their times together at the bedside, about thirty-six hours into Cassie's hospitalization—Tara occupied with her analysis, Gil working on a puzzle—that the quiet was broken by the alarm above Cassie's bed.

Gil instantly saw the problem: ventricular fibrillation. The normal, rhythmic and regular heart tracing had suddenly been replaced with a bunch of erratic lines on the EKG monitor. Cassie's heart was fibrillating like a bag of worms, twitching and writhing instead of pumping blood to her body.

"V-Fib!" he yelled to Tara. He sprang to his daughter's side and started giving her CPR.

The ICU Code Blue Team was next to him within seconds. Gil automatically started barking out orders.

"Dr Martin!" the team leader demanded. "Please step aside."

He hesitated. Years of training ingrained into him like a circuit board impelled him to act. His body, his muscles and nerves, knew exactly what to do and craved to be released to do it.

Tara tugged on his arm and he allowed himself to be led away. They retreated to a corner of the ICU. They could hear the sounds of the resuscitation going on behind the drawn curtains. All they could do was wait. And pray.

24

"First ask the patient,
Of what trade are you?"
Bernardo Ramazzini (1633-1714)
Father of Occupational Medicine

Dave Gardner loved the sound of fall leaves crunching beneath his running shoes. It was different from his South, where he had been used to palm trees, old Spanish moss, and frog-filled swamps. Here in Maryland's autumn, he deliberately headed for every little pile of leaves he could find.

In a sweat shirt and running shorts, he was on his usual lunch-time jog around Fort Detrick. The weather was brisk, bright with sunshine. There were scattered clouds. He had barely started out, but already his breathing had increased to match his stride. A warm glow spread over his face, his beard tingled, and a light sweat appeared on his forehead. He settled into the rhythm of it, barely aware of his surroundings, his feet leading the way, the rest of him following.

A widower, Gardner often envisioned on these runs his wife Jean's sweet face, her dazzling smile, the blond curls he had loved to nuzzle. When she passed away a few years ago, his grief was immeasureable. He hadn't known such pain was possible, even with the support he received from his three children and five grandchildren. But he had endured. He had gotten through bereavement. Time had healed the wound, and he had arrived at the point he was at now: comforted by work and family and relieved of stress by his life-long addiction to vigorous exercise. Running was his Valium, his Prozac.

He usually programmed his runs into the day's schedule. But sometimes, when the frustration got too much, he would simply change clothes and bolt out the door, heading for no place in particular, merely laying one foot down in front of the other.

Today had been an especially bad one. He was desperate to find a way to stop the epidemic. *Medusa* was still infecting almost 2,000 Americans each week. Sixty-five percent of them died, a higher death rate than in any U.S. foreign war. Something had to be done quickly before more perished. He had been thinking of nothing else since his meeting with the President.

Like Tara Martin, he thought the answer lay in discovering groups of people who were—for whatever reason—at high risk for the disease, then targeting them with every preventive strategy available. But he had gone through the same 11,000 case database Tara had and found no such groups either. Apparently, there were none.

He was into the second mile of the run when the idea hit him. The insight dragged him to a halt. He leaned against an old elm tree and had what the FBI after-action report would describe as a 'eureka' moment.

Wait a minute, he told himself. Maybe he and Tara were going about this the wrong way. Instead of searching for high-risk groups, maybe they should be looking in the other direction, for groups with a lower-than-normal risk. If any existed, it might be because they were protected, had some sort of barrier against the disease. Perhaps something to do with their work site or occupation. It was worth a look.

He spun around and headed straight back to his office, running hard. He didn't shower. He didn't change out of his running clothes. Instead, he wiped the sweat off his face, threw the towel around his shoulders, and logged on to the CDC database. He searched for occupational groups with fewer *Medusa* cases than expected. He made the selection criterium very restrictive: only work groups with 25 percent or fewer cases than would be expected. He didn't want any that were merely 'statistically' significant. He wanted those with big differences, differences which would make an impact on the epidemic.

He drummed his fingers on the desk while the computer sorted and classified the results. One occupational category— only one—popped up: agricultural workers. He had hoped for more. But at least it was a start. And it looked like a winner. This group, which should have accounted for 1160 cases, had only 220. This was a five-fold lower amount than expected.

He stared at the numbers for a long time, trying to understand what they were telling him. He then searched the database for individual job types within this category, such as tractor drivers, field workers, irrigation workers, etc. He found that those with the *least* involvement in farming—e.g., non-working family members—had the *greatest* percent of cases. And vice versa. In other words, farming was somehow protective against *Medusa* infection. And the more farming one did, the more protective it was. It was a clear correlation. But what did it mean?

He leaned back in his chair, rank with his own sweat, and pondered his startling discovery. What was there about the farm environment that was protective? The rural nature of farming— less exposure to sick people, for example—must account for some of it. But could this explain all the benefit? After all, today's farmers send their children to community schools along with city kids and regularly gathered in nearby towns to shop, dine and attend religious services with the 'townies.' And they often make the trip to the big city for theater and concert performances, to watch movies and to wander the malls, just like their urban cousins. Farmworkers were no longer as isolated as they once were.

Gardner looked out the window. In the distance he saw a flight of crows descend on the stubble of a corn field.

What else were farmers and farmworkers exposed to, besides the obvious ones of fresh air, dirt, manure? Insects! Insects in their crops.

Insects in their barns. Insects even in their houses. And where there were insects, there were bound to be what? Pesticides, by god! Virtually all farmworkers were exposed to some type of pesticide, weren't they?

He pulled at his sweat shirt. How best to follow this hunch? He started with the obvious, find out more about pesticide workers. He pulled a textbook from a shelf. It listed three distinct groups of them: *manufacturers,* who produced pesticides from raw materials; *formulaters,* who diluted the pesticides to the right concentrations; and *sprayers,* who dispersed the pesticides by airplane, ground, or hand-held equipment.

Armed with this, Gardner went back to the computer, this time searching for cases of *Medusa* in pesticide workers. He was stunned at the number which popped up: 6 cases. That was all, six cases out of more than 11,000. He couldn't believe it. This group of workers made up about 0.5 pecent of the workforce. Its statistical 'fair share' of cases, therefore—its expected number of cases—was 56. But there were only six actual cases. Now he was really excited.

He glanced again at the fat, black crows in the corn field. Then he started to read about pesticides. About the chemicals themselves. That's when his spirits began to droop like a rose in a Texas drought. There were more than 1,500 such products licensed for use. They included insecticides, fungicides, herbicides and rodenticides. There were dozens, even hundreds, of formulations for each type. Even the single category, 'insecticides' had: organophosphates, such as parathion and malathion; chlorinated hydrocarbons, such as Lindane; carbamates, such as Sarin; and naturally occurring products such as the pyrethrums and pyrethroids. And this didn't even include the arsenicals, the creosotes, the various rat and rodent poisons, and the termite toxins.

He folded his arms and stared at the computer screen. How to select from this jumble of chemicals the one or two which might be protective? His concentration was broken by the phone.

He snatched it up. "What?" he growled.

Twelve hours earlier, in the corner of Emory Hospital's ICU, Gil and Tara Martin had waited, eyes fixed on the drawn curtain around their daughter's bed. They both knew, could well imagine, what was going on. Their medical knowledge only exacerbated their worst fears. When they heard the order, 'Clear!' shouted from inside the curtain, they knew Cassie was getting doses of electricity into her heart. Tara dug her fingernails so tightly into Gil's arm she drew blood. He didn't feel a thing.

When they heard the words 'normal sinus rhythm' they knew Cassie's heart had returned to its regular rhythm again.

Gil stared at the blood smeared on his arm.

"Sorry," Tara said.

Soon the curtain was pulled back and the Code Blue team began to gather up its equipment. The team physician headed towards them.

"She's okay. She's out of v-fib. Her color's good, and her B.P. is back to normal. Sorry we had to shove you out."

"No problem," Gil said. "I deserved it. What caused the v-fib?"

The other physician shook his head. "Who knows? Maybe some toxic effect of *Medusa* on her heart muscle."

"Do you think it affected her…?" Tara asked.

"Her brain? Do I think there's been any brain damage?"

Tara waited.

"I do not. She was given CPR within seconds of the alarm. And we continued it until she was back to a normal heart rhythm, no more than a couple of minutes. She'll be fine."

"Thank you," Gil said.

They went back to their daughter's bedside. The nursing personnel had put everything back the way it was.

Once he was sure Cassie was safe again, Gil phoned David Gardner at USAMRIID. He couldn't shake the questions he had about his daughter's illness. Maybe Gardner would have the answers. He was the real expert.

"Hello, this is Gil Martin," he announced. But when he heard Gardner's growl, he hesitated. "This a bad time to call?"

"No, no. Heavens, no!" Gardner was mortified. "I'm sorry for being so gruff. How are you? Have you heard from Tara lately?"

"I'm with her now, at Emory Hospital. Our daughter was admitted here three days ago."

Gardner thought of his own children. "It's not *Medusa*, is it Gil?"

"I'm afraid it is. We just got back the blood culture report. It's definite."

"Gil, I'm so sorry. She's going to be alright, isn't she?"

"We had a big scare last night. But she's stable again, though still comatose." Gil pushed forward quickly into the awkward silence. "But I've a question about her illness, and I thought you could help me with it."

"Of course. Shoot."

He briefly described Cassie's clinical course. "Could that early URI—seven weeks ago—could it have been *Medusa*'s initial onset? And if so, why did it take so long to show up?"

"It could have been the onset. It definitely could have."

"Then why so long an interval?"

"A long 'tail.'"

"Huh?"

"The Sverdlovsk epidemic. You remember reading about that? It had a few cases—a long 'tail'— extending out many weeks past the major cluster."

"I didn't know that."

"And a 1956 British study of monkeys showed that, if inhaled deeply enough, anthrax spores could lie dormant in the lungs for weeks—even months—before germinating. We did a similar experiment at USAMRIID a couple of years ago and confirmed the British results. We had animal anthrax cases extending up to 58 days after exposure. The long 'tail.'"

"So, my daughter's initial URI could have been the onset of *Medusa* infection in her nose and throat. But it took this long for the spores in her lungs to germinate."

"That's my guess."

"Thanks Dave, that helps. Listen—before you hang up—I have another question for you."

"What?"

"Do you know anything about pesticides?"

Gardner was amazed. He was still in his sweat shirt and running shorts. He had just finished his computer and textbook search of pesticides and had given it up as a dead end. Until Gil's call.

"Are you kidding!"

Gil explained. "I didn't know about *Medusa's* long 'tail'. But I was convinced my daughter's URI seven weeks ago was the start of the disease. She probably caught it from a boy at school. That raised another question…"

"What are you getting at?"

"Why didn't Cassie's mother—Tara—get infected then? From Cassie."

"Good question. You'd make a good researcher, Gil."

"Thanks. I did some checking with Tara. Found out she *had* been exposed to pesticides—probably in high concentrations—right at the time of Cassie's initial URI symptoms. I figured they might have protected her."

Gardner laughed. "Christ! What a coincidence. I just came to the same conclusion about pesticides myself." He looked down at his long list of chemical names. It was probably too much to ask for, but he asked anyway. "You wouldn't happen to know which particular pesticide it was, would you, Gil?"

"Why, yes. I do have a name for you."

⬛

The information Dave Gardner got from Gil Martin was exactly what he needed. He wouldn't have to work his way through dozens of chemical compounds to find the most effective and safest ones. Instead, Gil had helped him narrow his search to just one compound: a single, silver bullet aimed straight at *Medusa's* heart.

He pencilled out the design for experiments to test this chemical. Normally, before a new drug is approved for human use, a complicated set of FDA protocols had to be followed. These typically took years to complete. But he didn't have the luxury of that kind of time. He needed to short-circuit the process. Skip the *in vitro* and small animal tests. Go straight to primates—monkeys—the closest animals to humans. If these were successful, he would recommend a large-population human clinical trial, an entire city or region of the country. The results should give the answer quickly.

He estimated he could be ready for human testing within three weeks. But he would need a lot of help to bypass government red tape. He played his only trump card.

"Good mornin', Mr. President," he said when his call was put through to the Oval Office. "I think I've found another rabbit for you."

"Really!"

"Yessuh. But I'm going to need all your help to pull it out of that ole hat."

"You name it, Dr. Gardner. Whatever you need, it's yours."

After his call to Dave Gardner, Gil returned to the ICU. He watched the staff go about their business. Very professional. He was impressed. He leaned back in the chair and looked at his daughter. She was still unresponsive. Tara had gone home for a shower and a change of clothes. He was reading a paperback novel he had found in the hospital's gift shop. He started to nod off, the book falling into his lap. Soon he was asleep. That's when the nightmare came.

The three of them—he, Tara and Cassie—were at a summer swimming pool party somewhere. It was a glorious day. The adults were all eating and drinking and gabbing, the kids splashing in the water. Cassie must have been about five years old.

Suddenly, he heard her voice through the noise of the crowd, high-pitched and frightened. "Daddy. Daddy."

He searched the water but couldn't see her among the other little tanned bodies.

Her calls rose in fear. "Daddy! Daddy!"

Then he spotted her. In the far corner of the deep end, holding on for dear life to the side of the pool, her face frozen in terror.

"Daddy! Daddy!"

He dropped his drink and started towards her. But his feet wouldn't move. They were stuck to the deck. He stretched out his arms and pulled with all his might. But he couldn't break free.

"Cassie! Cassie!" he screamed.

With a start, he awoke.

"Daddy. Daddy." the voice kept calling. It was softer now, barely above a whisper.

He shook his head and looked around the room, uncertain where he was. Then he remembered. Her eyes were open, she was looking at him and calling his name. Oh holy God!

He sprang toward her, knocking the paperback onto the floor. "I'm here, Cassie. Daddy's here."

He kissed and held her. Then he explained where she was and why she was here. She couldn't remember anything about her illness. Even the ride to the hospital in the ambulance, the siren blaring.

His medical training took over. He told her to move her arms and legs, which she did. Then he performed a quick neuro check and a test of memory and intellectual functioning. Everything seemed to be intact, everything had returned to normal. Except some amnesia for the past four days.

He kissed her one more time then called her mother.

Three weeks later, the first Monday in December.

A surprising, late-fall snowstorm had hit the Washington, D.C., area, catching the city off guard. It didn't last long and there was little accumulation. Just enough to snarl traffic and cause a few more fender benders on the beltway. But even after the snow had melted, the gloomy, overcast weather continued. The cherry trees, barren and stick-like along the banks of the Potomac, stood out stark against the leaden skies.

Dave Gardner could feel the city's mood during his taxi ride from the airport to the White House. Even the usually talkative cabbie was silent. In the Oval Office he shook hands with the President.

"Thank you for coming, Dr. Gardner. I hope this new 'rabbit' of yours works. I had to pull a few tricks myself to get you what you needed."

"I know, Mr. President. And I'm grateful."

The Chief of Staff was there and nodded to him from across the room. He was next introduced to the head of the Food and Drug Administration, the Mayor of Los Angeles, and Michelle Goad, L.A. County's Epidemiologist. She was dressed in a suit and a leather belt with a large silver buckle. She wore cowboy boots. Gardner blinked at the sight.

"Dr. Gardner," the President began when everyone was seated, "you have a proposal for stopping the epidemic. Let's hear it."

"Yessuh." Gardner told how he had searched for groups with low risk to *Medusa*, had discovered a presumptive benefit from pesticides, and how—pointed in the right direction by Gil Martin—he had isolated the safest and most effective of them.

"How did you test these…these?" The President looked at his Chief of Staff.

"Permethrins, sir. A common pesticide, I hear. Often used around the house."

"Right. How did you test them against *Medusa*?"

Gardner cleared his throat. "It was straight forward. First, to see what effect they had on animals who were already infected, I exposed healthy ones to an aerosolized spray of *Medusa* spores, waited until they became ill, then sprayed them with permethrins. None survived. They all died, all with the typical symptoms of *Medusa*."

"So, the permethrins didn't cure the *Medusa* infection?" Michelle Goad snapped. She was visibly irritated. "I thought that was why we were invited here. Because you had found a cure." She made some slashing notes on a notepad with her father's pen.

"Hear me out, Dr. Goad. I found something even better. Next, I sprayed another group of animals. Half got permethrins, the other half—the control group—just plain water. Then I exposed all of them to *Medusa*. Those who had been pre-treated with the permethrins survived, every one of them. None even developed URI symptoms. But all the control-group animals perished. I repeated the experiment four times, testing different concentrations of permethrins. I got the same results each time. The concentration I used in the last experiment was less than 25 percent of what you can buy over the counter at your local hardware store."

Michelle Goad understood. Her voice softened. "The permethrins prevented the infection from developing."

"Correct. They won't cure *Medusa* if you've already got it. But they will stop its spread."

"What about side effects?" she asked. She put her pen down and leaned forward.

"None. And I looked very hard for 'em. I wanted to be certain it was safe. However—" he raised his hand to hold off her next question "—these compounds are derived from chrysanthemums, the same class of plants as ragweed."

"What's that mean?" The Chief of Staff asked.

"People with ragweed allergy could develop hay fever symptoms from 'em, even trigger an acute asthma attack in highly sensitive folks."

Dr. Goad was surprised. "Even at the low concentrations you used?"

"Even the smallest dose can bring on a reaction in such people."

The President frowned. "Is this a show stopper?"

"I don't think so. Not as long as we warn the public that persons with ragweed sensitivity should use permethrins with caution. If they develop respiratory problems, they should seek immediate medical attention."

"Any idea how these permethrins work?" Dr. Goad asked. "To prevent *Medusa* infections."

Gardner shook his head. "I'm not certain. I can only guess that they somehow prevent the spores from germinatin' in a person's nose, mouth and lungs."

"What about people who've inhaled *Medusa* spores but haven't gotten sick yet?" Goad asked. "You know, the ones out there on the 'tail' of the disease. Could the permethrins prevent their illness as well?"

"Again, I don't know." Gardner answered frankly. "We'll just have to wait and see. But those are very rare cases…" He had a momentary flashback to his conversation with Gil Martin about his daughter. Then he continued. "Permethrins should prevent the illness in the majority of those using 'em."

"But you won't know for certain until you actually test them on humans," the FDA Administrator said pointedly. "And just how do you plan to do that?"

Gardner reached into his briefcase and pulled out a dozen small aluminum foil envelopes. "What do you think these are?" He held one up, turning it front and back. Something was written on both sides.

"They look like restaurant towelletes," the President suggested.

"Or alcohol swabs." Michelle Goad offered.

"Or betadine, an antiseptic swab used for wound care," the FDA Administrator volunteered.

"You're all correct," Gardner answered. "These little foil envelopes are used for a variety of purposes. Millions upon millions of 'em are produced each year." He waved his own packet in the air. "But these are special, very special."

He passed them around the room until each person had his or her own. "Will someone please read what's written on them?"

The Chief of Staff volunteered:

> *For the prevention of Medusa infections.*
> *Hay fever sufferers and asthmatics should*
> *use with caution.*

He turned the packet over and read the other side:

> *Use as directed twice a day.*

Gardner tore open his envelope. "Some of these packets have the directions and warning written in Spanish." He looked around the table. "Does anyone here have hay fever or asthma?"

No one answered.

"Good. Here's what you do." He removed the damp piece of napkin from the pouch, held it to his nose and mouth, and breathed deeply, once, then twice. Then he threw it into a nearby trash can. "Tell me what you think," he said, indicating that everyone should do the same.

When the President tore at his packet, a Secret Service Agent stepped up and grabbed his wrist. "Mr. President. Do you think this is wise?"

The President waved him off. "Are you kidding? Didn't you hear Dr. Gardner tell us this stuff comes from chrysanthemums?

Hell! I"ve had those flowers in my garden for years. Smell 'em all the time." Nonetheless, he brought the napkin to his nostrils gingerly. "I can't smell a thing."

"Me either," the FDA Adminstrator agreed.

The others—some with hesitation—followed suit, sniffing their own napkins.

"You just inhaled," Gardner informed them, "0.05% permethrin. This is one-fourth the concentration of what many of you have in the pesticides in your garages or under your kitchen sinks right now."

"I don't feel anything." the COS said, wrinkling his nose.

"No, and you won't. There should be no side effects. Except for those I've mentioned in hay fever patients and asthmatics. If you use one of these packets twice a day, you should be protected from *Medusa.*"

"And you say they're safe?" the President asked.

"Permethrins are the preferred treatment for scabies and head lice. There's no major side effects from them."

"What about in children?" the COS asked.

"They're used in kids every day. In much higher doses. Up to 5% in creams and shampoos."

"Aren't they used as insect repellents?" Michelle Goad asked. "Against ticks and mosquitoes?"

"Right."

"Where did you get these little packets?" Goad asked.

"From one of the manufacturers. I asked 'em to prepare a few demos for me. They also assured me they can turn out millions more within two weeks. Enough for every person in Los Angeles County to get started with. And millions more to follow."

"Ahhh!" the Mayor of Los Angeles said. He had been silent until now, not sure why he had been invited. "We're to be the guinea pigs. Now I understand why some are written in Spanish as well as English. But why us? Why L.A.?"

"The answer is right there next to you." Gardner pointed to Michelle Goad. "She and her contact investigators were the first ones to discover *Medusa's* contagiousness. She has the best information gathering team in the country: quick, reliable, accurate."

"Well, thanks for that," Michelle Goad said. "But LA's perfect for another reason. Our mild winters mean we can get medical services rapidly out to anyone who has a reaction. And we can use our existing system—the same one we've employed for distributing antibiotics and routing patients to medical facilities—for handing out these packets."

"You'll have to blitz the media like they've never seen, Mayor." the Chief of Staff warned. "Press conferences and briefings, TV, newspapers, the works. Coordinate the distribution of the packets with FEMA. Then set a start date a couple of weeks from now. You should be ready by then."

The Mayor raised his eyebrows. "Really?"

"I've personally spoken with the pesticide producers and the manufacturers of these packets," Gardner said. "They've all agreed to shift their entire factory output to producing the towelletes. I'm confident you'll be ready to begin handing them out within a couple of weeks."

"Who's going to pay for all this?"

The President was quick with reassurance. "Don't worry about that, Mayor. The White House has enough discretionary funds to get this operation started. If more is needed, Congress stands ready to pass an emergency appropriations bill. And National Guard and Army Reserve units will be at your disposal to help with distribution. You might also consider having the military set up smaller dispersal points at malls, school yards, and supermarket centers."

The President next turned to Michelle Goad. "How many cases of *Medusa* are you getting per week in L. A. now?"

"About 65. It peaked a few weeks ago and appears to have leveled off. But it's not shown any sign of dropping."

"So you should know fairly quickly if this is going to work or not."

She nodded. "If it's as good as Dr. Gardner says it is, we should have an answer for you quickly."

"How long a trial period are you thinking of?" the Mayor asked.

"One month," Gardner answered. "That should be enough time. One month after the packets are put into use."

The Mayor was still bothered by something and kept rubbing his temple.

"What is it, Mayor?" the President asked.

"If you think this is safe and effective, shouldn't you release it to the entire country right away?"

Gardner answered for the President. "Dr. Goad and I will be monitoring the results every week. If they show an immediate benefit, we'll cut short the clinical trial and alert the President to begin distribution nationwide."

The Mayor was still reluctant, "I'll have to discuss this with my own staff and get approval from the County Board of Supervisors."

"We don't have time for that Mayor," the President said with an edge. "Nor do I need your or anyone else's approval to start this trial. This is a national crisis. I have broad executive powers to deal with it as I see fit." He stared hard at the man. "And this is how I see fit."

"Then why was I invited here?" the Mayor shot back.

The Chief of Staff quickly intervened. "Because we want your cooperation, Mayor. We need your cooperation to pull this off."

After a tense but short pause the Mayor, a pragmatist, recognized he was politically out-gunned. "Very well, Mr. President, I will do all I can."

The FDA Administrator, who looked like Ichabod Crane, objected. Through pursed lips he said, "Mr. President, I really must protest. This violates all FDA procedures for clinical trials with new drugs. We must…"

The President cut him off with a chop of his hand. "Sir," he said firmly, "2,000 of our citizens are infected with *Medusa* every week. The majority of them die soon after. Despite everything we're doing, there's no end to this outbreak in sight. This is the only hope we have." He looked deliberately from face to face, his eyes challenging. "No more discussion, no more arguments."

"What shall we call this operation, Mr. President," someone asked.

Gardner held up his hand. "*Operation Clean Sweep*," he offered, "to sweep *Medusa* clean out of the country."

The Chief of Staff, an old Navy man, said, "I'll second that."

"Very well," the President said. "*Operation Clean Sweep* it is. Let's get on with it."

26

Gil Martin delayed his return from Atlanta as long as he could, both to watch over his daughter's recovery as well as to be with her mother. Cassie had been home barely a week, was still recuperating. She was unable to recall anything about those four critical hospital days. Probably never would. But, like the warming sun, her smile had returned.

One evening after dinner, when Cassie was resting on the sofa, Tara winked at Gil and said, "Care for a dip?"

"What do you mean?"

"The hot tub. I'll heat it up for us."

The moon was full, the sky clear, the air crisp. The steam rose off Tara's backyard spa like a veil. Gil wore an old pair of cut-off jeans as swim trunks. She was stunning in a bikini. Was that the same one in his old picture? Probably not. But it looked just as good.

They eyed one another through the mist.

"You've gained back some weight," she finally said. "That's the Gil Martin I remember."

"It's more than getting back what you remember."

"Oh?"

"I've changed, Tara. For the better."

Her toe came up and pressed against his knee. "Wanna talk about it?"

"Not really. Not now, anyway. But it has to do with you, with Cassie. What I lost."

"We lost too, Gil."

He hesitated. "Look, do you think we can—"

"Don't finish it. It's too soon. I know what you're thinking. I'm thinking it too. But let's not voice it yet."

Gil took hold of her toe. "When did you get the idea?"

"At the airport. When you mentioned *Serendipity*. You just hung there, Gil. I ached for you—and for me. I guess at that moment I thought maybe there was hope for us."

"I'm not much good on my own. Too many gaps."

"Me too."

Gil nodded. "There's no other woman."

Steam swirled and water rippled between them. "That's a damn big empty bed I sleep in, Gil. Lonely as hell."

"You look terrific in that bikini."

"I know. And I caught you looking at me."

"Maybe one day, right?"

Tara smiled. "One day."

<hr />

The next morning, Michelle Goad called from Los Angeles. Gil was still in his bathrobe.

"We're kicking off this huge clinical trial. The entire County. I need you here. I know your daughter's been ill, but I could sure use your experience."

He cupped his hand around the phone and explained to Tara. "They want me to come back. A big operation's about to begin."

She nodded. "Of course. You've got to go."

"But…"

She gave him a quick kiss on the cheek. "She'll be fine. We both will. The other thing can wait."

<hr />

The next day was emotional, the three of them saying their farewells.

Cassie threw her arms around his neck. "Bye dad. Call soon will ya?"

He looked down into her eyes and remembered how close he'd come to losing her. "That's a promise."

Tara said, "I'm thinking of subscribing to *Sailing* magazine."

He held her tight, nuzzling his face into her neck. He let go only when he heard the taxi's horn honking outside.

In Los Angeles, *Operation Clean Sweep* was set to go by the start of the traditional holiday season, December 20. Fifty million packets of permethrin had been dispersed to 250 major distribution centers. The Mayor and Michelle Goad had alerted the public by every means possible. Finally, all the pieces were in place. At a small ceremony in the Mayor's office, he threw a symbolic switch to put the Operation into effect.

It continued on through Christmas, New Years, and Hanukah. All the usual holiday sporting events had been cancelled. Not only for public health reasons, but because the Rose Bowl, Coliseum, Dodger Stadium and other major arenas were in use as distribution centers. FEMA's supply system now functioned efficiently, assisted by a small army of volunteers who went door-to-door to contact persons who were house-bound or without the means of getting to a distribution site.

Gil Martin's job was to scurry around to the county's major hospitals, clinics and medical centers, explain the purpose of the Operation to his colleagues, and enlist their aid. Soon, physicians were handing out the little foil envelopes right along with their prescriptions. Gil also emphasized the need for continued reporting of new *Medusa* cases. And of any side effects related to permethrin, particularly asthma or severe hay fever.

On January 4, exactly two weeks after *Operation Clean Sweep* began, Gil Martin, Michelle Goad, Jerry Essminger, Nathan Windsong and a few others gathered in Dr. Goad's office. All eyes were on the computer screen as the data was sorted and tabulated. By the end of the Operation's first week, there had been no significant change in the number of *Medusa* cases: 62 had been reported. Gil and Michelle Goad knew not to expect too much so soon. They had fixed a 30-day testing period to obtain reliable results. This was a trial which would determine whether the nation followed suit or not.

Now the numbers for the second week, the one just past, were popping up: 30 cases total. The rate had been cut in half. There were a few cheers in the room. Gil held up his hand for quiet.

"What's the probability these results are just due to chance?" he asked Jerry Essminger. "That they are just a temporary dip in the rate rather than a real downturn from the permethrins?"

Essminger did some quick calculations. "About ten percent."

Gil shook his head. "That's not good enough. Before we ask the President to commit the entire country, we need near certainty."

"I agree," Dr. Goad said. "Ten percent is not good enough. We'll stick to the protocol."

During the following week everyone doubled his efforts to get the foil envelopes distributed. The tension and rivalry between government agencies—the turf battles which had marked the early days of the epidemic—were gone, replaced with teamwork and cooperation.

Gil kept in contact with Atlanta. Cassie had returned to school, Tara to her duties at CDC.

"She misses you." Tara told him. "We both do."

"I'll see you when this is over," he promised. "I have something special to talk with the two of you about."

She tried to pry it out of him, but without success.

A week later, the same group gathered again in Michelle Goad's office. They watched while the new data was computed. There it was. This time it was unmistakeable. From 65 cases three weeks ago, to 30 the following week, the number had now dropped to 3. Only three new cases all last week.

The little group erupted in cheers.

"I think we can break the protocol," Gil shouted to Michelle over the noise.

"I agree." She swirled the scotch in her glass and drained it in one swallow. "Your permethrin works."

After a soda, Gil turned to go. But Michelle restrained him. "There's something I've been meaning to ask you. Been bothering me for weeks."

"What is it?"

"Dave Gardner referred to you as the father of this idea to fight *Medusa* with pesticides. What's that all about?"

Gil looked sheepish. "I wish I could tell you I got the idea from some blinding insight. Like Fleming's discovery of penicillin. But it was much less romantic."

"Tell me," she insisted. She kept urging until he finally relented.

"My motives were purely personal, purely selfish. My daughter was ill, and I had a number of questions about it. One of them was about *Medusa's* communicability."

He accepted another glass of cola. She waited.

"Cassie became infected during the first week of the epidemic. Long before we knew how it spread."

"Why didn't Tara get sick? Immediate family members are the first ones to become infected. The rate is over ninety percent."

"That was the question I had. I thought maybe Tara had been taking antibiotics for some other infection and they had prevented it. But she had not. Still, I couldn't shake the idea that she had been protected somehow."

"What did you do?"

"I asked Tara if she remembered anything special going on at home at the time of Cassie's initial symptoms. When she had that inital URI."

Michelle sipped more scotch and watched him. "And?"

"Nothing stood out, she told me."

"So, how did you finally stumble onto it?"

"I was standing in front of her refrigerator, drinking a glass of juice. I noticed her calendar. I flipped back a month to September. There it was. A clue."

"What?"

"A scribbled note for Friday, the 28th. I couldn't quite make it out. I asked Tara what it meant."

"'Oh, that,' she told me." 'I was having an ant problem. They were everywhere. I arranged for a local exterminator to come out that day and spray the house. Inside and out. I stayed home from work that day.'"

"She was exposed to the pesticides in the ant spray," Michelle said, draining another scotch.

"That's right. But it gets better. I asked her if she felt any ill effects from the spraying. None, she said. In fact, it had been a cool morning so she had closed all the windows and doors."

"She got the maximum pesticide dose. There was no ventilation."

"That's what I figure."

"What about your daughter?"

"She went to school. There was a new French boy there. A team of horses couldn't have kept her away."

"And when did your daughter get sick with the initial *Medusa* URI?"

"Two days later. Tara was certain there was a connection between the illness and the spraying. But I think it was the opposite…"

"Tara didn't get sick *because* of her exposure to the pesticides."

"Right. And by the time Cassie became really ill seven weeks later with toxic shock, that long-ago URI had been forgotten."

"But you figured it out. Good for you, Gil."

"I was elated. I phoned Tara's exterminator company to find out what was in that ant spray."

"Good follow up."

"They had stopped using the more dangerous pesticides long ago. Now they used much safer ones. Either naturally occurring ones from chrysanthemums. Or synthetic ones. Permethrin is one of these."

"And that's when you called Dave Gardner?"

"Yes. He couldn't believe his luck. Suddenly, those 1,500 dangerous pesticides on his list were down to just a couple."

Gil took a swallow of cola. "Permethrins are now the active ingredient in most general purpose pesticides. I found some in the storage shed of my apartment building. You'll find them in most pesticides at your local garden store."

"They're that universal?" She was amazed

"Go to the store and read the labels. See for yourself."

"Here's to 'em!" she said, slurring her words, happily intoxicated. They clinked glasses.

"Do you know, Gil, I used to smoke a pipe?"

Dave Gardner received Gil Martin's phone call just after lunch.

"It's succeeded, Dave. *Operation Clean Sweep* is a success. We've cut the clinical trial short. Congratulations."

Gardner then made a call to the White House. "Mr. President. About that rabbit..."

It took a month—February 1st—before *Operation Clean Sweep* was launched nationwide. And another two weeks before its effects were even detected. Part of the problem was the public's attitude to the little foil packets. At the national level, there had been no media preparation even close to what L.A. County had done prior to its clinical trial with permethrin.

Consequently, when it was first announced that a way had been found to stop the epidemic, John Q. Citizen was at first grateful and relieved. But that didn't last. Scepticism soon set in, followed by fear. It didn't seem possible to the man on the street that products which he had always been told were highly toxic (organophosphate pesticides had been used as 'nerve gas') were now beneficial. And he was supposed to breathe them twice a day. When a severe case of asthma was reported in a hay fever sufferer with ragweed allergy, it was trumpeted by unprincipled opponents of the Operation to raise the level of fear even further.

It was not until the entire First Family—the President, First Lady, and their two children—went on national television and breathed the permethrins that the fearmongers and skeptics were finally silenced. A dramatic increase in the use of the little towellettes occurred shortly thereafter.

Then the rate of new cases dropped dramatically. To around 1200 for the third week of February, and by the final week to less than 500. For the first week of March, only 32 cases were reported nationwide. *Medusa* was finally swept away, though a few delayed-onset cases were reported as late as the middle of March. But by the time of the vernal equinox, March 21, the country was finally rid of it for good.

In its *After-Action Report* the FBI prepared a list of 'Lessons-Learned' from the outbreak and a matching list of 'Recommendations'. At the top of the latter list was improved training to detect and manage future BW outbreaks. This training should emphasize bioterrorism rather than strictly military scenarios of biowarfare. Frontline physicians and nurses—ER docs and primary care specialists in particular—needed more training to recognize that these epidemics might be the work of terrorists rather than naturally-occurring ones. And since Acts of God—floods, earthquakes, tornadoes—often led to epidemics themselves from a lack of proper hygiene, poor sanitation and unsafe water supplies, more training was needed under realistic conditions to prepare health care providers to differentiate natural epidemics from man-made ones.

The second area of the *Report* dealt with recommendations to improve public access to preventative measures, such as properly-fitting face masks and prophylactic antibiotics. National Stockpiles of these supplies should be created at additional focal points throughout the country, not just on the two coasts. Distribution routes should be worked out well in advance. And the entire system should be periodically tested through disaster drills. Since terrorists with access to recombinant DNA technology may have designed BW agents with resistence to currently-used antibiotics, second-line drugs must also be developed, tested, and stockpiled.

The *Report* had much to say about the anthrax vaccine. It began with a scathing criticism of the failure to achieve universal military immunization. And it pointed out that PCR studies of the Sverdlovsk outbreak proved the Soviets had been experimenting with at least four different strains of anthrax. The current vaccine would probably not have been effective against all four strains, even if it had been available. Further, biological mutations of the anthrax bacteria into vaccine-resistant forms was always a possibility, as was man-made production of strains deliberately altered through recombinant DNA techniques into such vaccine-resistant forms.

Based on these sobering observations, the *Report* strongly urged greatly expanded research on anthrax vaccine development. This should include oral forms which could be stockpiled and quickly distributed to the entire country in an emergency. A priority as high as military vaccination should be routine anathrax immunizations for front-line health care providers.

Although the *Report* focused on anthrax, it noted that as a nation we are vulnerable to terrorist attacks with other BW agents: plague, cholera, smallpox, Ebola virus and botulism. Strategies for developing preventive measures and vaccines against these should go forward as well.

An expanded role for the U.S. Customs Service was vigorously recommended. This must include enlarged quarantine facilities, with appropriate personnel for medical evaluation, testing, and monitoring, at all international ports of entry. It was a foregone conclusion, the *Report* stated, that the current epidemic and the thousands of deaths it caused could have been prevented if Achmed Malabee and the five other Iraqi 'vectors' had been immediately isolated on their arrival into the country.

Finally, the *Report* had a few thousand choice words for the overall management of the outbreak. FEMA's early failures in the supply and distribution of prophylactic antibiotics were duly noted. Since FEMA's experience was mostly concentrated on natural disasters, the agency had little practice with deliberate biological ones.

Similarly, the public health establishment, from top to bottom, lacked the infrastructure and experience to handle a national disaster of this magnitude. Interagency rivalry and multiple chains-of-command made the problem worse. The *Report* recommended that a sub-cabinet level office—perhaps under the newly-created Department of Homeland Security—with a single person in overall command, should be established to train, drill and assume direct control over the response to any similar outbreaks in the future.

EPILOGUE

Gil Martin returned to his ER job in Los Angeles. But his thoughts were of Atlanta.

"I'll be there for your birthday," he told his daughter one evening on the phone. "Fourteen years old. I wasn't sure you were going to see this one, Cassie."

"Me either, dad. How long will you be here?"

"A few days…Maybe longer…We'll see…"

"Why all the mystery?"

"Put your mother on please."

"Where will you stay?" Tara asked.

"One of the hotels near the airport."

"My sofabed is still available. And cheap."

"Are you sure?"

"Yes."

After dinner, birthday cake and ice cream, and presents, the three of them lingered around the dining room table.

When they finally pushed their plates away, Tara asked, "Now what was it you wanted to tell us?"

"I've decided to leave L.A." He let the words hang in the air, satisfied from their looks that he had achieved total surprise.

"Where are you going, dad?"

"I thought I'd take a look in Atlanta. Do you think I can find a job here?"

"That would be great, dad!"

"You would do this for us?" Tara asked quietly.

"And for me."

The two looked at each other in a lengthening silence.

Cassie took the hint. "Hey, why don't you two go out and have some fun. I'll be okay."

He grinned. "A real date?"

"Sure," she smiled back. "Why not?"

Over dinner the next evening, Tara waited patiently. Finally, he got around to it, and it all came out in a rush. "I love you, Tara. I've never stopped loving you. Even when we argued, I loved you. I've been too damned blind to see it. Too full of self pity…"

"Or too drunk?"

"That too. But I've been sober for months. Look"—he held up his hands—"I've even got fingernails now."

She watched him.

"I think we should get back together."

"You're not just doing this for Cassie?"

"No."

"We're divorced, Gil. We can't just get back together."

"That's exactly what we'll have to do."

"You've got a ring, haven't you? In your pocket."

He pulled it out and balanced it on his fingertip. "You know me too well. You've got to marry me—again."

She took the ring but didn't put it on. "I can't go back to the old life."

"I know. I don't want it either." He looked at his plate. "Do you still love me?"

"Yes."

"Do you want us to be a family again?"

"Yes. But there must be room for two careers. For two independent personalities. Can we have a marriage with that?"

"I'm a different man today than I was a year ago. We can make it work this time."

She slipped the ring on her finger. "Then the answer is yes." For a moment she frowned. "What about our old rings, the one in my jewelry box, the one in that fake leather suitcase of yours?"

He grinned at her. "We'll take them out to sea. We'll have a ceremony."

That night, the sofabed in Tara's living room remained empty.

A Note on
Recombinant DNA

While 'The Medusa Strain' is about a fictional bacteria, the technology of cutting and splicing genes is not fiction. Growing bacteria, dissolving their cell walls, and harvesting their DNA is now routine. Enzymes known as restriction endonucleases, sometimes referred to as 'nuclear scissors,' are used to cut the DNA into discrete fragments. These, in turn, are separated and identified by a process known as gel electrophoresis, which makes use of the different weights, sizes and electrical charges of the fragments. The PCR technique (Polymerase Chain Reaction) is a tool for amplifying the quantity of selected fragments, which can then be recombined with other fragments by enzymes know as DNA ligases.

Non-chromosome loops of DNA found in bacterial cells— called plasmids—can be harvested, identified by what are known as monoclonal antibodies, and amplified by the PCR technique. Plasmids are fascinating. They contain, for example, the characteristics which make a bacteria or virus pathogenic: its virulence, antibiotic resistance, production of toxins, and the like.

Fictional character Dave Gardner's use of a bacteriophage (a virus which infects a bacteria) to carry his virulence-ending bit of DNA into *Medusa,* his *Perseus Factor,* is a technique also in actual use. The efficiency of this process is profound. If a DNA fragment —a plasmid, for example—is inserted into a phage, when the phage infects the bacteria, it forces it to reproduce this plasmid along with its own DNA. Furthermore, all the bacteria's offspring will carry the phage and the plasmid, driving the progeny's bacterial metabolism to produce even more of it. And while the phage infection, if left unchecked, will ultimately kill the bacteria, even that can be prevented by a repressor plasmid, which is harvested from another bacteria and introduced by another phage.

It may seem like science fiction. But recombinant DNA technology is all too real.

Check out these other fine titles by
Durban House at your local book store.

EXCEPTIONAL BOOKS
BY
EXCEPTIONAL WRITERS

Current Titles

BASHA   John Hamilton Lewis

DEADLY ILLUMINATION   Serena Stier

DEATH OF A HEALER   Paul Henry Young

HOUR OF THE WOLVES   Stephane Daimlen-Völs

A HOUSTON WEEKEND   Orville Palmer

JOHNNIE RAY & MISS KILGALLEN   Bonnie Hearn Hill & Larry Hill

THE MEDUSA STRAIN   Chris Holmes

MR. IRRELEVANT   Jerry Marshall

OPAL EYE DEVIL   John Hamilton Lewis

PRIVATE JUSTICE   Richard Sand

ROADHOUSE BLUES   Baron Birtcher

RUBY TUESDAY   Baron Birtcher

THE SERIAL KILLER'S DIET BOOK   Kevin Mark Postupack

THE STREET OF FOUR WINDS   Andrew Lazarus

TUNNEL RUNNER   Richard Sand

WHAT GOES AROUND   Don Goldman

Nonfiction

MIDDLE ESSENCE—WOMEN OF WONDER YEARS   Landy Reed

PROTOCOL   Mary Jane McCaffree & Pauline Innis
    For 25 years, the bible for public relations firms, corporations, embassies, governments and individuals seeking to do business with the Federal government.

BASHA   JOHN HAMILTON LEWIS

Set in the world of elite professional tennis and rooted in ancient Middle East hatreds of identity and blood loyalties, Basha is charged with the fiercely competitive nature of professional sports and the dangers of terrorism. An already simmering Middle East begins to boil and CIA Station Chief Grant Corbet must track down the highly successful terrorist, Basha. In a deadly race against time, Grant hunts the illusive killer only to see his worst nightmare realized.

DEADLY ILLUMINATION   SERENA STIER

It's summer 1890 in New York City. Florence Tod, an ebullient young woman, must challenge financier, John Pierpont Morgan, to solve a possible murder. J.P.'s librarian has ingested poison embedded in an illumination of a unique Hildegard van Bingen manuscript. Florence and her cousin, Isabella Stewart Gardner, discover the corpse. When Isabella secretly removes a gold tablet from the scene of the crime, she sets off a chain of events that will involve Florence and her in a dangerous conspiracy.

DEATH OF A HEALER   PAUL HENRY YOUNG

Diehard romanticist and surgeon extraordinaire, Jake Gibson, struggles to preserve his professional oath against the avarice and abuse of power so prevalent in present-day America. Jake's personal quest is at direct odds with a group of sinister medical and legal practitioners who plot to eliminate patient groups in order to improve the bottom line. With the lives of his family on the line, Jake must expose the darker side of the medical world.

HOUR OF THE WOLVES   STEPHANE DAIMLEN-VÖLS

After more than three centuries, the *Poisons Affair* remains one of history's great, unsolved mysteries. The worst impulses of human nature—sordid sexual perversion, murderous intrigues, witchcraft, Satanic cults—thrive within the shadows of the Sun King's absolutism and will culminate in the darkest secret of his reign: the infamous *Poisons Affair*, a remarkably complex web of horror, masked by Baroque splendor, luxury and refinement.

A HOUSTON WEEKEND   ORVILLE PALMER

Professor Edward Randall, not-yet-forty, divorced and separated from his daughters, is leading a solitary, cheerless existence in a university town. At a conference in Houston he runs into his childhood sweetheart. Then she was poverty-stricken, neglected and American Indian. Now she's elegantly attired, driving an expensive Italian car and lives in a millionaires enclave. Will their fortuitous encounter grow into anything meaningful?

JOHNNIE RAY & MISS KILGALLEN   BONNIE HEARN HILL & LARRY HILL

Johnnie Ray was a sexually conflicted wild man out of control; Dorothy Kilgallen, fifteen years his senior, was the picture of decorum as a Broadway columnist and TV personality. The last thing they needed was to fall in love—with each other. Sex, betrayal, money, drugs, drink and more drink. Together they descended into a nightmare of assassination conspiracies, bizarre suicides and government enemy lists until Dorothy dies…mysteriously. Was it suicide…or murder?

THE MEDUSA STRAIN   CHRIS HOLMES

A gripping tale of bio-terrorism that stunningly portrays the dangers of chemical warfare in ways nonfiction never could. When an Iraqi scientist full of hatred for America breeds a deadly form of anthrax and a diabolical means to initiate an epidemic, not even the First Family is immune. Will America's premier anthrax researcher devise a bio-weapon in time to save the U.S. from extinction?

MR. IRRELEVANT   JERRY MARSHALL

Sports writer Paul Tenkiller and pro-football player Chesty Hake have been roommates for eight seasons. Paul's Choctaw background and his sports gambling, and Chesty's memories of his mother's killing are the dark forces that will ensnare Tenkiller in Hake's slide into a murderous paranoia—but Paul is behind the curve that is spinning Chesty out of his control.

OPAL EYE DEVIL   JOHN HAMILTON LEWIS

From the teeming wharves of Shanghai to the stately offices of New York and London, Robber Barons lie, steal, cheat, and kill in their quest for power. Eric Gradek will rise from the *Northern Star's* dark cargo hold to the pinnacle of high stakes gambling for unrivaled riches. Aided by his beautiful wife, Katheryn, and the devoted Tong-Po, Eric fights for his dream and for revenge against the man who left him for dead aboard *Northern Star.*

PRIVATE JUSTICE   RICHARD SAND

After taking brutal revenge for the murder of his twin brother, Lucas Rook leaves the NYPD to work for others who crave justice outside the law when the system fails them. Rook's dark journey takes him on a race to find a killer whose appetite is growing. A little girl turns up dead. And then another and another. The nightmare is on him fast. The piano player has monstrous hands; the Medical Examiner is a goulish dwarf; an investigator kills himself. Betrayal and intrigue is added to the deadly mix as the story careens toward its startling end.

ROADHOUSE BLUES   BARON BIRTCHER

Newly retired Homicide detective Mike Travis is torn from the comfort of his chartered yacht business into the dark, bizarre underbelly of LA's music scene by a grisly string of murders. A handsome, drug-addled psychopath has reemerged from an ancient Dionysian cult, leaving a bloody trail of seemingly unrelated victims in his wake.

RUBY TUESDAY   BARON BIRTCHER

Mike Travis sails his yacht to Kona, Hawaii expecting to put LA Homicide behind him: to let the warm emerald sea wash years of blood from his hands. Instead, he finds his family's home ravaged by shotgun blasts, littered with bodies and trashed with drugs. Then things get worse. A rock star involved in a Wall Street deal masterminded by Travis's brother is one of the victims. Another victim is Ruby, Travis's childhood sweetheart. How was she involved?

THE SERIAL KILLER'S DIET BOOK   KEVIN MARK POSTUPACK

Fred Orbis is fat—very fat—but will soon discover the ultimate diet. Devon DeGroot is on the trail of a homicidal maniac who prowls Manhattan with meatballs, bologna and egg salad—taunting him about the body count in *Finnegans Wakean*. Darby Montana, one of the world's richest women, wants a new set of genes to alter a face and body so homely not even plastic surgery could help. Mr. Monde is the Devil in the market for a soul or two. It's a Faustian satire on God and the Devil, Heaven and Hell, beauty and the best-seller list.

THE STREET OF FOUR WINDS   ANDREW LAZARUS

Paris—just after World War II. On the Left Bank, Americans seek a way to express their dreams, delights and disappointments in a way very different from pre-war ex-patriots. Tom Cortell is a tough, intellectual journalist disarmed by three women-French, British and American. Along with him is a gallery of international characters who lead a merry and sometimes desperate chase between Pairs, Switzerland and Spain to a final, liberating and often tragic end of their European wanderings in search of themselves.

TUNNEL RUNNER   RICHARD SAND

Ashman is a denizen of a dark world where murder is committed and no one is brought to account; where loyalties exist side-by-side with lies and extreme violence. One morning he awakens to find himself paralyzed in a mental hospital. He escapes and seeks vengeance, confronting old friends, the Pentagon, the Mafia, and a mysterious general who is covering up the attack on TWA Flight 800.

WHAT GOES AROUND   DON GOLDMAN

Ten years ago, Ray Banno was vice president of a California bank when his boss, Andre Rhodes, framed him for bank fraud. Now, he has his new identity, a new face and a new life in medical research. He's on the verge of finding a cure for a deadly disease when he's chosen as a juror in the bank fraud trial of Andre Rhodes. Should he take revenge? Meanwhile, Rhodes is about to gain financial control of Banno's laboratory in order to destroy Banno's work

Nonfiction

MIDDLE ESSENCE—WOMEN OF WONDER YEARS   LANDY REED

Here is a roadmap and a companion to what can be the most profoundly significant and richest years of a woman's life. For every woman approaching, at, or beyond midlife, this guide is rich with stories of real women in real circumstances who find they have a second chance-a time when women blossom rather than fade. Gain a new understanding of how to move beyond myths of aging; address midlife transitions head on; discover new power and potential; and emerge with a stronger sense of self